Gore in the Garden

DATE DUE

Hayner PLD/Large Print
Overdues .10/day. Max fine cost of
item. Lost or damaged item: additional
$5 service charge.

GORE IN THE GARDEN

COLLEEN J. SHOGAN

WHEELER PUBLISHING
A part of Gale, a Cengage Company

Copyright © 2019 Year by Colleen J. Shogan.
A Washington Whodunit.
Wheeler Publishing, a part of Gale, a Cengage Company.

ALL RIGHTS RESERVED

Wheeler Publishing Large Print Softcover Cozy Mystery.
The text of this Large Print edition is unabridged.
Other aspects of the book may vary from the original edition.
Set in 16 pt. Plantin.

LIBRARY OF CONGRESS CIP DATA ON FILE.
CATALOGUING IN PUBLICATION FOR THIS BOOK
IS AVAILABLE FROM THE LIBRARY OF CONGRESS.

ISBN-13: 978-1-4328-9181-7 (softcover alk. paper)

Published in 2021 by arrangement with Camel Press, an imprint of Epicenter Press, Inc.

Printed in the United States of America
1 2 3 4 5   25 24 23 22 21

For my brother Greg,
a tireless supporter of my writing
who does not resemble Sebastian
in any way.

CHAPTER ONE

"Has he arrived yet?"

I fired off the question to the reliably omniscient concierge of my upscale condo building while ransacking my purse to locate the keys of my residence.

"Yes, Ms. Marshall," he said while checking his wristwatch. "I let him into the apartment at half past five."

"You're a lifesaver, Charlie." I placed my hand lightly on his shoulder. "I don't know what Doug and I would do without you."

He tipped his hat in my direction. "Not a problem, ma'am. All in a day's work."

"I wish Capitol Hill shared your attitude," I muttered under my breath.

"Excuse me," he said. "I couldn't hear what you said. Do you require additional assistance?"

"Absolutely not. I was simply admiring your willingness to help out in a pinch, Charlie. Not everyone in the workforce is so accommodating."

He lowered his voice and stepped closer to me as I waited for the elevator to arrive. "This is Washington, Ms. Marshall. If someone isn't living up to your expectations, you can show them the exit." He pointed in the direction of our building's ornate lobby for emphasis. "And I'm not just saying that because I'm a doorman."

I chuckled. "Thanks for reminding me. I'd better get upstairs now."

The elevator dinged, and I exited on the fourth floor. As I approached the door to our condo, I braced myself for the inevitable onslaught. No, we didn't keep a secret tiger or exotic pet in our two-bedroom apartment. But we did have a chunky beagle mutt named Clarence whose exuberance exceeded the stock market after Trump's election.

After putting the key in the lock, I immediately shifted my body to cover the crack in the door as I opened it. Clarence had an uncanny knack for anticipating my arrival. If the door remained open for more than a second, he'd take advantage of the situation and run down the hallway, barking in glee to celebrate his newfound freedom. The situation presented no real danger because Clarence had nowhere to escape.

But Mrs. Beauregard, who occupied a unit several doors away, seemed to have a dog radar fixated on poor Clarence. If he as much as set one paw on the common hallway space without the benefit of a leash, she immediately called the condo board and demanded Clarence pay an obscene fine for his transgression. Since our dog was currently unemployed, it fell upon us to cover his expenses.

I braced myself for Clarence's enthusiastic greeting. Nothing happened. Nada. This was indeed a mystery. I flung open the door and found Clarence on his back, receiving a belly massage from my brother, Sebastian Marshall.

Both he and Clarence reacted immediately. Sebastian got up and ran to give me a hug. Not to be outdone, Clarence followed behind him and issued several licks punctuated by a staccato series of excited barks.

I squeezed Sebastian back. "Long time no see, little brother," I said. "Let me get a good look at you."

Sebastian took a step backward. He was still tall and lean, just as I remembered him. Pushing thirty, his youthful face had been replaced with a more chiseled appearance, but he still had a headful of dishwater blond, wavy hair. Like a fine wine, his good looks had improved with age.

Sebastian shrugged. "You look the same to me."

"Yeah, we could be twins." We both laughed. I was almost the physical opposite of my only sibling. With long, brown, straight hair, average height, and perennially ten pounds to lose, one of us might have been switched at birth.

Clarence gave a polite bark. He didn't like to be neglected. Sebastian rubbed his neck. "When did you get this little guy? He's adorable."

"A few years ago, from a local shelter. Clarence is friendly, but I have to warn you. He can be quite a handful."

"Never." Sebastian was an animal lover, one of the few traits I shared with my brother and parents.

Clarence seemed to agree. He barked again.

"Clarence has developed a bit of a mouth lately. You'll have to excuse him. Please, have a seat." I gestured to the couch in our living room. "I'm afraid we won't be here for long. We need to go back to the city soon. I have a congressional reception I can't miss. But I made sure you were on the guest list so you can join me."

Sebastian wrinkled his nose. "You want

me to go to a congressional reception?"

I groaned inwardly. "You do remember my place of business, right?"

"It's your choice to work for the man. But I don't need to be part of it."

Now I remembered why I'd let three years lapse since my last brotherly visit. "Come on, Sebastian. I need to go to this reception. My boss, Representative Maeve Dixon, is on the committee which oversees the United States Botanic Garden. And tonight's reception is a special event for members of Congress and staff to view the blooming of an extremely rare flower." I took a breath. "Surely a hippie can appreciate nature."

Sebastian squared his shoulders and ran his fingers through his beautiful locks. "I'm not a hippie. I'm an activist."

"Sorry. An activist. Forgive my mistake." The sarcasm dripped from my voice.

Sebastian opened his arms. "Kit, I don't want to fight. We're on the same team. We just play the game differently."

I nodded, even though Sebastian's comment was the understatement of the day. My brother had a unique approach to life. A brilliant computer programmer, he worked on contract to make enough money to finance his true passion: protesting. No left-leaning cause was too harebrained or idealistic for Sebastian. Picketing the World Trade Organization? No problem. Occupy Wall Street? Sebastian lived in Zuccotti Park for months. Combatting climate change? He'd gladly march alongside the penguins and polar bears.

I didn't disagree with his beliefs. But I had chosen a divergent path that involved working within the system of government to affect change. Sebastian didn't like that my route often involved compromise. He failed to comprehend the meaning of the word. It was the primary reason I'd let our relationship slide.

"Then you'll come with me to the reception?" I asked.

Sebastian sighed. "I suppose so. I'd like an opportunity to speak with Maeve Dixon."

I pursed my lips. "Sebastian, I can introduce you to her. But you can't embarrass me, remember?"

"I'm not a juvenile. But there's no harm in talking about a few issues, right?"

"Maeve Dixon is a reliable vote for many of your causes. But she represents a district in North Carolina. She's got to be careful or she'll lose the seat. Would you want that to happen?"

Sebastian didn't speak for several seconds.

Then he took a deep breath. "I suppose you're right. your way of thinking has value in these troubled times."

"That's the most reasonable thing I've heard you say in a decade," I said. "Come on. You need to get changed before we head out."

Sebastian looked down at his khaki shorts, faded Greenpeace T-shirt, and classic two-strapped sandals. "Aren't we going to a botanic garden?" he asked innocently.

"If all we were doing was visiting plants, that would be perfect attire. But we're also having drinks and appetizers with important members of Congress and dozens of other dignitaries from the legislative branch. You need to step it up."

Sebastian gave me an empty look. "How? I don't have a suit. Remember, I'm against corporate greed."

How could I forget? I thought for a moment.

"You'll have to try on something from Doug's closet," I said. "We don't have time to hit up Brooks Brothers before the reception. Come on." I grabbed his arm and dragged him from the couch into our guest bedroom, where Doug kept his business couture.

My husband was a professor of American

history at Georgetown, but luckily his wardrobe didn't consist of stereotypical ripped jeans and tweed jackets with elbow patches. He'd never shed his conservative upbringing from a Boston Brahmin family. Most days, he wore a suit and tie. The problem was that Doug was a good three or four inches shorter than Sebastian. Unfortunately, my husband made up for those inches around his waistline.

I flipped through his suits and finally spotted one near the back that might work. "Here you go," I said, thrusting the outfit into Sebastian's hands. "I haven't seen Doug wear this in a while. He bought it several years ago, when the slim fit trend was all the rage." What I left unsaid was that Doug probably couldn't fit into the suit these days. Who was I to judge? I kept several outfits in the dark recesses of my closet that I vowed to wear again in an imagined future state of thinness.

I left Sebastian in the guest room to change into his fancy duds. Clarence's dog walker would arrive shortly, so no worries about having to take him out for a spin. Did I need to do anything else before leaving for the reception? As I wracked my brain, my iPhone dinged. A text message had arrived from my best friend and work colleague

14

Meg Peters.

Should I come to this reception to-night?

Meg was weighing whether this was worth her time. Previously obsessed with the opposite sex, Meg was a reformed serial dater. In the past six months, she'd altered her boy-crazy routine and focused the reclaimed attention on herself. The result had been positive, even though I wondered how long her apartment vegetable garden and Netflix addiction could substitute for male affection. I punched a reply.

Yes. Come meet my brother Sebastian.

Three dots indicated she was writing back.

I keep forgetting you have a brother. C U there.

Meg's words stung. Sure, Sebastian and I hadn't been terribly close in the past. In fact, he'd only met Doug once before, and that was only for an espresso at a cafe as he breezed through D.C. for one of his infamous marches. The next few days would be telling. Doug wasn't quick to judge, but I frankly didn't know if he and my brother

15

would hit it off.

Sebastian appeared at the door of my bedroom, where Clarence had made himself at home on his favorite spot in the middle of our mattress. Of course, Clarence had a perfectly suitable dog bed on the floor, yet he predictably preferred our king-sized memory foam mattress. Whoever said dogs lacked intelligence had never witnessed Clarence's discerning tastes.

"What do you think?" Sebastian asked. He turned around and pointed both hands at me like a gun.

"Nice model pose. You might have a future on the runway if you get tired of fighting for a reduced carbon footprint," I said.

"Seriously, Kit. Does it pass muster for your fancy pants crowd?"

I scrutinized my brother. The pants were short, but dark socks would help mask it. On Sebastian, Doug's suit appeared more relaxed than slim. No one would know the difference, especially amongst the congressional crowd. Capitol Hill bore no resemblance to Fifth Avenue.

"It'll work. Follow me. Let's find a tie to finish it off," I said.

After providing Clarence with his dinner of reduced calorie dog food, we headed downstairs to procure a ride. "There's nowhere to park near the Botanic Garden," I explained. "It will be easier if we grab a ride with Uber or Lyft."

Sebastian frowned. "I prefer using taxis. I support unionized labor in this country."

I sighed heavily. Sebastian had already agreed to attend my boring work reception, and I rarely saw my brother. Playing along for a short time wouldn't hurt. I pulled out my phone and dialed the local Arlington taxi number.

"I'm not sure how long this will take," I said. "I haven't called a taxi in five years."

Sebastian put his hand on my arm. "Kit, should we really judge ourselves based upon instruments of time? Isn't fairness what matters most?"

"Not where I work," I muttered.

"Did you say something?" he asked.

"Never mind, Sebastian." I buried my nose in my iPhone. "I'm sorry, but I have a lot of emails to catch up on."

The gods of transportation were with us, and our taxi showed up five minutes later. Before we knew it, we were speeding along the George Washington Parkway and the Arlington Memorial Bridge toward the District of Columbia.

"So why are we going to a garden to drink beer tonight, Kit? Has Doug's trust fund dried up?" Sebastian gave me a playful punch on the arm to let me know he was yanking my chain.

"Doug is currently on leave from Georgetown. He's a senior fellow in American history at the Library of Congress's research center. He'll meet us tonight," I said. "And the answer to your question is no. His trust fund has not disappeared. But we both still prefer to work for our living."

"How proletariat of you," said Sebastian. "But you still haven't told me why you've forced me into this monkey suit to meet elected officials who have sold their souls to corporations in exchange for political power."

It never ceased to amaze me how my brother managed to squeeze such an impressive amount of invective into one measly sentence. He was a man fueled by a deeply felt mission. Long ago, I'd traded the polemic for the art of the possible. It was this divide that fueled the estrangement with my brother.

I sighed for the umpteenth time before responding. "It's my job, Sebastian. I'm the chief of staff for a member of the House of Representatives. She's been assigned to a relatively obscure committee called House Administration. It oversees the legislative branch agencies, the Capitol Grounds, and the operations of Congress. I know you're not interested in this, but Capitol Hill is like a small city. And the members of House Administration are the town council."

Sebastian considered my answer for a few moments before speaking. The snide tone was gone. "That's actually kind of cool. So, your boss helps run Congress?"

"Partially. The Speaker appointed her to this committee because she's smart and asks intelligent questions. The nice part about the assignment is that she gets invited to the best events on Capitol Hill. Like tonight."

We'd just driven past the Washington Monument, on our way due east toward the Botanic Garden, which was situated at the base of the Hill between the Hirshhorn Museum and the Capitol Building.

"Why is tonight so special again? There's a special flower you want me to see?"

I punched his arm playfully. "Trust me, Sebastian. Aren't you a fan of the Earth and everything natural? You'll be right at home at the Botanic Garden," I said. "But you're right. You'll see something amazing at the reception this evening."

He cleared his throat. "And what exactly is this awe-inspiring specimen of the plant kingdom?"

In my most ominous voice, I answered my brother. "The corpse flower. We're going to see the corpse flower."

CHAPTER TWO

Sebastian sputtered. "Did you say corpse? As in a dead body?"

I laughed. "You got it. Its name comes from the odor it gives off during its bloom, which is extremely rare. The Botanic Garden is lucky to have one of these plants as part of its collection."

"You mean we're going to a congressional reception that smells like garbage? Truth really is stranger than fiction." Sebastian grinned.

"Good one," I admitted. "I'm not really sure how pungent it will be. All I know is that the flower is only in bloom for two days. And we scheduled this special reception so members of Congress could experience it. The public lines to get a glimpse today were around the block!"

For once, Sebastian seemed impressed. "This is a special privilege?"

"Yes," I said slowly. "Like I said, my boss

is on the oversight committee for the United States Botanic Garden. She'll be there this evening, and since I'm her chief of staff, I was invited."

"Will you know anyone else?" Sebastian asked.

"Doug will attend. Plus, my best friend Meg Peters. I'm not sure you met her before. She works for Representative Dixon as her legislative director. We've worked together for years on Capitol Hill."

"A Kit Marshall acolyte?" he asked coyly.

"Not in the least," I said. "Meg is her own woman. You'll understand once you meet her. She's a force of nature."

Sebastian raised an eyebrow but said nothing. Our cab driver dropped us off on Independence Avenue. That meant we had to walk around the building to enter the conservatory via the vehicular-unfriendly Maryland Avenue entrance.

"Let's walk through the National Garden," I suggested. "It's faster than walking up Third Street."

Sebastian dutifully followed me. My iPhone buzzed. I pulled it out of my purse and swiped it open. Text message from Doug.

Arriving in 5 minutes.

I typed a response.

Here. We'll meet @ bar.

Three dots appeared.

10-4, good brother :)

Doug thought it was funny I was nervous about my brother's visit. I'd tried to warn him that he'd only experienced him once before and it had been a brief encounter. He underestimated the potential impact of Hurricane Sebastian.

We walked through the outdoor section of the complex, which included a rose garden, the First Ladies' water garden, and butterfly garden. We emerged adjacent to the conservatory's entrance.

"That was quite impressive," said Sebastian. "I had no idea there was such a pleasant outdoor area in the middle of Capitol Hill."

"I wish more people took advantage of it," I said as we turned onto the walkway leading to the limestone facade of the main building.

Sebastian looked at the stone greenhouse from top to bottom. "This looks like something you'd see in Europe."

I nodded. "It was built in 1933 by the Architect of the Capitol, the office which is still responsible for the Botanic Garden today. The building's design was modeled after the orangerie at Versailles, and the symmetry of the building mirrored George Washington's greenhouse at Mount Vernon."

"Did you say there's an architect in charge of the Capitol?" asked Sebastian.

"You heard me right. The Architect of the Capitol oversees the maintenance and preservation of the United States Capitol buildings and grounds. That includes all the congressional buildings, the Capitol itself, the visitors center, and even the Supreme Court," I explained.

"That's one headache of a job," murmured Sebastian.

We opened the door to the conservatory and walked inside the greenhouse. Almost immediately, a pungent odor hit us.

"Ugh," said Sebastian. "Is that coming from the flower of death or whatever you called it?"

A young woman wearing a "USBG" baseball hat walked up to us. "Good evening. Welcome to our congressional reception." Then she turned to Sebastian. "Sir, you are correct. The odor you detected is from

Amorphophallus titanum, popularly known as the corpse flower." Smiling widely, she'd either grown accustomed to the smell of rotting flesh or her excitement about the rare bloom had overtaken her senses.

"Why does it smell so bad?" I asked.

"The stench attracts pollinators, such as beetles and flies," she said. "It's part of the natural life process of the plant."

Sebastian and I approached the flower for a closer look. Over eight feet tall, a long rod resembling a telephone pole had emerged from the unfurled bloom. "It smells even worse now," said my brother.

I wrinkled my nose. "Sort of like rotting vegetables, fish, and garlic all rolled up in one."

Our friendly botanist had followed behind us. "Excellent description!" she exclaimed. "That's exactly how many people describe the smell."

"No offense, but can you tell us why this is so special?" We moved several feet away from the flower.

"The corpse flower is the largest unbranched inflorescence in the world. The bloom is so large, it requires years for the plant to store up energy through photosynthesis," she said. "This is not an annual occurrence by any stretch of the imagination."

"I take it we don't have too many of these plants in the United States," said Sebastian.

The USBG employee vigorously nodded. "Absolutely. The plant is from the island of Sumatra. There's not many opportunities to see one outside the tropics."

A crowd of reception attendees had begun to gather behind us. Sebastian and I thanked our guide and moved to the side so others could examine the unusual plant. I noticed a few members of Congress were posing in front of the plant with staffers snapping away on their iPhones. No doubt Twitter would be deluged tonight with the hashtag **#corpseflower.** Most politicians didn't ask questions when they spot an opportunity for a catchy social media photo.

"A flower that smells like a corpse. It's a bit creepy, if you ask me," I said.

Sebastian laughed, his blue eyes twinkling. "I agree, big sister. Let's get a drink."

We made our way along the west side of the garden court, stopping to examine specimens as varied as coconut trees and cacao plants. Finally, we came upon the bar. I spotted Doug standing to the side, glass of wine already in hand.

I grabbed Sebastian's hand and scurried over. Doug gave me a kiss on the cheek and offered his hand to my brother. "Good to see you again, Sebastian. I'm glad you're spending some time with us."

Sebastian shook Doug's hand. "Thank you for hosting me," he said. "Kit tells me you're working on Capitol Hill these days, too. I guess politics runs in the family."

Doug shook his head. "I don't work for a member of Congress. I'm a scholar in residence at the Library of Congress, which is nearby. But it is a lot of fun to work near Kit. Isn't it, darling?"

I managed a smile. "It has been, um, interesting."

"What's so interesting?" I heard a familiar voice behind me.

We turned abruptly. Doug spoke up. "Good evening, Meg. How's your summer going?"

My best friend and colleague was clearly enjoying the warm D.C. weather. She wore a fitted white halter dress with a blue piped trim. In the office today, Meg had worn a blazer over the dress to reflect the House of Representatives rules that sleeveless dresses didn't satisfy the requirements for "professional female attire." However, this was an evening reception and all bets, including the blazer, were off. Meg had the figure and guts to don almost any outfit of high couture. And when she had the chance, she often did.

Meg narrowed her eyes as her gaze fell on Sebastian. "It's suddenly taken an upward turn," she said softly. "You must be Kit's brother she's told me so much about."

Sebastian flashed a thousand-watt smile. "And you must be the best friend she's told me almost nothing about."

Meg offered her hand to Sebastian. Instead of shaking it, he grazed his lips over her palm. They locked eyes for what seemed like an eternity.

"I hate to break up this moment, but would anyone like a drink?" I asked, not bothering to hide the impatience in my voice.

Doug raised his glass. "Already have one."

"Count me in." Meg linked arms with both me and Sebastian.

Meg ordered a glass of bubbly, her favorite libation. I went for a Chardonnay and Sebastian selected a local IPA.

We rejoined Doug at a high-top table adjacent to the bar. "At least the Botanic Garden was sensible enough to put the refreshments far away from the corpse bloom." Doug held his nose in disgust.

"This whole thing is overblown," said Meg. "But it's Capitol Hill and I'm glad they decided to host a reception for those of us who toil away on that blasted committee."

I put my right hand on my hip. "Meg, you know it's an honor to serve on House Administration. The Speaker of the House handpicks the members to serve in the majority."

"It's more like a punishment than a reward," said Meg. "What kind of campaign money can you raise from being on it? I'm telling you. It's penance because our boss has been involved in more than one murder investigation on Capitol Hill."

"Murders?" asked Sebastian with raised eyebrows.

"You heard Meg correctly," said Doug. "Your sister has a penchant for dead bodies."

"Not just dead bodies," explained Meg. "She also has a knack for finding the killers."

I made a "T" signal with my hands. "Timeout for a second. Meg and Doug are right. But these circumstances are nothing more than happenstance. I can't help it if I've stumbled across a few crimes in the past couple of years."

"It's a debatable proposition, Kit," said Doug. "Whether you've stumbled across these crimes or conveniently involved yourself in their resolutions."

I pursed my lips and then smiled. "Guilty as charged."

Sebastian put one arm around me and clinked his glass to mine with the other. "I'm learning a lot about you, Kit Kat. But it sounds like you haven't changed much. Always out to preserve law and order."

I made a face as Meg laughed. "I'll make sure to call you Kit Kat when we're engaged in a serious legislative negotiation someday."

With friends like this, who needs enemies?

I was saved by the bell, better known as Congresswoman Maeve Dixon from North Carolina. She snuck up behind us and announced her presence. "Hello, team!"

On cue, Meg and I turned around and straightened our posture automatically. Maeve was a great member of Congress, personable and generally affable, but she was still our boss. Meg and I never forgot that basic fact. What she said, we did.

Dixon examined our group. She'd met Doug numerous times previously, so it was no surprise her gaze stopped on Sebastian. She extended her hand in his direction and smiled warmly. "I'm Maeve Dixon. You must be Kit's brother."

I held my breath and prayed Sebastian would behave.

My brother flashed his pearly whites in return. "Pleased to meet you. I'm Sebastian Marshall."

Maeve clinked her wineglass to his. "Welcome to Washington, Sebastian. I'm glad you were able to join us this evening to experience the Botanic Garden and the rare bloom of the corpse flower."

I interjected myself into the conversation. "Thank you again for making sure all of us were on the invitation list tonight."

Maeve waved her hand. "We might as well enjoy some sort of benefit from my committee assignment, right?"

Sebastian leaned in. "That's pretty much how our nation's capital works, isn't it? Tit for tat? You scratch my back and I'll scratch yours?"

Maeve wiggled her eyebrows. "Sometimes. After all, the system was built on the premise of compromise. As a member of Congress, I often have to give a lot to get a little." Her eyes twinkled.

My boss's answer was accurate, but I didn't like the direction this was headed. I shot Doug a desperate glance. He fiddled with his glasses and spoke up. "Congresswoman, I'm greatly enjoying my fellowship at the Library of Congress. I thought you'd like to know," he said flatly.

At least Doug had tried, although it hadn't been a riveting conversation changer. Meg hadn't picked up on the awkward chatter. She was too busy enjoying her drink and scrutinizing Sebastian. My best pal hadn't taken her eyes off him since they were introduced.

"That's nice to hear," said Maeve politely. "The Library of Congress is a national treasure."

Unfortunately, Maeve had given Sebastian yet another opening. "Speaking of national treasures, Congresswoman, what do you think we should do about climate change? In fifty years, Miami and southeastern Florida might be under water due to rising sea levels."

If Dixon was caught off guard by Sebastian's probing questions, she didn't show it. Without batting an eyelash, she said, "We should take sensible steps now to prevent it from happening, of course."

Sebastian took a deep breath. I knew where this was headed. He was about to barrage her with a litany of facts and end his diatribe with a condemnation of national leadership on the issue. I'd heard it before, and so had my boss.

I beat him to the punch. "Thank goodness the Botanic Garden is doing its part.

There's solar panels on the roof, making them a leader on Capitol Hill for conservation. I think we should celebrate the initiative."

Doug picked up on my diversion. "I second Kit's toast. Let's all drink to the Botanic Garden!"

A female voice spoke over our clinking of glasses. "Congresswoman Dixon is leading a toast and neglected to ask me to join?"

Rhonda Jackson, the chair of the House Administration Committee, stepped forward. Maeve moved aside to make room for her.

"Not on purpose," said Maeve. "I was just enjoying a drink with my staff."

Jackson, an African American woman in her early seventies who'd served in Congress for decades representing Cleveland, gave a polite nod. "Good to see everyone here," she said. Then she pulled Dixon to the side. "You need to mingle and meet important people. Follow me."

Jackson's firm tone hadn't given Maeve the option of staying. Our boss followed dutifully after the chairwoman.

Meg giggled. "It's fun to see her get bossed around every once in a while."

"I have to agree, Meg," I said. "Do you think I should have followed?" As Dixon's chief of staff, I tried to keep track of who the congresswoman met and where.

Meg stood up on her tiptoes so she could see where they'd gone. "Nah, I don't think so. It looks like they're talking to the Architect of the Capitol. Maeve doesn't need any introductions there."

Melinda Masters had been named to the prestigious position earlier this year. Since House Administration maintained oversight over the Architect of the Capitol, Masters made the rounds with current members of the committee before her confirmation process concluded in the Senate. In her mid-forties, Masters was the first woman in American history to be named Architect of the Capitol. It was quite an honor, and our boss had been eager to support publicly the ground-breaking nomination.

"Is Masters actually an architect?" asked Doug.

"As a matter of fact, Melinda Masters is an architect," said Meg. "She's also had a lot of management experience in the private and public sector. An impressive person, as I recall."

I nodded. "Her nomination sailed through. No one voted against her."

"That's highly unusual these days," said Doug. "She must have made quite a positive impression."

"Some people just have that certain *je ne sais quoi,*" said Meg. "It enables them to tackle herculean tasks, like charming Capitol Hill." She smiled mischievously.

"Speaking of impossible feats, can you tell me if you made any progress on the staff picnic?" I asked.

Meg sighed. "Really, you had to ask?"

"I did put you in charge of the planning as our legislative director."

"I'm not sure picnic planning fits neatly into my job description," said Meg. "But don't worry. Our picnic will happen. And it will be a lot of fun."

"Have you resolved the conflict between our two young staffers?"

"If you mean the May–December romance, then yes."

"I don't care if they're dating or not, but I want to make sure we have a picnic with burgers, hot dogs, and refreshing drinks for the entire Maeve Dixon staff this Saturday," I said. "Can you assure me that will happen?"

Meg crossed her fingers in an "X" over her heart. "I promise. Even if I have to man the grill myself."

"No lady should have to do that," said Sebastian.

Meg batted her eyelashes. "What a gentleman," she said. "You'd like to come to the picnic and do the honors."

"He's not sure if he'll be in Washington that long," I said quickly. "Right, Sebastian?"

My brother cleared his throat. "That's true," he said slowly. "It's not certain."

Meg, who loved to live for the moment, brushed off his comment. She flashed a toothy smile. Spotting that Sebastian's glass was empty, she asked, "Anyone like to join me for a refill?"

"Sure, why not? I did my burpees and push-ups today," he said.

Meg touched his upper arm. "I see you have. Very muscular. You'll have to tell me about your strenuous exercise regimen." They took off for the bar, which now had quite a line. Apparently, the corpse flower was not to be missed.

Doug leaned in and gave me a peck on the cheek. "Sebastian doesn't seem so bad, Kit."

"Give him a little time. He's just getting his bearings. Then he'll swing into action," I said. "Believe me."

"He is your brother, so I suppose you know best," said Doug. "Try to enjoy the time with him."

36

"I know. We haven't seen much of each other recently." I mustered a smile. "Good advice."

Our chat was interrupted by a trim older man dressed in a light blue perfectly fitted seersucker suit. Obviously not one to shy away from making a fashion statement, he also wore a matching cobalt bow tie. "Excuse me for interrupting," he said with a southern accent. "But aren't you Maeve Dixon's chief of staff?"

Doug took a step back. He knew the drill when he crashed my receptions, dinners, and happy hours.

"Yes, I am." I extended my hand and reached inside my suit pocket for a business card.

"Kit Marshall, a pleasure to meet you, ma'am," he said. "I'm Grant Dawson. I wanted to personally welcome you to the Botanic Garden this evening."

"How nice of you," I said. "This is my husband Doug Hollingsworth. We were delighted to see the corpse flower."

Grant waved his hand. "It's a good gimmick for us. Every couple of years, they break the doors down to see the darn thing bloom and smell up the entire place."

"I'm guessing you work here," I said.

"I'm the executive director," he explained.

"Oh," I said, blushing. "I'm sorry I didn't recognize your name. I apologize. Representative Dixon is new to the House Administration committee, as you know. We're getting up to speed on all the important people."

"No worries, darling. That's why I came over to say hello," said Grant, who smoothed the remaining hairs on his mostly bald head.

"I appreciate your understanding." I scanned the crowd. "You've got a full house this evening."

"Not only a full house, but the right people showed up, too," said Grant. "We have some heavy hitters tonight, including your boss."

I wasn't sure a two-term congresswoman qualified as a heavy hitter, but I didn't protest. After all, Grant Dawson had come over to make a good impression.

Doug looked over Grant's shoulder. "Who else of note is here?" he asked.

Grant rubbed his chin. "Well, you've got the Comptroller General of the United States here. He's the bulky guy standing next to the Architect."

I turned to catch a glimpse. "Wait a second," I said. "I remember his name. It's Italian . . . I know it sounds like a cheese I like."

Doug narrowed his eyes. "Mozzarella? Provolone?"

I snapped my fingers. "Romano! Gordon Romano, right?"

Grant laughed. "You got it. He's been the head of the Government Accountability Office for a while. But he still has a few more years left on his fifteen-year term."

"That's one of the most important Washington jobs no one knows anything about," said Doug.

"I'd have to agree with my husband," I said. "G-A-O helps Congress assess government performance and hold executive branch agencies accountable. Without their work, we'd have no idea what was going on in the bureaucracy."

"No argument there," said Grant. "Let's put it this way. We make sure Mr. Romano gets the plants he wants to decorate his office suite."

"Smart move," I said. "Anyone else I should know?"

Grant craned his neck to survey the crowd. He leaned closer and whispered. "Of course, there's Representative Cartwright. She's not a favorite in our neck of the woods."

"She's not a favorite anywhere," I said. "I don't know too much about committee politics, but I know Cartwright can be a troublemaker. Thankfully, she's not on our side of the aisle." Cartwright served in the minority on House Administration and often liked to cause a ruckus in hearings.

"I'll say," said Grant. "She keeps my boss Melinda hopping."

"Now I understand," said Doug. "The Architect of the Capitol is your supervisor."

Grant pulled his shoulders back. "Absolutely. Technically, the Architect is the Acting Director of the Botanic Garden, too. But in practice, I'm in charge of the daily operations as the executive director."

"That seems like a sensible arrangement," I said.

Grant took a big sip and finished his glass of wine. "Most days, I suppose."

Doug and I exchanged a knowing glance. No surprise there was trouble in paradise. Whether it was guns, butter, or plants, there was bound to be a debate in Washington over it. Nothing escaped controversy.

Grant motioned toward the bar. "There's Steve Song," he said. "The distinguished, fit gentleman with greying hair and a blue tie."

I craned my neck to spot him. "I see who you mean, but I don't know his position."

"You wouldn't know Steve unless you were deep in the weeds." He grinned devilishly. "Pun intended, given our location."

Grant's wit was entertaining, to say the least. "Who is he?" I asked.

"He's the deputy Architect. Lifelong employee of the A-O-C." Grant fingered his empty wineglass. "Steve got passed over when they appointed Melinda Masters to the big job."

"You didn't approve?" asked Doug.

Grant scratched the back of his head, probably trying to decide how much he wanted to reveal to a congressional staffer charged with oversight of his operation. "I don't make those calls," he said evenly. "The President appoints and the Senate confirms. They must have seen something they liked in Melinda. Steve is a good soldier, but oftentimes that's not enough."

I decided to let Grant off the hook. It wasn't my intent to interrogate a senior official during a reception. On the other hand, I did need to get up to speed on the important players in the committee's jurisdiction.

I offered Grant my hand. "Thank you for the conversation. I appreciated the warm welcome tonight."

He straightened his bow tie. "It was an honor and a pleasure, Ms. Marshall." He took my hand and gave me a peck on the top of it. "I look forward to working with you and Representative Dixon. I'm right happy to have a fellow southerner on our oversight committee."

"Thank you," I said. "You certainly have impeccable manners."

His eyes twinkled. "Don't be a stranger, now. You walk down that hill every once in a while, and come see what we're doing here at the garden." He waggled his fingers at us. "Ta ta. Gotta make the rounds!"

I turned to face Doug. "What a card. You never know who you're going to meet at these receptions."

My husband ran his fingers through his bushy hair. "No kidding. I felt like he was straight out of casting for *Midnight in the Garden of Good and Evil.*"

"Well, you know what rule number one is, right?" I asked.

"You got me," said Doug. "I haven't read that book or seen the movie in years."

I raised my empty glass. "Always stick around for one more drink."

"That's my cue to get you a refill," said Doug. "I'll be right back."

In the meantime, I took off to locate Meg and Sebastian. They'd been gone for a while, and I wasn't sure what to make of that pairing. After two tumultuous relationships, Meg had forsworn men for a spell.

Her respite had worked out quite well, much better than I had anticipated. She'd taken up jogging and had found time to focus more on herself. Several hipster hobbies, such as canning, beekeeping, and knitting, had already gone by the wayside. Nonetheless, I was confident Meg had emerged on the other side of the forest as more grounded, mature, and self-aware.

I found Meg and Sebastian in the corner of the garden courtyard, hovering over cacao plants like they might yield a carton of Hershey bars any moment. I cleared my throat while approaching. "Hmm . . . excuse me, I hope I'm not interrupting?"

Their heads were plastered so close to each other, they might as well have been sharing a state secret about the nuclear codes. Within a second of the question, they split apart and turned in my direction.

"Not at all," said Meg sheepishly.

"Meg was explaining . . ." stuttered Sebastian. "How Congress works."

"Amazing," I said. "If Meg was able to do that, she should win a Nobel Prize."

Meg put her right hand on her hip. "I was providing Sebastian with a basic understanding. There's nothing wrong with that."

"Certainly not." Doug handed me a glass of white wine. Without indulging in any of the pedestrian cheese, rubbery crackers, uninspired hummus, and semi-wilted fruit available at a run-of-the-mill federal government reception, I couldn't have much more than a few mouthfuls before growing tipsy. I cautiously sipped my drink.

"Sebastian, what are your impressions of your first congressional event?" Doug asked.

I shot my husband a sharp sideways glance. I'd tried to warn him about Sebastian and his predilections.

My brother ran his fingers through his sandy locks. "It's impressive, of course." He scanned the room warily. "There aren't any photographers here, are there?"

Meg touched his arm lightly. "If there were, I'd ask them to get a closeup of us." She winked mischievously.

"I haven't seen any," said Doug. "Private congressional events are usually off the record. Aren't they, Kit?"

I nodded. "I suspect Sebastian doesn't want anyone else to know he was hobknobbing with the insider Washington crowd."

Sebastian stuttered. "One photo on Twitter can really go a long way. After all, I've got a reputation to uphold."

Meg chimed in. "Don't we all? I hate it when a photo of me goes online and I don't approve."

Meg didn't realize Sebastian could care less about his appearance. I had a strong suspicion his close circle of friends wouldn't approve of a wine and cheese reception at the Botanic Garden to celebrate the blooming of a rare flower. Before my luck ran out, it was time for our departure.

"Time for dinner?" I asked. "We can head somewhere on Capitol Hill or even Eastern Market." The nearby neighborhood next to the Hill had exploded in recent years, resulting in a number of trendy bars, restaurants, and nighttime entertainment.

"Absolutely," said Meg. "I'm starving."

I sighed inwardly. My best friend had been blessed with rare genetics that enabled her to eat and drink whatever she pleased and never add an ounce to her slim frame. The fairy godmother who had bestowed this gift upon Meg had undoubtedly passed me over. If I smelled a chocolate chip cookie, I gained three pounds.

"Let's hit the road," said Doug as he wrinkled his nose. "The corpse flower has run its course, I think."

As we moved toward the exit near the center of the garden court, I noticed the crowd had thinned considerably. Representative Dixon was headed for the door. I waved to get her attention before she left.

"Everything go okay this evening, Congresswoman?" I asked.

"Sure," she said. "But there's only so much time you can spend inside a confined space with a huge plant that smells like dirty diapers."

I chuckled. There was a lot I liked about my boss, not the least her sharp wit.

"I'll see you tomorrow morning," I said. "Don't forget to read that memo on your upcoming committee hearing."

Maeve waved her hand to acknowledge my admonition and then leaned in closer and lowered her voice. "Be sure to spend some time with your brother, Kit." She looked me straight in the eye. "Work is important, but so is family."

My boss's remark caught me off guard since she rarely commented on personal matters. I managed a barely audible, "Yes, ma'am" before rejoining the group.

"Everything alright?" Meg asked.

"She's headed out now, so it's all clear for us to leave," I said. "Looks like it's wrapping up."

We walked out of the conservatory and headed in the direction of the butterfly garden. Doug pointed toward the center of the park adjacent to the conservatory.

"What's that area over there?"

We walked in the direction he indicated, and we came across a large shallow water fountain surrounded by a two-toned granite esplanade. Tables and chairs provided a quiet place to relax.

Meg's forehead wrinkled. "I've never seen this place before in my life. And I thought I knew everything about Capitol Hill."

"Correction," said Doug. "You know every restaurant and bar in Capitol Hill. Outdoor gardens without booze don't qualify."

Meg crossed her arms. "Very funny, Doug."

My husband and best friend were polar opposites. Occasionally, their diversity of views led to verbal repartee. Hopefully they'd keep it civil for Sebastian's sake.

Meg found a small plaque near the edge of the fountain. "Welcome to the First Ladies' Water Garden," she announced. "It commemorates the contributions of our nation's First Ladies. The design of the fountain mimics the classic Martha Washington quilt pattern."

"That's pretty cool," said Sebastian. "I usually don't get to see these sights when I'm in Washington."

"Why's that?" asked Meg. "I thought everyone who visited D.C. went sightseeing.

Most days I could count a hundred tour buses in ten minutes on Independence Avenue."

"That's because he's usually carrying a sign and avoiding arrest when he's here," I said. "My brother is a professional protestor."

I thought my revelation might dampen Meg's interest in Sebastian. Instead, she gave him a playful nudge. "Activists are so sexy."

"Time to eat," I said, pointedly changing the conversation. "Where should we go? We're dressed too nicely to walk. Let's find a ride to Eastern Market."

"Wait a minute," said Meg. "Before you do that, I need to go to the bathroom."

Doug sighed. "Really? You couldn't have gone before we left the reception?" Meg's sometimes scatter-brained demeanor grated on his nerves, particularly when he hadn't eaten. Doug's picture should be included in the Oxford dictionary's definition of "hangry."

"Sorry," she said. "My mind was focused on other things."

"Like ogling Kit's brother," said Doug underneath his breath.

Meg put her hands on her hips. "What did you say?"

I answered for Doug. "Nothing. Why don't you head back to the reception and see if you can use the restroom there? Then we'll go to dinner. But make it quick." I wiped moisture off my forehead. "It's hot out here."

"Good idea." Meg sprinted off in the direction of the conservatory. "Meet me on Maryland Avenue," she called over her shoulder.

Sebastian, Doug, and I drifted back to the sidewalk outside the butterfly garden. "Tell me more about your friend Meg," said Sebastian. His eyes sparkled with interest.

"She's not dating these days," I said quickly. "Let's not go there."

"Meg is attractive," said Doug. "But I'm not sure she's your type. I don't see her taking to the streets anytime soon to protest the world's injustices."

"Not unless the protest was taking place inside Nordstrom's," I said. "If you could arrange that location for a demonstration, then you could persuade her to make an appearance."

Doug and Sebastian both chuckled. But their laughter was interrupted suddenly by a bloodcurdling scream from inside the conservatory.

"That sounds like Meg!" I exclaimed.

"Come on."

We rushed over to the entrance, pulled open the door, and entered the garden court. Meg was standing next to the blooming corpse flower. I didn't even notice the odor because I was fixated on her terrified face.

I ran to her and put my hands on her shoulders. "Meg, what's wrong? It looks like you've just seen a ghost."

"Worse than that," she sputtered, gesturing wildly behind her.

"Is something wrong inside the tropical rainforest?" I asked.

"You could say so," Meg gasped. "Someone's dead."

CHAPTER THREE

Meg froze in front of the glass door, immobilized by whatever she saw on the other side. I yelled to my brother. "Sebastian, stay with her. I'm going inside to find out what happened."

The lush greenery surrounding me was usually delightful, a peaceful refuge bursting with bright, colorful flowers and verdant plants underneath a glass dome. This evening, there was no one inside the indoor tropical forest, and the thick fauna and flora felt like a blanket threatening to suffocate me. It didn't help that the Botanic Garden set the humidity at over ninety percent. Combined with the July heat, I was sweating the moment after stepping inside the leafy sauna.

My eyes adjusted to the lower light levels at the bottom of the green canopy. A long fountain pool ran the entire length of the rainforest, a miniature river winding through the vegetation. The reception had been confined to the exterior garden court area, so the tropics exhibit hadn't been open for guests. Why had Meg wandered into the off-limits area?

I walked slowly down the path alongside the pool. The gurgling from the water, which normally added to the tranquil ambiance, unnerved me. I studied the fountain. Was the body in the water? Nothing seemed amiss. I reached the end of the walkway and looked to my right. I jerked backward. A human hand stuck out at the path's bend.

I took several deep breaths. At least I'd found what I was looking for. I walked cautiously toward the hand, undoubtedly attached to the dead body Meg had discovered.

Before rounding the corner, I mentally prepared myself for what I might see. I'd come across dead people before, but it wasn't an everyday occurrence. Looking back on it, no amount of time would have psychologically equipped me for the gruesome spectacle.

Melinda Masters lay on her back. However, Melinda hadn't died a natural death. A long, brown vine was tightly wound around her throat like a necklace. I bent down on my haunches to see if she was breathing. She was perfectly still, so I doubted she'd survived the vicious attack. I couldn't detect any sign of life, but just in case, I grabbed the makeup compact out of my purse. I stuck the mirror underneath her nose. After confirming there was no sign of respiration, I grabbed her wrist. Ditto for a pulse. The Architect of the Capitol had been strangled inside the Botanic Garden of the United States. I dropped her wrist and fell backward on my butt, bumping into something. I turned around to see what I'd hit, and I did a double take.

It was a small exhibit sign, identifying the plant species on display. They were all over the garden, both inside and outside. The label might as well have been in neon lights. It read, *"Ficus aurea"* in large italicized letters at the top. It was the words in capitals underneath that startled me. "STRANGLER FIG."

I was staring at the sign when I heard footsteps coming my way and then Doug's voice. "Kit, where are you?"

I yelled. "At the end of the fountain path. Come quickly!"

I brushed off my clothes and stood. Doug appeared with Grant Dawson right behind him. I gesticulated wildly. "Over here! It's Melinda Masters. She's been murdered!"

The three of us surrounded the body and stared at poor Melinda. Grant pulled out a handkerchief from his breast pocket and wiped the sweat off his forehead. "Heavens to Betsy," he muttered. "What in the hell happened here?"

"That vine didn't wind itself around her neck," said Doug. "Someone killed her. But when?"

Grant shook his head. "I have no idea. The reception ended about fifteen minutes ago. It must have happened sometime around then."

"Her hand was still warm when I checked for a pulse," I said. "She hasn't been dead for long. Besides, we saw her at the party." I turned to Doug. "Do you remember when we spotted her?"

"It was before we talked to Grant," said Doug. "I'd say between thirty and forty-five minutes ago."

I checked my Fitbit for the time. It flashed 7:15. "That means the murder probably took place between six-thirty and seven."

"That seems right," said Doug. "Not a big window of time."

Grant backed away from us. "You'll have to excuse me. This is a little too much for my delicate southern senses."

I put my hand on his arm. "I'm sorry,

Grant. We're being insensitive. This is your boss and someone you knew well."

He pointed in the direction of Melinda's body. "How she died," he choked. "I can't believe someone used one of our plants as a murder weapon."

I didn't dare touch the vine wound around Melinda's neck. Instead, I walked over to the tree adjacent to the crime scene. "This is *ficus aurea*?"

Grant nodded numbly. "It's called the strangler fig for a specific reason."

We waited for him to continue. Finally, Doug prodded him gently. "Which is what, Mr. Dawson?"

"In order to grow, it strangles a host tree." Grant gulped. "The only way it survives is by encircling its victim and killing it."

The terrible reality of Grant's words reverberated within the otherwise peaceful tropical garden.

CHAPTER FOUR

We couldn't dwell upon Grant's revelation for too long. Silence was interrupted with a familiar, booming voice.

"Step away from the victim!"

Our eyes followed the command. A paunchy, middle-aged man stood at the edge of the fountain. He was dressed in khakis and a button-down shirt, but I knew from past experience he was no civilian.

I took several steps toward our latest arrival. "Detective O'Halloran. It's been a while since we've seen each other." I extended my hand to the beefy cop.

O'Halloran scrunched up his face in a half-hearted grimace as he shook my hand lightly. "Ms. Marshall. Why am I not surprised you're involved when there's a dead body found on Capitol Hill?"

"I don't go looking trouble," I protested.

"And yet a cloud of chaos seems to follow you." The glint in his eye indicated he was only partially serious. A detective serving on Congress's own police force, O'Halloran would have jurisdiction on the crime. We'd worked together previously to solve murders on Capitol Hill. A sensible detente seemed to govern our relationship. As long as I didn't overstep my bounds and kept him informed about the case, he'd grown to appreciate my amateur sleuthing. Maybe "appreciate" was too strong. In reality, he tried unsuccessfully to keep me out of harm's way.

"Detective, you remember Doug Hollingsworth? We're now married." I flashed O'Halloran my wedding ring.

"Congratulations. Read about it in the *Washington Post.* Did you go on one of those murder mystery weekends for your honeymoon?" he asked wryly.

I ignored his question. "And this is Grant Dawson, the executive director of the Botanic Garden."

Dawson nodded politely to O'Halloran.

"I assume you discovered the body?" O'Halloran motioned toward me.

I shook my head vigorously. "Nope. It was my friend Meg Peters."

O'Halloran rolled his eyes. "Not blondie. She's involved in this mess, too?"

"I'm afraid so, Detective," I said.

57

"Well, it looks like the gang's all here," he said. "It's a bonafide party, except for the deceased here." He motioned toward the ground. "Do we know who she is?"

Grant spoke up. "Yes, Detective. It's my boss, the Architect of the Capitol, Melinda Masters."

Detective O'Halloran let out a low whistle and bent down to examine the body. "No kidding, you're right. I thought she looked familiar." He looked up at us. "This is going to make a lot of headlines in Washington."

O'Halloran's comments put my political instincts in gear. I'd better let my boss know what had happened.

"Excuse me, Detective. May I step outside to make a phone call?" I asked.

"That's fine. I'd like everyone to give us some space," he said. Several other uniformed Capitol Hill police officers had arrived on the scene.

"We'll leave you to it," I said.

O'Halloran spun around. "But don't leave the Botanic Garden. I'll need official statements. And tell your best buddy Meg that I need to speak with her immediately."

I gave O'Halloran a mini-salute to let him now I understood his instructions. Doug, Grant, and I hustled out of the tropics

58

exhibit and returned to the garden court area. The pungent smell of the corpse flower had grown stronger.

"Ugh," I said. "I can't stand near that plant for one more second. Where's Meg and Sebastian? Hopefully they didn't go far."

Grant stared at the corpse flower. "As it blooms and opens up, the odor will intensify. I never thought we'd have an actual corpse inside the Botanic Garden."

"The victim probably wanted to get away from the stink," I muttered, almost to myself.

Doug must have heard me. He tapped my arm and pointed to the left. "Let's retrace our steps from this evening."

The reception area was now empty. A few waitstaff were picking up dirty glasses and plates left behind. "Detective O'Halloran will want to speak to everyone here," I said.

Doug nodded. Meg and Sebastian were still nowhere to be found. Then I heard high-pitched sobbing coming from the direction of the East Gallery.

We pushed through the glass door to find Meg huddled in the corner with Sebastian. My brother's arm was lightly draped over her shoulder, but the look on his face indicated he'd already gone above and beyond the call of duty.

Sure enough, as soon as he saw me, he disentangled himself and rushed over. "Meg is very upset. I didn't want to leave her to go look for you. Did you see the dead person?" He leaned closer to me, whispering, "Or was she imagining it?"

"She wasn't imagining," I said in a low voice so only he could hear. Louder, I said, "I found the body, Meg."

My best friend had a reputation for occasionally acting like a drama queen. Actually, well before I met her, she apparently was an actual drama queen. The star of many high school and college plays, Meg could really play to a room — or, in this case, to an unattached and handsome guy named Sebastian.

I didn't need to go into all of this with my brother. Still, it was time to let him off the hook. After all, he hadn't come to Washington to solve a murder. I'm sure there was a protest or rally he would join tomorrow. No doubt, our sojourn this evening had turned into more than what he'd bargained for.

I put my arm around Meg. "Are you okay?"

Her eyes were moist, her makeup showing the earliest signs of damage. She wiped the small tears away from her eyes, carefully avoiding her eyeliner so it wouldn't streak. Even in a crisis, Meg found a way to preserve her impeccable appearance. You had to hand it to a gal who didn't mess up her eyes after finding a dead body.

She sniffled. "I'm calming down. I think I was in shock for a bit."

"Completely understandable," I said. "What happened, Meg? When you left us, you were headed inside the Botanic Garden to use the restroom."

Meg nodded. "I went inside, but I realized I didn't know where the facilities are located. Then I saw a sign for the restrooms on the glass door for the tropics exhibit, so I just decided to walk in and find them there."

"Ah," I said. "I wondered why you'd gone inside. That area wasn't open during the reception."

"I know," said Meg. "But I figured no one would mind if I used the restroom quickly and left. I walked down the path and that's when I saw that poor woman's body lying on the ground with something around her neck."

"Did you recognize the victim?" I asked.

She shook her head vigorously back and forth. "I got one glimpse and ran out of there as fast as possible. You know the rest of the story."

I squeezed Meg tighter before giving her the bad news. "The woman you found was Melinda Masters."

Meg edged backward from my one-armed embrace. "The Architect of the Capitol?"

"I'm afraid so. This will be a high-profile investigation."

"And she was murdered?"

Grant stepped in and explained the strangler fig around her neck. Meg shuddered. "Someone ripped a vine off a tree inside the Botanic Garden and killed the Architect of the Capitol?"

"Not quite sure if it was ripped off the tree or not," said Grant. "Those vines are damn strong. It's more likely someone grabbed a long one, wrapped it around her neck, and strangled her. Sort of like a lasso attached to a tree."

Our mouths dropped open at Grant's horrific depiction of the murder. Meg looked as though she might burst into tears again. Sebastian held his stomach, as if he'd suddenly become nauseous. Only Doug appeared unfazed. On the contrary, I detected the glint of excitement in eyes.

My husband turned to me. "Kit, didn't you want to make a phone call? To Maeve Dixon, I presume? And shouldn't Meg speak with Detective O'Halloran?"

"O'Halloran?" asked Meg. "He's here?"

"I forgot to mention it," I said. "It seems as though he's the investigating detective for the case."

Meg rolled her eyes. "I guess it's better to deal with the devil we know," she murmured.

"I think so. At least you'll be dealing with a familiar face." I added, "He was looking forward to talking with you." She didn't need to know about the "blondie" comment.

"Why don't I take Meg to the detective," offered Doug. "You stay here with Sebastian and make your phone call."

"Thank you, Doug," I said. "We'll meet back here as soon as the police have spoken with Meg."

"I appreciate you rescuing me from your friend," said Sebastian. "She was flipping out."

"It's traumatic to find a dead body, Sebastian," I said.

My brother tilted his head to the side. "And how would you know that, Kit Kat?"

"You remember the conversation from earlier tonight. I've been involved in a couple murder investigations in Washington."

"In which you stumbled across dead people?" he asked, his eyebrows raised.

"A few times, yes. I understand what Meg is going through."

Sebastian snorted. "Here I thought you were living a boring life in D.C., toiling away on behalf of faceless politicians to no avail."

I winced at Sebastian's description of my job.

He continued. "But now I know the true story. Your congressional position is simply a cover for your real vocation as an amateur sleuth."

I pursed my lips. "I'm an amateur sleuth for a reason, Sebastian. People want my help to solve these crimes, and I'm in the position to provide it. But it's not how I make my living."

"Until Detective whomever hires you to help him solve all the big crimes that come his way," said Sebastian.

I waved my hand. "I don't have time for this nonsense. I need to call my boss." I reached inside my purse for my iPhone.

"Why are you so uptight about checking in with her?" Sebastian asked indifferently.

"Sebastian, she's an elected official, and she was just at a reception where a high-ranking government official was strangled. I think she needs to know about it." I didn't bother to hide the annoyance in my voice.

He put his hands up defensively. "Geesh. Sorry I asked about it."

I shouldn't have been so short with him. It wasn't his fault he didn't understand the challenges of my job. I'd apologize later. Right now, I needed to get Maeve on the line. I punched her number, saved in my "favorites" contact list. Besides Doug and Meg, there was no one else I called more frequently.

Thankfully, she picked up immediately. "Is something the matter, Kit?" My boss didn't mince words.

I recounted the unfolding crisis, including the identity of the murder victim. The phone went silent for several seconds.

"Ma'am, are you still there? Did you hear what I said about Melinda Masters?" I asked.

"Yes, I heard. Let me think for a moment," said Maeve.

Thirty seconds later, her voice came back on the line. "Kit, please stay at the Botanic Garden. I'll call you back in five minutes or so."

I responded affirmatively and clicked off the call. She must have something up her sleeve.

"Everything okay?" Sebastian asked.

"She's going to call me back shortly. Listen, I'm sorry I snapped at your earlier. The job I have. . . ." I paused to find the right words. "It's demanding, Sebastian. And it's a lot of responsibility."

His face softened. "I get it. You're in the belly of the beast. It's not easy."

"No, but I enjoy it. By the way, are you sticking around Washington for a while? What are your plans?" When Sebastian had emailed to let me know about his visit, he hadn't mentioned how long he planned to stay.

Sebastian pushed a stray hair out of the way. "Not sure. There are a few organizations I'm touching base with this week."

Organization was a Sebastian code word. He meant a protest was brewing.

"Be careful," I warned. "I can't take any time off work to bail you out of jail."

He grinned sheepishly. "Don't worry, sis. Remember, this isn't my first rodeo."

He had a point. Sebastian had been demonstrating for causes since he was in high school. Bringing attention to his pet issues was in his blood, much like politics was in mine.

"How's Mom and Dad?" I asked softly.

Our parents had sold the family home a

couple years ago. They traveled the world, staying in different places for varying amounts of time, dependent on how much fun they were having and how many vineyards they could visit.

"Oh, you know. They're the same," said Sebastian, shrugging half-heartedly. "Every once in a while, we happen to find ourselves in the same city. We touch base then."

"They didn't make it to my wedding," I said. "Of course, neither did you."

Sebastian rubbed the back of his neck. "Sorry about that. I got your email about it. But there was a big global justice rally in Seattle."

"Don't worry about it. I understand." I forced a smile. Years ago, I'd learned to accept Sebastian and my parents for who they were as opposed to conventional ideals of familial bliss. It had made me a fiercely independent woman, for better or worse.

Sebastian looked me square in the eye. "Mom and Dad are really proud of you, Kit."

"I know they are." My parents valued self-reliance more than anything. Mumbling, I added, "Still would have been nice to make an appearance at my wedding."

Before Sebastian could comment, my iPhone rang. Shanice's "I Love Your Smile" interrupted our conversation.

"That's a catchy ringtone, Kit Kat," joked Sebastian, breaking the heaviness of our conversation.

"It does the trick," I said, with a smile on my face.

I swiped open my phone and answered, "Congresswoman, I'm here."

After listening carefully to Maeve, I squeezed my eyes shut. My boss's instructions were not going to play well.

"Are you sure that's what you want me to do?" I asked.

Maeve Dixon's voice raised an octave. I held my iPhone away from my ear so her increasingly loud response wouldn't damage my eardrums.

After she was done, I returned the phone to my ear. "Yes, ma'am. You've made yourself absolutely clear. I will meet the Chairwoman in ten minutes."

I punched the button and ended the call, shaking my head.

Sebastian wrinkled his forehead. "What was that all about?"

"My boss spoke with the chair of the House Administration committee, Rhonda Jackson," I explained. "She wants to keep a close eye on the investigation of Melinda Masters's death."

"That's understandable," said Sebastian slowly. "That committee has oversight over the Botanic Garden, right?"

"You're a quick learner," I said. "I guess my boss volunteered me to serve as the liaison between the police and the committee."

"Why you?" He hit his forehead. "Of course. Because you've helped to solve murders before."

"You got it," I said. "Chairwoman Jackson jumped at the offer for me to run point on this. In fact, she's returning to the Botanic Garden shortly to tell Detective O'Halloran personally." I tried to hide the excitement in my voice. Another fortuitous opportunity to solve a crime on Capitol Hill had presented itself, and I'd managed to become involved in another murder.

"I bet that will go over like a lead balloon," said Sebastian.

"He won't love it. But I've worked well with O'Halloran before." I turned toward Sebastian. "The bad news is the investigation might tie me up the next couple of days. I'm not sure how much time we'll get to spend together."

So much for my boss's pronouncement earlier in the night that family was important. Of course, she'd said in the same breath that work was important, too.

Sebastian put his arm around me and gave me a hug. "Don't worry about it. Maybe I can help with the investigation."

"In between your demonstrations?" I asked jokingly.

"Touché," he said. "I guess we'll both be pretty busy."

"I need to head back to the main door so I can greet the Chairwoman and take her to O'Halloran," I said. "Let's head that way."

We exited the East Gallery and walked down the long corridor toward the corpse flower. As soon as we arrived at the entrance to the Botanic Garden, the door opened, and Chairwoman Jackson emerged.

Despite her age, Jackson had a reputation of being a real firecracker. She didn't let anything slow down her agenda.

"Madam Chair," I said tentatively. "I'm Kit Marshall, chief of staff for Maeve Dixon. My boss called me a few minutes ago and asked that I introduce you to the lead detective on the murder investigation."

Jackson pushed her glasses up and studied me. "So, you're the congressional staffer turned detective." By the way she said it, she didn't seem impressed.

"Yes, I've assisted in several cases in the past year or two," I said.

70

"Well, I don't have anyone on my staff who has a shred of experience in murder," she said. "You're the best we have to offer. At least you understand the relationships on Capitol Hill and how they work."

Not a ringing endorsement, but it would suffice. And she was right, I did know how Capitol Hill worked after over five years in various jobs. "Would you like to stay here while I ask Detective O'Halloran to step out to speak with you?"

"Is Melinda inside there?" She pointed toward the tropics exhibit. Through the glass doors and walls, it was obvious that's where the flurry of activity was focused.

"Unfortunately, yes. Another staffer from our office found her when she returned to the reception to use the restroom," I explained.

Jackson rubbed her chin as she considered my explanation. "I think I'd like to see it with my own eyes."

I nodded. Jackson was as tough as nails. I motioned for Sebastian to stay behind as I escorted the Chairwoman to the crime scene. This was highly unconventional, but Jackson's committee also oversaw the Capitol Hill police force. I doubted O'Halloran could refuse her request to survey the scene.

We made our way down the fountain path,

but we didn't get very far before a police officer stopped us.

"Sorry, ladies. This is a crime scene, and I can't let you go any further," said the young cop.

Jackson took it in stride and introduced herself. Even after she explained who she was, the rookie was having none of it. He refused to let us through. Then I spotted Meg, standing to the side. She had either just spoken with O'Halloran or was waiting to do so.

"Meg, over here!" I motioned with my arms to attract attention.

She looked our way and realized Rhonda Jackson had accompanied me. Always a woman of action, Meg marched over to the veteran detective and tugged on his sleeve. She pointed in our direction, and O'Halloran's gaze followed. The portly police officer inhaled deeply and sighed. In Washington, even a murder investigation couldn't evade politics.

Despite his apparent annoyance, he ambled toward us. "Officer Burns, these two are with me."

As soon as he heard his supervisor's comment, the diligent cop moved out of our way, and we continued to walk down the path to meet O'Halloran.

The detective ignored me for the moment and extended his hand to Jackson. "It's an honor to meet you. I'm Detective O'Halloran, and I will be the lead on the homicide investigation of Melinda Masters."

Jackson accepted his hand and shook it vigorously. "Always pleased to meet one of Capitol Hill's finest." The muscles in Jackson's face tensed. "I had the pleasure of working with Melinda Masters for the past several months. I strongly supported her nomination as the first woman to serve as Architect of the Capitol. You can understand how upset I am to learn about her death."

"Of course, Representative Jackson," said O'Halloran.

Jackson set her jaw. "That's Chairwoman Jackson, Detective."

I gulped as O'Halloran winced. It was a minor faux pas, but obviously one that our esteemed chair took seriously.

"Chairwoman Jackson," repeated O'Halloran.

"And as you know, I lead the committee which oversees the Capitol Hill police," said Jackson. "I want to make it quite clear how important this investigation is to me and my staff."

O'Halloran blinked rapidly. "Yes, ma'am." Realizing his mistake, he quickly corrected himself. "Yes, Chairwoman Jackson."

"Very good. I'm glad we understand each other." Then she motioned toward me. "This is Kit Marshall, who works for Congresswoman Maeve Dixon, a valued member of our committee."

O'Halloran glanced my way. "I know Ms. Marshall," he said evenly. "Our paths have intersected before."

"Yes, I'm quite aware," said Jackson. "That is why Kit will be my eyes and ears on this matter. Make sure she stays in the loop concerning the developments of the case. And you might want to consider any insight she's able to provide. Representative Dixon tells me she's been quite an asset in past investigations."

O'Halloran crossed his arms. "Not a problem," he said through clenched teeth.

"I'll be sure to speak with Ms. Marshall tomorrow." She might as well have told him he'd been demoted to metal detector duty at the Capitol Visitors Center. "Kit will keep Representative Dixon informed, and in turn, Dixon will keep me informed. I hope you will be able to bring the monster who did this to justice." Then she added, "Swiftly."

O'Halloran leaned forward with a steely

gaze. "I couldn't agree with you more, Chairwoman Jackson."

CHAPTER FIVE

Jackson and I retreated to the main hallway with Meg trailing behind. We stood next to the corpse flower as I introduced Meg to the Chairwoman.

"Meg has helped in several investigations," I explained. "If you don't mind, both of us will keep our eyes and ears open."

Behind me, I heard someone clear his throat. I turned around and realized it was Doug. "Aren't you going to introduce me?" he whispered.

I pulled him next to me. "This is my husband Doug Hollingsworth. He's a professor at Georgetown and is currently on a fellowship at the Library of Congress."

Jackson smiled politely and offered her hand, which Doug accepted.

"I've also assisted Kit with several criminal inquiries," he said. "Since I'm working on Capitol Hill these days, I can play a bigger role."

Jackson's brow furrowed. "Well, I can see you will have no shortage of help when it comes to finding out who did this to Melinda Masters. Please keep Congresswoman Dixon informed about the progress." She nodded politely and headed swiftly for the exit.

"I remember a time when you used to try to stop Kit from sleuthing," teased Meg.

Doug tugged on his suit jacket to straighten it. "It's easier to make sure both of you stay out of danger if I'm involved."

"And we appreciate your . . ." I wracked my brain for the right word. "Protection."

Meg snorted but said nothing.

"Have you already spoken to Detective O'Halloran?" I asked her.

"All done," she said. "There wasn't too much to tell. I didn't see anyone else inside when I discovered the body. I'm afraid my statement wasn't much help."

"You never know, Meg. I'm sure someone must have seen a detail that will point us in the right direction," I said.

Meg swiveled her head around. "Did we lose Sebastian?"

"I left him behind when I took Jackson to meet O'Halloran," I said. The area where the reception had been held was empty.

"I bet he's outside," said Doug. "The

smell from that corpse flower is nauseating."

I took another look at the blooming behemoth of a flower. "You're right. Let's get out of here. That thing is a bad omen, as far as I'm concerned."

We hustled outside and found Sebastian sitting on a bench, his phone in hand.

"Sorry about that, Sebastian. We didn't know where you'd gone," I said.

He finished typing on his phone and stood up. "I was just communicating with friends about plans for tomorrow."

"I don't even want to know what you're involved with." My stomach rumbled. "Should we get something to eat?"

"Tell you the truth," said Meg. "After discovering that body, I'm not sure if I'm up to it."

I did a double-take. Meg never lost her appetite. "Are you sure? I didn't think you ever turned down a meal."

She wavered. "Well, I might be able to stomach a milkshake."

"An adult milkshake?" I teased.

"Maybe that would be okay," she said tentatively.

"What's an adult milkshake?" asked Sebastian, clearly confused by our exchange.

"It's preferred vernacular for a milkshake

with liquor in it," said Doug.

"Sign me up." Sebastian lightly placed his hand on Meg's arm. "Only if you're up for it, of course."

Meg batted her eyelashes. "I think I can manage."

I suppressed rolling my eyes. Meg might have sworn off men for the past several months, but old habits die hard.

"Let's get a ride to Ted's Bulletin," said Doug. "I assume that's where you want to go, right?" I glanced at Sebastian. Deep in conversation with Meg, he didn't protest about preferring a taxi this time. Even activists succumbed to distractions of the female persuasion.

"Of course," I said. Ted's Bulletin was a throwback classic diner situated a few blocks from Capitol Hill in the nearby Eastern Market neighborhood.

I was about to schedule our car when my phone dinged. After glancing at the screen, I asked Doug if he could take care of our transportation. I pointed to my phone. "Gotta answer this text message."

Doug nodded and complied with my request as I typed a reply on my phone. As we got into the car for the short ride to Ted's, Meg asked, "Who messaged you?"

I hesitated before answering, but decided

honesty was the best policy. "It's Trevor. He'd like to meet with us."

Meg scowled. "Isn't it too late for Trevor to be out and about?"

"Who is Trevor?" Sebastian let nothing get by him without a probing question. Maybe we were more similar than I liked to admit.

"This guy Meg and I have known for a long time," I explained. "He worked in the Senate with us, became a lobbyist, and then wrote a tell-all book about living and working in Washington, D.C."

"Which was a flop," goaded Meg.

"That's a bit of an exaggeration," said Doug. "It may have underperformed according to Trevor's standards, but I know it was on the *Washington Post*'s non-fiction bestseller list for a week or two."

"Big deal," said Meg. "Even your boring history books make that list."

I rubbed my forehead, trying to stave off a migraine. "Enough! Trevor is meeting us so we can brief him on the murder. Remember, he works for the C-A-O these days. He heard about it through the Capitol Hill grapevine and suspected we might have been at the reception."

Sebastian started to ask another question. "What is . . ."

I cut him off before he could finish. "The C-A-O, right?"

"I feel like I need a handbook to understand what you're talking about," Sebastian grumbled. "It's barely English."

"Welcome to Washington where everyone is above average and acronyms reign the day," I joked. "Chief Administrative Officer. It's the office that manages the technology, human resources, and financial operations of the House of Representatives. Sort of like a chief operating officer in a company."

"Sounds absolutely fascinating," said Sebastian in an obviously bored tone.

Our ride arrived, and we climbed inside. Thankfully it was a spacious sedan, and we didn't have squeeze like sardines.

Meg refused to let go about Trevor. "Why does he always want to ruin our fun? We could tell him what happened tomorrow morning."

"Trevor has shown a lot of personal growth in the past couple of years," said Doug. "He's not nearly as ornery as when you worked with him in Senator Langsford's office."

Despite the passage of time, it wasn't easy to hear Senator Langsford's name in the past tense. Meg and I had met working for Langsford. His murder was the first case we helped solve on Capitol Hill. Even though the killer was brought to justice, the loss of our beloved Senate boss still stung.

Meg pursed her lips. "I suppose you're right."

"Well, now I've seen everything," I said.

"Because of what happened tonight?" asked Doug.

"Nope. Because I witnessed Meg conceding a point to you," I said.

Meg shook her finger at me as she reapplied her lip gloss. "That's not fair, Kit. I'm a reasonable person."

However exaggerated her self-description was, Meg provided the opportunity for a change in conversation. "Speaking of reason, let's talk about Melinda's murder after we order our shakes and nibbles. I have a feeling that Chairwoman Jackson means business. We need to come up with a game plan."

Ten minutes later, we were seated in a spacious booth at Ted's Bulletin. We passed around the menus and were studying the options when we heard a man's voice.

"Ahem," he said. "This is the table du jour, I presume?"

Our heads swiveled to find our former colleague standing next to us, tapping his fingers impatiently on our table.

I scooted over so Trevor would have room to sit. "Everyone, this is Trevor. Trevor, you know everyone except my brother. This is Sebastian."

Sebastian offered his hand. "Hey, man. Nice to meet ya."

Trevor's upper lip curled. As fastidious as Felix Unger, Trevor clung to formalities and structure. Sebastian's renegade lifestyle would not jive with our Type A consort. However, he accepted Sebastian's hand and shook it politely. "A pleasure to meet Kit's brother."

"We're getting ready to order. Take a look at the menu and see if you'd like anything." I shoved a menu in Trevor's direction.

"Delightful." The way he said it, he meant anything but.

Our waiter came to our table. "Ready?" he asked.

Everyone was silent until Trevor suggested I order first.

"Sure. I'll have a Toasted Coconut milkshake and a strawberry tart."

"Well, it's good to know you're diversifying your fruit intake," said Trevor sarcastically.

I knew better than to take the bait from Trevor. His *modus operandi* included goading his interlocutors into an argument.

Doug naturally went for the Nutty Professor milkshake and a salted caramel tart while Sebastian opted for the Bananas Foster with a piece of carrot cake.

The waiter looked at Meg. "And you?"

"It's so hard to decide," she said. "How about the Key Lime Pie milkshake?"

"Good choice," the waiter said. "Anything for dessert?"

"Actually, I'd like a meat loaf sandwich," she said.

Sebastian did a double-take. Given her killer physique, Meg's appetite surprised most strangers.

"Good to know you're feeling better," I teased.

"Well, a girl has to keep up her strength, especially if we're going double-time with the sleuthing," she said.

Last time I checked, detective work didn't rank highly on the list of calorie-burners. But I was glad Meg had returned to normal after her nasty discovery earlier this evening.

Trevor handed the menu to our server. "I'll just have some coffee, please."

"Want anything in that?" asked the waiter. "Like Kahlua? Amaretto?"

"No liquor. Just black with a touch of cream. Thank you." Trevor folded his hands neatly on his lap.

The moment the waiter departed with our order, Trevor spoke up. "I'm ready to be briefed on the homicide of Melinda Masters now."

"That sounded more like an order than a request," said Meg.

"In a manner of speaking, it is," said Trevor. "I need to speak with the Chief Administrative Officer tomorrow, and he'll want to know what happened."

"Why wasn't he at the reception tonight?" I asked. "He should have been invited."

"He was," said Trevor. "But he had a more pressing engagement. Not everyone has time to wait around for a malodorous flower to bloom."

This was definitely the Trevor we knew and loved . . . and sometimes detested.

"There's not too much to catch you up on," I said. "Meg found Melinda Masters on the ground inside the tropics exhibit on her way to the ladies' restroom. She was dead, but not for long."

"I take it the reception transpired outside the area in which the body was discovered?" asked Trevor.

"Yes, how did you know?" I asked.

"I thought it unlikely that guests were noshing on canapés and swilling wine in the same space in which the murder of the

85

Architect of the Capitol took place," Trevor said.

"Good point," I said. "Actually, you could be a real help to us, Trevor."

He straightened in his seat. "And what do you mean by that statement?"

Our milkshakes arrived, and we started slurping them. "This is fantastic," said Sebastian. "Do you mind if I order another?"

"Be our guest," I said.

As Sebastian flagged down the waiter, Meg smiled broadly. "A man after my own heart."

I groaned inwardly. So much for trying to quash the brewing attraction between my best friend and younger brother.

I turned toward Trevor. "You're always helpful when we investigate. Can you keep your eyes and ears open?"

Trevor sipped his coffee and carefully placed the mug back on its saucer. "Certainly. My boss wants this murder solved by the end of this week."

"Of course, he does," said Meg, who had moved on from her milkshake to the meat loaf. "No one wants a killer loose on Capitol Hill."

"I'm afraid it's more than general concern for the welfare of others," said Trevor.

"Really? There's something more important to the Chief Administrative Officer than safety and security?" she asked snidely.

Trevor patted his mouth with a napkin. "The Cannon Building renovation."

I took a bite of my homemade strawberry pop tart, a Ted's Bulletin favorite. "Delicious," I murmured.

Doug narrowed his eyes. "An office building renovation is motivating your boss to solve a murder? I'm not sure I follow."

Trevor sighed. "I forget I need to explain everything for this crowd. The Cannon Building renewal project is our top priority. Cannon is the oldest office building on the campus, dating back to 1908. Its structure has never been updated."

"Duh, we know that, Trevor," said Meg. "Remember, we work in the House of Representatives."

"What you fail to realize, *Megan,* is that the entire project will take over a decade to complete. Delays will end up costing the American taxpayer more money," he said.

Meg clenched her fists. She detested it when Trevor used her full name.

"And the reason you want Melinda Masters's killer caught is because the Architect of the Capitol is leading the renovation project," I said.

"At least someone is paying attention,"

said Trevor. "Obviously, we can't think about a permanent replacement for Masters until her murderer is apprehended. The sooner that happens, the better for everyone."

"We can certainly all agree to that," I said.

"What happens next?" asked Doug, leaning forward in his seat.

"We'll talk to Maeve Dixon tomorrow morning," I said. "I mean, Meg and I will speak with her."

"Okay," said Doug, with a touch of disappointment in his voice. "Let me know if I can help. Remember, I'm not far away these days."

"How could we forget?" murmured Meg.

I ignored my best friend's commentary. "We'll need all the help we can get. I don't know much about the Architect of the Capitol's operation."

"You might consider following the money," said Trevor. "Maintaining the grounds and all the buildings on Capitol Hill isn't cheap. And there's a lot of players that make it happen."

"We met Grant Dawson tonight," I said. "He's the head of the Botanic Garden, so Melinda Masters was his boss."

Trevor finished his coffee and placed the cup back on its saucer. "There's your first suspect."

"Grant? He seemed genuinely surprised and disturbed by Masters's death," I said.

"He wasn't in agreement with his boss about the direction of the Botanic Garden," said Trevor. "They didn't share a common vision of the future."

"And you think that's a motive for murder?" asked Sebastian. "Because they disagreed about how to arrange the flowers?"

Trevor fixed a downward gaze on my brother through his wire rimmed glasses. "You're obviously new to Washington. People take their jobs quite seriously in this city. No matter if it's plants or public policy."

"Sounds intense," said Sebastian. "I can see why Kit fits in so well here."

Meg patted Sebastian's hand playfully. "Don't let Trevor scare you. Washington isn't all work and no play." With a seductive look that made me feel slightly uncomfortable, Meg sucked the last of her milkshake through the red straw in her tall glass.

"Was it a serious disagreement between Grant Dawson and Melinda Masters?" I asked. Trevor was right. If a career was at stake, it could be a legitimate motive for murder.

Trevor threw down a few dollars on the

table and stood. "You'll have to use your best detective skills to find out." In a flash, Trevor, who possessed the uncanny ability to appear and disappear almost instantaneously, was gone.

Sebastian threw back his head and drained the remainder of his second milkshake. "What an odd man," he said.

"Trevor is like scotch," said Doug.

"What do you mean?" I asked.

"He's an acquired taste," he said, laughing.

I threw down my credit card. "Shall we call it a night? Tomorrow will be a busy day."

Sebastian pushed the card back in my direction. "I got this, Kit."

"Are you sure?" I asked skeptically. In the past, Sebastian had never been flush with cash.

He chuckled. "Don't worry, sis. I just got paid for work on a big tech job."

My face relaxed. "Thanks, Sebastian."

This was music to Meg's ears. "I hope I can thank you in some small way during your visit."

That was enough for my ears. "Ready to go?" I asked Doug and Sebastian. It was more of a command than a question.

Outside the restaurant, we said our good-byes to Meg while Doug secured a ride home for us. After we greeted our driver and squeezed into the back seat, Sebastian nudged me. "Life as Kit Marshall is more exciting than I thought," he said.

Of course, too much of a good thing can be dangerous.

CHAPTER SIX

The next morning, I awoke to the harmonious snores of Doug and Clarence. How they managed to orchestrate a perfectly synched symphony when they were both unconscious, I do not know. On a good day, they gave Yanni a run for his money.

With practiced dexterity, I managed to extract myself from the bed without disturbing either my husband or canine. Before confronting any challenges, including the obligatory email check to make sure nothing earth shattering hadn't happened overnight, I made a beeline for the kitchen. The day couldn't start properly without coffee.

To my surprise, Sebastian was already sitting on a stool in our breakfast nook. "Good morning," I said. "You're up early."

"In the technology world, we get started at the crack of dawn," he said. "I already exercised and read the paper. I hope you don't mind I used your espresso machine.

What a behemoth, by the way."

Sebastian referred to our large, industrial-grade coffee machine. Besides Clarence, it was my prized possession. It ground fresh coffee and spewed out almost any possible brewed caffeinated combination, mimicking barista-style quality. I never faced the morning without its assistance.

After punching a few buttons, the machine sputtered to life and provided me with a freshly brewed latte with three shots of specially selected espresso, which Doug had recently purchased at our locally sourced shop. Washington was no Seattle, but it had recently developed a coffee culture, and Doug was leading the charge.

"It's good to hear your work is going well," I said, sipping my steaming drink. "Your paid employment, I mean." With Sebastian, work was a touchy subject. He'd always considered his protesting and advocacy as his true calling. His tech jobs paid the bills, but never meant more than a means to an end.

Sebastian looked up from his phone. "It is. Turns out when you have a decade in the tech world, you start to garner some respect. I'm not just the low-level grunt they bring in to do the heavy lifting anymore."

I kept my face neutral to hide my surprise.

I'd never heard Sebastian speak positively about his professional career. His lack of focus was one characteristic we didn't share as siblings. The newfound enthusiasm for his tech work led me to wonder about his visit to Washington. "What are your plans during the visit, Sebastian?"

He rose and helped himself to another coffee. "You know. A little of this and that. I want to talk to some people here and get the lay of the land."

Could he speak in any more generalities? I tried another tack. "How about today? What are you doing?"

"Oh, yeah. Well, I've got this climate change thing today," he said, pointing to his "IT'S NOT EASY BEING GREEN" T-shirt. "I thought I'd spend some time with Clarence and then head out to it."

It wasn't exactly the level of specificity I'd hoped for, but at least it was something. "I need to get ready for work. It'll be a busy day with everything that's going on."

"Like the murder?" asked Sebastian.

"Mostly," I said. "Plus, my regular duties."

"Kit, I don't mean to pry into your life, but why are you so obsessed with solving murders these days?"

I thought about my brother's question for a moment before answering. "The crimes seem to find me. But I usually figure out a way to become involved in solving them."

Sebastian raised his eyebrows. "And the reason for that is?"

"The authorities sometimes jump to conclusions," I said. "They want to solve these murders as quickly as possible because they're high profile. But the most obvious suspect isn't always the guilty party. I know how politics works, and that makes me uniquely capable when a murder happens in my orbit."

Sebastian nodded. "Don't work too hard, Kit. It seems like you have two demanding jobs."

I smiled. "I'll try to keep it under control. I'll be busy all day, but let's try to meet later for dinner. There's a good Vietnamese restaurant in Arlington. Sound like a plan?"

Sebastian gulped his coffee before answering. "Where's the pooch? I'll take him for a jog around the neighborhood."

"Still sleeping with Doug," I said. "I'll get them up momentarily. But didn't you say you already exercised?"

"I did. But that was just my normal routine of strength exercises. You know, the basic stuff. Sit-ups, push-ups, planks, tricep dips."

"Wow, you'll have to show me sometime.

I'm always trying to get in shape."

"The best exercise you can do is a burpee." In an instant, he flattened himself on the floor, then pushed his legs up to a squat. He followed it up with a jump and a clap above his head.

"Looks excruciating, Sebastian."

"Come on, Kit. You try it," he urged.

Reluctantly, I put down my coffee. I managed to lie flat on the floor, but then it was impossible for me to get back up. After a few tries, I got it.

"Good job. Keep at it and you'll be cranking out twenty in no time." Sebastian smiled. "It's good to spend time with you, Kit. Just like the old days when we were growing up."

Twenty minutes later, Doug and Clarence had been roused out of their slumber, and I was almost out the door. Doug had just made his first cup of coffee and was sitting on the couch, reading today's headlines on his iPad. Sebastian had fastened Clarence's leash to his harness in preparation for their morning sojourn.

"See you both tonight for dinner," I said.

In a synchronized chorus, Doug and Sebastian said, "Be safe!"

I was used to dealing with Doug's trepidations about my sleuthing. Now my brother had added another voice of concern to the mix.

During my subway ride, I considered my next move concerning Melinda Masters's murder, although admittedly it was hard to concentrate when squished like a sardine between a portly bureaucrat and a perspiring tourist. A few potential suspects already surfaced, like Steve Song, the deputy Architect who lost out on the big job when Melinda got appointed. Of course, it was worth remembering that Grant Dawson had mentioned Song specifically and managed to assign a motive to him. Was that just petty cocktail gossip or had Dawson deliberately tried to plant a seed of suspicion before he killed Melinda?

At nine o'clock sharp, I opened the heavy door to Representative Maeve Dixon's congressional office inside the Cannon Building. The renovation hadn't made its way to our floor yet. How much would the murder investigation delay the mammoth project? It wasn't the only reason to figure out who killed Melinda Masters. But with millions of dollars at stake, it wasn't peanuts, either.

I greeted staff while making my way to the corner of the open office suite where my desk was located. A Dunkin' Donuts

Styrofoam coffee cup sat on my desk. I picked it up. It was still half full. Borderline disgusting that it had remained there most of yesterday and then overnight. I dumped it out in our small kitchen area and tossed it in the trash bin. I aspired to find a perfectly clean desk upon my arrival to work in the morning. Would I ever get there? Doubtful.

I turned on my computer and started to think about my options for securing another cup of coffee when I looked up. Meg was standing directly across from my desk.

"A minute to chat?" she asked pointedly.

Did I really have a choice?

I mustered a smile. "Good morning, Meg. Please sit down." I motioned toward the single chair adjacent to my desk, which barely fit in my tiny hovel. Congressional suites, particularly in the House of Representatives, were tight on space, except for the boss's lair. Maeve Dixon's wood-paneled office included a stately desk and sprawling landscapes from the North Carolina district she represented. My office had enough room for one guest and a framed photograph of Clarence and Doug. Some days, I debated whether there was room for the picture.

"How's Sebastian settling in?" Meg asked coyly.

"There hasn't been much change since we left you last night," I said. "Today's agenda involves an environmental crusade."

"Such dedication to worthy causes," sighed Meg. "It's so romantic."

The notion of protestors in sweaty T-shirts occupying city squares for weeks at a time didn't sound like a contemporary version of *Gone With The Wind*. Sebastian was no Rhett Butler, although Meg did occasionally remind me of Scarlett O'Hara.

"I thought you'd foresworn men," I said, tapping my fingers on the desktop.

Meg leaned closer. "It was a good solo run. It made sense to focus on me for the past six months." She examined her perfectly manicured red fingernails. "But now I'm getting lonely. Don't you think it's time to get back in the saddle?"

"Yes, but I'm not so sure the first horse you should ride is Sebastian."

Meg stared at me for several seconds. Then she burst into laughter. "Kit, you are so funny. I swear to God I don't know what I'd do without you."

"Maybe focus on our work," I said. "Not to mention solving Melinda Masters's murder. I assume you're feeling better after last night's adventure?"

"Oh, you know me," said Meg. "I'm highly resilient. But that reminds me about what I wanted to tell you. Maeve wants to see you pronto. She has a lead for you on the murder investigation, and it concerns Congresswoman Cartwright."

I made face. "Cartwright? I know she was there last night. But why would I start with her?"

"Don't know," said Meg. "But she made it seem like it was important."

I stood and smoothed the wrinkles out of my suit jacket. "I'd better check in with her, then."

Meg snapped her fingers again. "Hold it. There's something else we need to talk about."

I was secretly relieved Meg had legitimate reasons for commandeering my office so early in the morning. For a minute, I'd thought her apparent obsession with Sebastian had motivated it.

"Let's make it quick," I said. "Don't like to keep the boss waiting."

"It's the picnic," she said. "Jess and Oliver refuse to work together. And I need them to collect the money this week, go to the store, and buy the food."

Now it was my turn to sigh. "Meg, we

talked about this last night. You need to assert yourself here. You're their boss. It doesn't matter they used to date and it didn't work out. They need to organize the staff picnic for Saturday. Everyone is counting on it." Not to mention I'd shelled out fifty bucks to reserve the pavilion in an Arlington park.

"Okay, okay. Relax. I'll figure it out. It's just difficult to get them to remain civil. I arrived this morning, and they were already yelling at each other about whether we should budget for veggie hotdogs or not."

Regular hot dogs were composed of unknown meats. I didn't even want to know what ingredients were in the veggie variety. "Tell them to poll the staff," I said reasonably. "Then we can pick the three or four most popular items to grill. After all, the United States is still a democracy."

Meg, who disliked the current president, wrinkled her nose. "I suppose so. At least nominally." Then she turned away and scuttled out of my office.

I glanced at my computer. My screen was a sea of bold, unread messages. Why some people thought it made sense to capitalize the subject of their emails was beyond my comprehension. SUPPORT FARM BILL NOW! wasn't exactly a Miss Manners invitation to co-sponsor the legislation in question. A sure sign of tumultuous times, there was anger all over the Capitol these days, including my beleaguered mail inbox.

There was no time to wade through the digital morass. Maeve Dixon needed to speak with me, and she was my number one priority. I took five long strides to reach her closed door. The congresswoman's scheduler sat outside Dixon's office and only left for a twenty-minute lunch and a few potty breaks (if she was lucky). She squinted at her computer screen, probably trying to perform some heroic maneuver concerning Maeve's calendar that involved her being in two places at once.

"Patsy, is Maeve busy? Meg told me she wanted to speak with me," I said.

One of the most important staffers on the congressional team, the scheduler often knew the whereabouts, mood swings, and mental state of the boss. As the chief of staff, I outranked Patsy, but I depended heavily on her judgment and discretion.

Patsy pushed her screen aside so she could focus on me. She moved her rolling chair closer in my direction, squeezing her ample bosom against the edge of her desk. Thank goodness Patsy was better at scheduling than she was at applying cosmetics. I noticed she'd only used eye-shadow, mascara, and eyeliner on her right eye this morning. Who knows what had happened to prevent her from turning her attention to the other one? Quite frankly, it didn't matter one bit to me. As long as her work was competent and Maeve was happy with her schedule, the last time I checked, I didn't work for Maybelline. Besides, it wasn't prudent to point fingers. Routinely the fashion equivalent of a hot mess, I somehow persevered.

"Good morning, Kit. The congresswoman does want to see you. She told me to let her know when you'd arrived for the day." Patsy grabbed the phone and buzzed Maeve's direct line. After she exchanged a few words with Dixon, she turned back to me. "She's ready for you."

I bent over Patsy's desk so she could hear my whisper. "Is she in a bad mood?"

Patsy's round face crinkled as she thought about my question. "I wouldn't say a bad mood. It's something else."

"Angry?" I asked. That was even worse than bad.

"No," said Patsy quickly. "More like sad."

"Interesting," I said. "That must be related to Melinda Masters's death."

Patsy pushed back into position in front of her monitor. "I'd say so. It's all over the news this morning. I hope they catch the person responsible for it. We don't have enough women in government leadership positions on Capitol Hill. Losing one to murder seems doubly unfair."

Boy, wasn't that the truth? "Thanks, Patsy. See you later." Then I added, "Maeve might have me out of the office a lot today. Keep an eye on things."

Already focused on her computer, Patsy gave me a salute. I opened Maeve's door and walked inside, uncertain about what my boss might have in store. Of course, the unpredictability of solving a murder was no different than my day-to-day job as a congressional staffer. Twists and turns, untruths, and false leads were common pitfalls of Capitol Hill. Hercule Poirot might have excelled, although I doubted his epicurean tastes could have survived the House of Representatives cafeteria fare. Deadly didn't even begin to describe it.

Maeve Dixon was sitting behind her stately desk, poring over today's edition of *Roll Call*. Not many people outside the Beltway knew about the paper, but its notoriety on Capitol Hill was legendary as the paper of record for those who lived and breathed Congress. Melinda Masters's photo was predictably plastered above the fold on the front page. Her murder was the equivalent of the D.C. press tsunami.

Maeve ran her fingers through her shoulder length brown hair. My boss resembled Andie MacDowell from her heyday in the mid-nineties. Toned with excellent bone structure, Maeve's overall look was accentuated by her minimalist, yet professional, makeup and elegant jewelry. Dixon had served abroad in the military after the nine-eleven terrorist attacks, so her resume spoke for itself. The total package had been constructed and perfected afterward. She was the ideal political candidate: good looking, even-tempered, moderate, cautious, and pragmatic. After surviving a difficult electoral challenge last fall, Maeve Dixon had once again become bullet-proof, albeit metaphorically.

"Congresswoman?" I said softly. She'd failed to acknowledge my presence, under stably ensconced in the newsprint before her.

She looked up immediately, a faint smile appearing on her lips. "Kit, good to see you. Let's talk over there." She pointed to the sitting area of her office, which consisted of a formal couch and several high-backed chairs.

My stomach clenched. Maeve was rarely

so proper. Why was she calling me to the couch? Had I done something wrong last night? A rash of bad thoughts flew through my head. Unlike other federal employees, congressional staff weren't covered by civil service protections. We were "at-will" employees, which meant dismissal by the boss without just cause was perfectly permissible and legal. If I'd done something to annoy Maeve, she could certainly terminate me. Dixon didn't seem like that type of boss, but there was a first time for everything.

I sat down on the couch because I knew Maeve preferred the aqua-colored wingback chair facing her desk. The last thing I wanted to do in this situation was breach protocol.

"I understand you spoke with Rhonda Jackson last night," she said.

I nodded vigorously, happy that the first words out her mouth weren't "you're fired." Despite my best efforts, Donald Trump had managed to infiltrate my psyche.

"I accompanied Chairwoman Jackson to the crime scene," I explained. "And she spoke with Detective O'Halloran about the case."

Maeve pursed her lips. "He's in charge of the investigation?"

My boss knew O'Halloran from a previous murder that occurred on Capitol Hill. She'd been a suspect in the case and didn't have fond memories of O'Halloran trying his best to pin her to the crime.

"Yes, and Chairwoman Jackson made it clear he's supposed to keep me in the loop about his progress. I need to check in with him sometime today."

Maeve smiled wryly. "I'm sure that news was received well by the good detective."

"He seemed to take it in stride, ma'am."

"I hope so, because Rhonda is expecting me to keep her informed about this investigation, and I'm counting on you to serve as my conduit. Do you think you can handle this?"

"Of course, I can," I said quickly. "After all, it's not my first murder investigation."

Maeve rubbed her hands on her pantsuit. "I understand, but please be careful. We expect you to keep us informed. You don't need to single-handedly catch the culprit."

"I expect to have help from Meg," I said. "Maybe even Doug. He works nearby these days."

"That's not what I meant, Kit. Let the police do the heavy lifting," she said, shaking her finger at me. "It would be quite inconvenient if I had to search for a new chief of staff because something happened to you."

Maeve had a roundabout way of showing concern, but I understood what she meant. "I'll be cautious." I crossed my fingers over my heart. "I promise."

Maeve sat up straight in her chair. "I'm glad that's settled. I have a lead for you to track down this morning."

I narrowed my eyes. Maeve never offered help in my investigations. "Which is?" I tried to keep any trace of skepticism out of my voice.

"Bridget Cartwright," she said definitively.

"You mean Representative Cartwright?" I asked. "The Republican from Virginia who's on the House Administration committee with you?"

"The one and only," said Maeve. "She had a beef with Melinda Masters. I'm not sure why, but I know she wasn't happy with her. There might be a motive there."

"And she was at the reception last night," I said.

Maeve nodded. "I saw her in passing, but I didn't speak with her. She's not known as the friendliest member of the House of Representatives."

That rumor was well traveled. I hadn't dealt with her personally, but I knew plenty of people who had. Cartwright's unfavorable reputation preceded her.

"Given that she's from the other political party, how do you expect me to investigate her?" It was a legitimate question. I couldn't simply march inside Cartwright's office and demand a meeting with her. If I took that approach, I'd garner more laughter than clues.

"Good point," said Maeve. "I guess I'm out of my league in this murder investigation business."

After a moment of silence, my boss snapped her fingers. "I got it. I'll call Rhonda Jackson to arrange a meeting with you and Cartwright."

I wrinkled my nose. "Would Cartwright listen to her?"

"Believe me, Kit. No one turns down a request from Rhonda Jackson. Even someone as brazen as Bridget Cartwright."

I shrugged my shoulders. "You would know. It's worth a shot."

"Hang tight," said Maeve. "I'll let you know when it's arranged."

I nodded and shuffled back to my desk. The last weeks of session before Congress fled town for the long summer recess were always a bear. The Speaker of the House often tried to jam as much legislation as possible on the schedule so rank-and-file members could return to their districts and claim credit for all the wonderful laws they'd just passed. No doubt my boss and Chairwoman Jackson also wanted Melinda's murder solved before they departed for home, too. Adding Sebastian into the mix made it even more complicated. I dutifully opened my email inbox and started triaging messages, deleting those that required no action and forwarding others that required the attention of staff members. If my prime responsibility was the homicide investigation, then the Dixon legislative team would need to step up to the plate.

I'd waded through a good chunk of the most important emails before I heard Dixon's office door open. She motioned for me to follow her back inside the office and then closed the door firmly behind me.

"You're all set," she said. "You have a ten o'clock appointment with Representative Cartwright."

I gulped. Truthfully, I hadn't thought Jackson would be able to secure the meeting. I also hadn't imagined it would happen so quickly. I tilted my wrist to check the time. I had twenty minutes to prepare.

"What does she think this meeting is about?" I asked.

"She knows it's about Architect of the

Capitol issues," said Maeve. "Cartwright wants some statue replaced. Hear her out and then try to see what you can find out."

"But you don't want me to promise her anything, right?"

Maeve waved her hand. "Use your judgment, Kit. Just try to figure out if Cartwright had a motive to kill Masters."

"Okay. Is her chief of staff also attending the meeting?"

"Nope," said Maeve firmly. "Rhonda wanted it to be just the two of you. It's more likely she'll be forthcoming if there's no staff in the room."

"This is pretty unusual circumstances. Usually members of Congress meet with other members of Congress," I said, biting the inside of my cheek.

Maeve took my arm and gently guided me toward the door. "I understand, but I've got an appearance on MSNBC and a North Carolina radio show this morning. You can handle it."

Before I knew it, I was staring at the other side of my boss's office door. Maeve Dixon had many virtues, but patience wasn't one of them. She'd instructed me to handle the situation, and I'd better figure it out. Now I was due at Cartwright's office in fifteen minutes. With the House of Representatives floor now open for business, our office had started to buzz. There was no sense in sitting at my desk trying to come up with a game plan. Instead, I grabbed a notebook and a pen, fired off a text message to Meg to inform her I was headed out for a meeting, and began the trek to the Rayburn House Office Building to Cartwright's office.

Every month, it seemed as though the Cannon Building renovation project claimed another victim. Several corridors were closed, rendered inaccessible by temporary walls and friendly signs such as "KEEP OUT." No wonder Trevor wanted to see a new Architect of the Capitol installed as speedily as possible. Such a massive modernization project required leadership. Without it, cost overruns would likely ensue. Eventually, our office would be impacted, since the renovation work was scheduled to rotate until the four sides of the Cannon office rectangle were completed. But any temporary move was still years away, and quite frankly, surviving the week was often hard enough, let alone worrying about the distant future.

Ten minutes later, I stood outside Bridget Cartwright's congressional suite. There hadn't been much time to prepare for our chat, so I'd have to trust my instincts. Cartwright was as broken up about Masters's death as my boss and Chairwoman Jackson. I took a deep breath and pushed open the glass door.

A clean-cut staffer in his early twenties sat behind the main desk. He wore a neatly pressed suit and a crimson tie, the epitome of congressional staff attire. The west coast laid-back clothing trend hadn't made its way to Washington yet, and I seriously doubted if it ever would.

"Good morning. Can I help you?" He adjusted his headset, which allowed him to take calls from adoring constituents while he also managed the traffic coming in and out of the office. Staff assistants didn't make much money, and they certainly earned every last penny.

"Kit Marshall, chief of staff for Maeve Dixon. I'm here to see the Congresswoman," I said.

Mr. Clean Cut tilted his head to the side. "Ah, yes. This meeting was just added to the schedule." Almost under his breath, he added, "Highly unusual."

I didn't know if he wanted me to comment, but I figured what the heck. "What's highly unusual?"

He did a double take. "Oh, nothing."

I stared at him and drummed my fingers along the countertop. The silent treatment usually made people nervous. Mr. Clean Cut succumbed easily.

"I mean, Representative Cartwright rarely changes her schedule," he said. "Especially for a meeting with staff."

Mr. Clean Cut had said too much, a common pitfall of young congressional types. He caught himself and attempted a recovery. "Of course, given the circumstances, an exception makes perfect sense." He flashed his pearly whites.

I decided to let him off the hook. "Not a problem. I'll take a seat until Representative Cartwright is available."

He nodded and turned his attention back to his computer, no doubt relieved I hadn't scolded him for his faux pas.

My gaze turned to the framed photos on the wall of Representative Cartwright's reception area. I guessed that Bridget Cartwright was in her early fifties. Tall, blonde, and slim, she definitely knew how to put herself together. She sported a different designer suit in each photograph, although the smiling expression on her face was unchanged. She resembled one of those paper dolls dress-up sets I played with as a kid. The face and body remained the same while the outfits could be swapped out.

I was pondering whether a congressional line of those dolls might be financially lucrative when a female voice interrupted my daydream.

"Ms. Marshall?"

I snapped to attention. Standing in front of me was the real-life Bridget Cartwright. She wore a tailored light green pastel suit jacket over a matching sheath dress. Gold stud earrings and a layered chain necklace completed the outfit. She smiled, precisely the same expression displayed on her office portraits.

I jumped to my feet. "Congresswoman, a pleasure to meet you." I thrust my hand in her direction, and she accepted it with a light touch.

"Let's adjourn to my private office." She motioned for me to follow her through the door that led to the rear of the suite.

I shuffled past several staffers, who shot curious glances my way. They must have wondered why a chief of staff from the other side of the aisle had the privilege of meeting with their boss without supervision present. I would have been similarly suspicious if the circumstances were reversed.

I sat down on a fancy beige settee. It was more ornate than comfortable, and I longed for the relaxing couch in Maeve Dixon's office. It was a good reminder I wasn't in Kansas anymore.

"Ms. Marshall, I have fifteen minutes to chat with you." Cartwright smoothed her blonde hair with her manicured hand, but I noticed it didn't move when she touched it. I had a feeling not much moved out of place on the congresswoman.

"As I understand it, Chairwoman Jackson requested your help with the homicide investigation," I said.

"Yes, Rhonda called me this morning. Who can say no to her?" Cartwright laughed nervously.

"Not many, I gather. But I understand you had a problem with the Architect of the Capitol." It was a bit brash, even for my tastes. But I figured Jackson's interest in the case would give me additional latitude, and I intended to use it.

Cartwright bristled. "You've been misinformed, Ms. Marshall."

"Your relationship with Melinda Masters was perfectly fine?" I pressed. There had to be some grain of truth in what I was told. Neither the Chairwoman nor Maeve Dixon would send me on a wild goose chase without cause.

"Let me be perfectly clear," said Cartwright, as she smoothed her dress over her shapely legs. "I had cause for concern with the A-O-C, not Masters specifically."

Politicians were famous for splitting hairs. It didn't bother me when we were engaged in our regular business. Murder was an altogether different story.

"What was your problem? Didn't like the way the agency was operating?" I asked.

Cartwright shifted in her high-back chair, resembling a queen sitting on a throne. I imagined her yelling "off with her head" and several eager staffers scrambling to find a way to execute her wishes.

"Much more serious than that, I'm afraid," she said. "Ms. Marshall, I have no idea what your boss or Chairwoman Jackson think of me. But I'm happy to set the record straight with you." She paused a moment to take a sip from a glass of water. "I'm no lightweight. I didn't come to Congress to make friends or get my photograph in newspapers. I'm not a show horse. I came here to reform government, starting with Congress."

"Okay," I said slowly. "I still don't understand the connection to Masters."

Cartwright leaned forward in her chair, her face illuminated. An excitement in her eyes appeared that I hadn't seen in the pictures on the lobby wall. Maybe there were two Bridget Cartwrights. One who put on a fake smile to look pretty for the camera, and one who was deadly serious about enacting her agenda in Washington.

"Let me spell it out for you. The Architect of the Capitol is responsible for the construction and maintenance of all properties and grounds on the Hill. Some of the work is done by those who work for the A-O-C, but the big stuff gets done by contractors." She stared at me. "You understand?"

I nodded. I didn't want to interrupt her speech with any questions.

"A lot of money, I'm talking hundreds of millions of dollars, rolls through that office every year. A few years ago, there were reports about malfeasance in the Architect's office. Companies started to complain they weren't being considered fairly in the contracting process." She paused to take a deep breath. "When I got assigned to the House Administration committee, I decided I'd make it my business to find out what was going on. After all, some of those contractors who'd cried foul were Virginia residents."

"You asked Melinda Masters about it," I said.

"Of course. When I met with her before

she was confirmed for the position, I brought it up. She promised to get back to me after she had a few months on the job," she explained.

"And did she?" I asked.

Cartwright smirked. "There's no way someone is going to offer that type of information willingly. It didn't matter. I kept bringing it up with her."

"And what did she tell you?"

Cartwright waved her hand dismissively. "She was vague. Gave me all kinds of excuses and promised she was digging as hard as she could. In the meantime, I'd requested a G-A-O investigation."

"Was Gordon Romano moving forward with it?" I asked. Romano, the Comptroller General, was the head of the Government Accountability Office.

"What do you think, Ms. Marshall?" She looked at me pointedly. She was getting tired of me asking all the questions.

"You're a member with low seniority, and you're also in the minority party," I said. "Unlikely that Romano would pay attention to you."

"Precisely," said Cartwright. "He gave me the runaround. But it didn't mean I was going to drop the issue."

I glanced at my Fitbit. Time was running

out. Pretty soon, Cartwright was going to politely show me the door. Then I remembered what Maeve told me.

"Were you upset about a statue?" I asked. "I heard you had a beef with Masters about it."

Cartwright grimaced. I'd hit a nerve. She shifted uncomfortably in her chair. "I was discussing the replacement of a statue on the Capitol grounds with Ms. Masters. But it's a long process, requiring Congress to pass a law."

"Which statue do you want to replace?" I asked.

"I suppose it doesn't hurt to tell you, and I'm going to need members of Congress from across the aisle to support me," she said nervously. "It's James Garfield."

"Garfield? He has a statue near the Capitol?" Ninety-nine percent of my time on Capitol Hill was spent inside. If I went outside, it was usually to head down Pennsylvania Avenue to have a drink with staff, a lobbyist, or someone I was trying sweet talk into a deal. Unfortunately, my eyes rarely left my iPhone. I missed a lot when it came to my surroundings, statues of former presidents included.

"See? You wouldn't even miss it if he was gone," she said. "He's at First and Maryland, not far from the Botanic Garden entrance. In fact, I met Ms. Masters at the base of the statue before the reception last night."

I blinked rapidly. "Why did you do that?"

"I wanted to discuss the possibility of replacing Garfield with James Madison," said Cartwright. "As the father of our Constitution and a member of the First Congress of the United States, it makes perfect sense for a statue of Madison to be included on Capitol grounds."

I had to concede Cartwright's point on the merits. "But isn't one of the Library of Congress buildings named Madison?"

"Yes, of course," she said. "But that's hardly comparable to a statue in front of the United States Capitol."

Then it clicked. When a member of Congress behaves in a puzzling way, approximately ninety percent of the time, the behavior can be traced back to the district he or she represents.

"You're from the Virginia Seventh District, right?" I asked, with my eyebrows conspicuously raised.

"Yes, of course." Cartwright uncrossed and crossed her legs.

"If memory serves me correctly, that district includes Montpelier, the home of

James Madison. Is that right?"

She pursed her lips. "That's correct." Her voice was only slightly above a whisper.

"You want to replace Garfield's statue with Madison so you can make your constituents happy? Not a bad win to take home to your history buffs," I said.

"It's not a state secret, Ms. Marshall," Cartwright hissed. "I met Melinda Masters at the Garfield statue before the reception so we could discuss the matter. But instead of listening to reason, she gave me a thousand boring reasons why she wouldn't get behind my effort."

Now we were getting somewhere. "Masters didn't want to exchange Garfield for Madison?"

Cartwright lurched forward in her seat, like a lion getting ready to pounce. "The woman wouldn't listen to reason. She went on and on about how Garfield's assassination was a national tragedy in 1881 and funds were raised to build this statue after his death."

"Not too many people think about James Garfield these days," I said.

Cartwright's face lit up. "Exactly! But everyone knows James Madison. No matter how historically significant that statue was at the time, you can't tell me people wouldn't appreciate having the father of our Constitution preserved on Capitol grounds."

"The Architect of the Capitol must have had her reasons," I said. "I take it you didn't make any headway with her?"

"Of course not," said Cartwright. "I don't know if you knew Melinda Masters, but she could be bullheaded."

Frowning, I asked, "Did her opinion really matter? Doesn't the Architect of the Capitol do what Congress wants? A law demanding a statue of Madison on Capitol grounds would have superseded her opinion."

"Technically speaking, you're right," she said. "But it would have been near impossible for me to convince other members of Congress about the replacement if the Architect of the Capitol opposed it. Most of my colleagues would defer to her expertise and opinion."

Representative Cartwright had a point. Melinda's opposition would have made it a steep mountain to climb. Most bills that got drafted never got voted on in the House of Representatives. With formidable opposition coming from the Architect herself, the chance of James Madison seeing the proverbial and literal light of day on Capitol Hill was slim to none.

"Wasn't James Madison a slaveowner? And Garfield an ardent abolitionist?" I asked. "That also seems like a big hurdle to overcome."

Cartwright smoothed her blonde hair with her hand. "You sound like Melinda Masters. And look what happened to her."

I wasn't sure if that was a veiled threat or merely an observation. Either way, this conversation was coming to an end. I sprang up and stuck out my hand. "Thank you for the information. Chairwoman Jackson will be in touch if needed."

Cartwright nodded tightly as she pumped my hand, aware she'd said too much. "I'm not sure what's going on in the Architect of the Capitol's office, but I'm going to find out. For the benefit of Virginians and all taxpayers." She took a deep breath. "Even if I have to wait for a new appointee."

Spoken like a true House member who someday aspired for higher office. Did Cartwright have her eye on the Senate or the Governor's mansion? Either way, she wanted to make her time in her current position count. She didn't plan on remaining a backbencher for long.

I turned to leave her office and then spun around. "By the way, after you looked at the Garfield statue outside, did you speak to

Melinda Masters again at the reception?"

Representative Cartwright hesitated. A hint of despair flashed across her face. But she recovered almost immediately. "No, I don't think so. We went our separate ways after looking at that smelly flower."

"Do you have any idea who would have wanted Melinda dead?"

She considered my question before answering in a measured voice. "Not specifically. But something was not on the up and up inside that office." Then she looked me directly in the eye. "Ms. Marshall, you've done some detecting around Capitol Hill so I think you'll agree with me. Where there's smoke, there's fire."

I couldn't disagree with the Congresswoman. "Thank you for your time. I'll be sure to let Representative Dixon know about our meeting."

As I closed the door behind me, I caught a last glimpse of Bridget Cartwright. She'd sat down again in her highjack chair. From across the room, I could spot the worry lines creased across her face. Botox couldn't fix everything, particularly the agitation caused by murder.

CHAPTER SEVEN

Five minutes later, I was riding the escalator connecting Rayburn to the Longworth Building. This part of the House of Representatives basement corridor resembled an old department store building. Who put an escalator in the middle of an office complex? Without my Macy's shopping bag, I felt naked.

Like most politicians, Bridget Cartwright was a complicated character. She definitely had a reformist streak within her, thus her strident insistence something was afoul inside the Architect's office. She also had a solid motive for wanting Melinda Masters dead. Without her endorsement, Madison wouldn't set foot on the Capitol lawn anytime in the near future. I wondered if the latter might have led her to kill Masters. If she'd just left a frustrating meeting with the Architect of the Capitol, she felt as though her options were dwindling. Maybe she did speak with the Architect of the Capitol subsequently, and Masters told her to take her Madison statue and shove it. That could have certainly ignited the mercurial Cartwright to shift into overdrive and strangle Masters. A crime of passion, not over sex, but sculpture. I could only imagine the headlines.

The area around the Longworth elevators bled into one of the busiest areas of the congressional buildings. It was the House of Representatives crossroads, where staff housed in all three office buildings and even the Capitol might meet. The big cafeteria was right around the corner, as well as the gift shop, stationery store, and credit union. The House of Representatives even had its own post office, also conveniently located at this particular intersection. Throw in wandering tourists, lobbyists, and eager constituents, and you had the Washington equivalent of Star Wars' Mos Eisley. Thankfully, I hadn't seen any bounty hunters, at least lately.

It made perfect sense that I would find Trevor standing next to the credit union ATM machine, his face buried in his iPhone. I snuck up on him. "You'd better watch it. I heard those things are addictive."

He kept texting and didn't bother to look

up. "Hello, Kit. Have you solved the murder of Melinda Masters yet?"

I sighed and put my hands on my hips. "What do you think, Trevor?"

He stopped fiddling with his phone and met my gaze. "I think the clock is ticking. You've got pressure from your boss and your boss's boss to solve this one. If I were you, I'd get cracking."

"In fact, I was investigating this morning. I just came from a meeting with Representative Bridget Cartwright," I said.

Trevor swiveled his head left and right. "Best not to talk about this subject in one of the busiest corridors in Congress, don't you think?"

"You're right," I conceded. I glanced at my Fitbit. It was almost eleven o'clock. "Are you free for lunch in an hour?"

Trevor adjusted his glasses. "That sounds suitable. But the Longworth cafeteria is as bad as this hallway for a confidential discussion."

Sharing a secret inside the main cafeteria was about as private as posting it on Twitter. "How about the Library of Congress?" We were only a short walk away from the main cafeteria, located inside the Madison Building.

Trevor wrinkled his nose. "Typically, I

eschew cafeteria food. But it's an acceptable alternative. Are you going to invite your husband?"

"I'd better. If he finds out I ate there today and didn't let him know, his feelings will be hurt."

"Ah, the complications of a modern urban marriage," said Trevor.

Ignoring his editorial comment, I typed out a text message to Doug and told him about our lunch plans. I didn't know if he would be able to join us, although it seemed as though his schedule was wide open as a research fellow.

We agreed to meet for lunch in an hour. It made no sense to return to the office for such a short period of time, so I made a beeline for the sixth floor of the Madison Building. The Library of Congress cafeteria offered a pleasant view of the southern portion of the city, including the freeway and the distant Navy Yard. Considering the House of Representatives cafeteria had no natural light, it was definitely an upgrade. It was also a good place to accomplish work, since interruptions from lobbyists and other congressional staff were minimal. I answered a multitude of emails before Trevor showed up at my table.

"Ready to eat?" he asked.

"Yes, please," I said.

"Did I really need to inquire?"

I ignored Trevor's predictable sarcasm. Last night's dinner had been unsatisfactory. The milkshake was delicious, but despite the high calories, it hadn't really stuck with me. A salad would be best, yet I was drawn to the display of pizza slices. I resisted, and opted for a middle of the road option, a turkey sandwich on whole grain.

Trevor had already found a seat by the windows, so I joined him after paying for my food. I glanced around the busy cafeteria. There was no sign of Doug. Maybe he was busier than I thought.

Trevor didn't waste time. "What did you learn from Bridget Cartwright?"

I told him about her desire to replace Garfield with Madison on the west lawn of the Capitol. He shook his head. "We're sitting inside the monument to Madison on Capitol Hill. He's got a whole building named after him."

"I tried to tell her that, but she wasn't convinced," I said. "That gives her a concrete motive for murder. Melinda Masters wanted nothing to do with her scheme."

Trevor sipped his soup as he considered my comment. "It does. Especially if she'd promised the statue to constituents in her district. I could be wrong, but I think she might face a challenger from within her party in the next election."

Only eight months had passed since the last election. That didn't stop anyone from thinking about the next one. With two-year terms, House members perpetually ran for reelection. It was a never-ending, vicious cycle that drove some good politicians to abandon Congress and elected public service.

"The statue wasn't the only interesting thing we discussed." I leaned across the table. "Cartwright had something else she wanted to share about the Architect of the Capitol's office."

From behind me, a familiar voice interrupted. "I hope you're not talking about the case without me!"

Doug suddenly appeared at the side of our table. He had a plastic container filled to the brim with a taco salad.

Trevor motioned to the empty seat. "Please sit down, Dr. Hollingsworth."

My husband did as he was told. "You know Trevor, you can call me Doug. We've known each other for a while now."

Trevor wrinkled his nose. "You earned a doctorate. Why shouldn't I call you by the salutation you deserve?"

"Most people think it's a little snooty, Trevor," I explained. "We try not to be so elitist."

With a half-smile, Trevor said, "I find it ironic that you work so hard to create an image that negates your achievements. But that's your choice, I suppose."

Trevor was super smart, yet somehow the common-sense gene eluded him. I decided to shift us back on track to the murder investigation.

"Doug, I was just about to tell Trevor about what I learned this morning from Representative Cartwright," I said.

"Please proceed, Kit. I don't have much more time to devote to this sojourn," said Trevor.

I crossed my arms. "Very well. Cartwright hinted there was malfeasance within the Architect of the Capitol. She wasn't able to give me specifics, but she said it was potentially big."

With his mouth full of salsa and guacamole, Doug still managed to ask a question. "What did she mean by malfeasance? Where?"

"It has to do with contracting. She mentioned there were reports a while back about the process being unfair." I looked at Trevor. "Do you have any idea what she means?"

My lunch invitation had an ulterior motive. Trevor was like a walking encyclopedia of knowledge. Annoying as he was, his remarkable memory often proved handy.

He nodded. "I think so, but I'm going to have to check some files I have back in my office."

My face brightened. "I knew I could count on you, Trevor."

He rose to leave. "I'll be in touch. In the meantime, may I offer a suggestion?"

I'd just taken the last bite of my turkey sandwich. Instead of talking with my mouth full, I made a sweeping motion with my hand to indicate Trevor should proceed.

"Perhaps you should do some homework on the A-O-C," he said. "So, you can understand its function and operations. You might need it to solve Masters's murder. Furthermore, your boss now sits on the committee charged with its oversight. It's time to educate yourself, Ms. Marshall."

I set aside the know-it-all tone. After all, Trevor would sound condescending in pretty much any circumstance, even if he was standing next to Larry David. Beneath his veneer of snobbery, Trevor often had a valuable point to convey. This time was no different.

"Fair enough," I said. "I'll do some legwork to make myself conversant."

"Can't you talk to someone at the Congressional Research Service?" asked Doug. "The staff are located in this building. At least, I think they are."

"Great idea, Doug. Although C-R-S is supposed to help staff with legislative work, not solving mysteries." I felt guilty using congressional resources for the wrong purpose.

"As I stated clearly, you should educate yourself about the Architect of the Capitol for a number of reasons, including your boss's work on the committee," said Trevor. "Now I really must return to my office. I will contact you later today."

In a flash, Trevor was gone. His uncanny ability to appear and disappear almost instantaneously used to unnerve me. Now, I was used to it, although I still wondered how he managed to move so fast.

"Well, it looks like you have your next lead," said Doug. "Shall I accompany you to C-R-S?" His eyes glowed with eager anticipation.

"Better not," I said. "I want to stick to the learning about the Architect of the Capitol due to Maeve Dixon's committee business. If you came with me, it would arouse unnecessary attention."

Doug's shoulders slumped. "I guess that makes sense."

I didn't like to disappoint Doug. "Cheer up. I'll be sure to fill you in tonight. I promised Sebastian we'd take him out to dinner in Arlington."

His face relaxed. "Sounds like a deal."

After saying our goodbyes, I headed to the elevator and pushed the button for the second floor. I'd previously used the La Follette Congressional Reading Room when I needed assistance in a pinch. There was no time today to phone in a request or submit it over the web, which was the typical way to receive help. I'd have to take my chances that a trusty librarian would be available in person.

Several congressional staffers were reading newspapers or consulting library materials. It gave me great solace that others found the pursuit of knowledge valuable. With fake news and tweets du jour reigning the day, I often wondered if verifiable facts were going the way of the dodo. Apparently, visiting the nation's library was still considered a worthy use of time.

A younger woman manned the front desk. She didn't look like the stereotypical bookish librarian. She had on funky dark pink glasses and wore a small black and white zebra bow in her hair. Grinning, I walked up to her.

"Hello, my name is Kit Marshall and I'd like to learn more about the Architect of the Capitol," I said.

After looking me up in her computer system and verifying I did indeed work in Congress, she asked me a few more questions. A few minutes later, I settled in a desk to read a report, which covered the selection process for the Architect and overview of its functions. There was no mention of financial impropriety or problems. Research could be exhausting. I'd have to try again with my fashion-conscious librarian.

"Thanks for this background material," I said. "But I'm looking for something more juicy."

She fiddled with her oversized black chain link necklace. "Juicy?" she asked. "That word usually isn't used in the same sentence as the Architect of the Capitol."

"Fair enough," I said. "But I heard there were allegations of problems in contracting a few years ago. I didn't see that covered in the report."

She raised her eyebrows. "Was it in a congressional hearing? What's your source?"

I didn't want to offer Representative Cartwright's name. I wasn't sure if our conversation was confidential. The worst thing you could do in Washington is blab when it's better to keep your mouth shut.

"I'm afraid I can't say who told me," I said. "Sorry I'm not much help."

"Was it in a newspaper?" she asked.

"Maybe," I said. "I get the sense my source found out about the problem before getting elected to Congress."

My helper repositioned her computer monitor directly in front of her. With the intense focus of an air traffic controller, she studied the results on her screen. Then her fingers danced across the keyboard like Beethoven playing his fifth symphony. I was mesmerized. This librarian was no joke.

A slow smile spread across her face. She turned the monitor so I could see her discovery. "Nexis isn't always easy to use, but if there's information to be found, I can usually find it."

"You're a real sleuth!" I said enthusiastically.

She pushed up her pink glasses, repositioning them so they fit squarely on her face. "Actually, I'm a librarian. I just got my Master of Library Science degree and now I'm working here on a fellowship."

"My husband is here on a fellowship, too," I said. "They should hire you permanently!"

She lowered her voice. "Can you tell my boss that? It might mean a lot, since you're a chief of staff for a member of Congress."

"Certainly," I said. "Can you write your name down and who I should email? I promise I'll do it before the end of the day."

After writing scribbles on a Post-it note, she stuck her hand out. "I'm Grace, by the way."

I shook it vigorously. "Grace, the sleuth posing as a librarian. Pleased to meet you. Maybe our paths will cross again one day."

As I turned to leave, Grace waved her hands. "Wait a second, Kit. Didn't you forget something?"

I showed her the scrap of paper. "Nope, I have your info. Don't worry. I'll be sure to contact your boss. I hope it helps."

Grace pointed to the computer monitor. "You didn't read the article I found about the Architect of the Capitol!"

I thumped my forehead with the palm of my hand. How could I be so forgetful? I was always juggling multiple tasks, so it was inevitable that I'd make mistakes here and there. But forgetting the purpose of my visit to the reading room altogether signaled a new level of absent-mindedness. I used to think Doug was a scatterbrain. Now, it would be like the pot calling the kettle black.

"Of course," I said. "Thank you for reminding me. Please show me what you found."

"It was in the *Washington Examiner* a few years ago." Grace clicked on the article. "At least I think this might be what you're looking for."

Sure enough, Grace had found an obscure article on the Architect of the Capitol's office. I scanned the headlines and first several lines of copy. There was no doubt in my mind this article was the source of the "report" that Representative Cartwright had referenced. The Examiner had a conservative political following, so it made sense she might have seen the article years ago and remembered it after she was elected to Congress.

"Can you print a copy of this for me?" I asked.

"Not a problem," she said. "And I can send you a copy of it on email."

"That would be perfect," I said. "My boss is a new member on the House Administration committee. It's good background reading for her."

Grace stiffened. "I can't say this article is true. It might just be sensational journalism."

"Understood," I said. "I won't present it

as such. This is more about chasing down a lead." Grace didn't need to know that "lead" was really a code word for "murder suspect."

The librarian's face relaxed. "Oh, that's good to hear. We don't like to endorse sources we can't evaluate fully." She straightened her glasses and handed me the printout of the article.

"Don't worry," I said, heading out the door. "I won't jump to any crazy conclusions!"

At least not this afternoon. But I couldn't promise restraint if a break in the case didn't happen soon.

I sat down on the bench next to the elevator and read the article. It had been written as an expose, an obvious effort by the reporter to shine attention on the Architect of the Capitol. As the story went, several contractors had submitted bids for various projects, some high dollar. They were competitive proposals, often offering to complete the advertised work for a lower dollar amount than the winning bid. Of course, the lowest bid didn't always win in government contracting. Other factors were often in play, specified in the up-front terms. But the article made it seem as though this was happening too often in the Architect of the

Capitol's Office, intimating there was a nefarious pattern. Although there was no hard evidence in it, the article suggested that a senior official, the Architect himself, had been profiting from making sure the contracts got awarded to certain companies and not others. The term "kickback" failed to appear, but the reporter did everything but spell it out.

I wasn't paying attention to the Architect of the Capitol a few years ago when I worked in the Senate. But I couldn't remember any high-profile hearings or attention devoted to the issue. There were scandals no one on Capitol Hill forgot, like the Jack Abramoff lobbying fiasco or the Walter Reed Army Medical Center neglect crisis. This article might have gotten minor attention when it was written, but then Congress moved on to the next problem, most likely without a hearing or further consideration.

Who'd written this article, anyways? I used my finger to scroll to the top of the article. Marty Buchman. The name wasn't familiar. That didn't mean much, since I left press relations to our communications experts. Trevor could help with the situation. I forwarded him the link to the article as I hit the button for the elevator.

Before it arrived, my phone buzzed. It was

a text message from Meg. Hopefully she was just checking in.

WHERE ARE YOU???

The capital letters and multiple punctuation marks were not an auspicious sign.

Headed back now. Something wrong?

Three dots appeared. Meg was replying immediately.

GET BACK HERE

Then three more dots.

PRONTO!

I didn't really need the last text. I could have figured the request for my return had an immediacy to it. Meg was a lot of things. Understated wasn't one of them.

I jumped in the next descending elevator and double-timed it back to the Cannon Building. The late summer crush before recess had begun. Every lobbyist, tourist, well-wisher and naysayer had swarmed the nation's capital to press their sworn representatives into action. Anything not accomplished would have to sit until Congress assembled again in September. Heaven forbid if someone would have to wait five whole weeks for action.

Due to the crowded hallways filled with warm bodies and summer humidity, beads of sweat began to glisten on my forehead as I hustled back to the office. I wiped above my brow with the back of my hand while turning the hallway corner by our suite.

I'd been so fixated on navigating the crowds, I hadn't bothered to think what the crisis might be. Had Maeve accidentally voted incorrectly on an amendment? That had happened before, and although it was lamentable, it could be remedied with a statement for the record to establish her correct position. Or she'd said something damaging to the media? I looked at my phone. Twitter hadn't blown up, and if she had made a gaffe, no doubt it would be trending by now.

After opening the door to our reception area, I realized the problem had nothing to do with legislation or the press. It was much, much worse.

CHAPTER EIGHT

Our compact waiting room was filled to capacity. Granted, it only took ten people to fill up our entrance lobby. Some were sitting on the floor, others were standing with large signs. The lowly staff assistant who answered the phones was still trying to do his job, although his telephone headset was slightly askew on his head. I surveyed the room and stopped when I saw a tall, lanky guy with dirty blond hair holding a leash with a familiar beagle mutt at the end. As if on cue, my head started to throb at the exact moment Clarence barked.

I couldn't restrain myself as I marched across the room. "Sebastian, what are you doing here?" I wasn't even going to ask why he had Clarence with him.

His chin lowered as he averted my piercing gaze. "Sorry, sis. We didn't plan on coming to Representative Dixon's office. Or at least no one told me this was the plan."

Sebastian's merry band of protestors were obviously focused on the environment today. One sign read, "Want more cancer? Then deny climate change." Another said, "Treat the planet like it's Earth and not Uranus." However, a bookish-looking woman with thick glasses had the winner: "Without science, it's just fiction."

Before I could respond to Sebastian's pathetic attempt at an excuse, a guy with bushy brown hair and a shaggy beard pushed his way toward me. "Hey, that's the chief of staff. I saw her photo on Instagram with Dixon!"

Damn social media. Our communications team was way too effective. I needed to have a word with them when this was all over.

After taking a big breath, I turned my attention to the interloper and thrust my hand in his direction. "That's correct, sir. My name is Kit Marshall, and I am the Congresswoman's chief of staff. Can I ask why you and your friends are occupying our reception area this afternoon?"

"We need to save our planet," he bellowed. "And Maeve Dixon doesn't seem to care one bit."

The merry crowd of eco-protestors suddenly realized their leader had engaged in a conversation with a person of authority.

They stopped chattering and turned their attention to the unfolding drama.

"Wait a second," I said. "Where do you get the idea that Representative Dixon doesn't care about environmental issues?"

A woman behind the ringleader yelled out. "She voted against public lands!"

A skinny guy to my left joined in. "And she didn't join the amendment to protect streams!"

"And she's doing nothing to enact a carbon tax," said a mousy-looking girl wearing an "Earth Matters" T-shirt standing behind me.

That was enough. I pivoted with the speed of Michelle Kwan. "Did you say carbon tax?" I asked.

She blinked rapidly. "Yes. It's a top priority on our agenda."

I sighed. "I'm sure it is. But that's not going to happen anytime soon. The congresswoman needs to focus her efforts on initiatives that have a fighting chance."

Shaggy beard reengaged. "Spoken like a true bureaucrat." He paused to point directly at me. "This is what's wrong with Washington."

The crowd, which was closing in like an anaconda that hadn't eaten in a month, started murmuring all kinds of expletives and condemnations. The situation was going from bad to worse — and fast.

Just when I thought I was going to have to yell for the staff assistant to call the Capitol Hill police, a familiar female voice rose over the din. "Everyone take five steps backward. Right now."

Meg emerged from the rear of the lobby. Everyone's heads pivoted in her direction, but no one moved.

She put her left hand on her hip and pointed at the unruly crowd with the other. "You heard me. Back the hell up!"

Miraculously, our merry band of protestors did as they'd been told. "You can write your name on this sheet of paper with your email," said Meg. "As the legislative director, I'd be happy to send you information about Representative Dixon's positions on the environment."

One by one, our garrulous guests marched up to Meg and wrote their information on the piece of paper. After the last person had finished, they stood silently and stared at Meg.

"You can go now," Meg commanded. "After all, we have a congressional office to run here and constituents from North Carolina to serve." As she turned to leave, she issued one last missive. "Next time,

147

make an appointment. Better yet, make an appointment with the member of Congress who represents you!"

Without a word, the crowd exited our suite. Sebastian held back. His friends might have gotten off easy, but I wasn't done with my little brother.

"Sebastian, what were you thinking?" I asked.

"Like I said, I'm sorry. I knew we were headed to Capitol Hill today to draw attention to climate change, but I didn't know Dixon was on the list of offices we were going to visit," he said, chin quivering.

"That was really embarrassing. What if Meg hadn't been able to calm them down? I would have been forced to call the cops and have my own brother arrested!" I shook my head in disbelief.

Clarence looked up at me with big eyes, his tongue lolling out of the side of his mouth. Why are you yelling? Aren't you glad to see me?

When I bent down to pet him, I noticed he was wearing a green kerchief around his neck. "What's this?" I asked. Then I looked closer. "BARK TO SAVE THE PLANET" was printed on the scarf.

Removing it, I shook the bandanna at Sebastian. "And now you've even corrupted

Clarence!"

I stomped off, opened the door to our offices, and slammed it behind me. A moment later, Sebastian and Clarence followed me.

"What are you doing? You can't follow me back here!" I exclaimed.

The legislative team, which sat in small carrels in a cramped area of the suite, immediately looked up. Our office hummed throughout the day, filled with chitchat and discussions concerning our work. But loud voices were largely verboten. Maeve Dixon liked an orderly, calm office. I attributed these preferences to her military training.

Meg hadn't gone far. "Hello, Sebastian. Were you amongst the *hoi polloi* out there? I hadn't noticed." She smiled seductively. What a cunning minx Meg was.

"Umm . . . Yeah, I was," stuttered Sebastian. "Although I gather from Kit I shouldn't have been."

Meg waved her hand. "Water under the bridge, isn't it Kit?" She linked her arm underneath mine. "It's all in a day's work. And we love a visit from Clarence." She reached down to pet our mutt, who gladly licked Meg's hand.

I sucked in my breath. What a load of malarkey. If Sebastian hadn't been involved, Meg would have been the first person to complain bitterly about the mess. And while she liked Clarence, doggie drool was definitely not on her list of preferred substances.

Now it was Sebastian's turn at the charm offensive. "You certainly knew how to handle the situation, Meg." He flashed his pearly whites and ran his fingers through his sandy locks as he turned toward me. "You're fortunate to have someone like Meg as a colleague, Kit."

"I thank my lucky stars every day," I said, through clenched teeth. No one noticed the hint of irony in my voice.

Meg squeezed her arm tighter around mine. "Aww. You're so sweet. Isn't she, Sebastian?"

Before he had a chance to respond, Clarence barked. Everyone laughed, including me. Leave it to Clarence to ease the tension.

"Well, at least I have one vote of confidence, even if it comes from a canine," I said. "By the way, you did a great job in handling the situation, Meg. You didn't need me."

"I had a plan, but I had no idea if they'd listen. I figured if someone was going to get arrested, the chief of staff ought to be here," she said.

"That's probably a good rule of thumb.

Arrests can only be sanctioned by the chief of staff," I said. Turning to my brother, I asked, "Sebastian, are you still available tonight for dinner? Or are you going to be too busy leading the environmental revolution?"

"Very funny," he said. "I think I can take a break from demonstrating and dissenting. I'll see you later this evening."

Meg perked up. "I'd love to join you for dinner."

There was no use in mentioning she hadn't received an invitation. After all, she was my best friend and we did have a murder to solve.

"Most likely in Arlington," I said. "Are you sure you want to venture out to Virginia?" Meg lived in the city and only traveled to the surrounding suburbs when absolutely necessary or something really struck her fancy. I gathered Sebastian was enough of an inducement for Meg to make the trip.

"Of course," said Meg. "I simply love Arlington."

Enough was enough. I steered Sebastian and Clarence toward the door. "I don't know when I will be home tonight, but I'll text to let you know where to meet us."

Sebastian waved goodbye, and Clarence

eagerly followed his new friend, likely off to cause trouble in a host of other congressional offices. On impulse, I opened the door and called out to them just as they were about to leave our suite. "Do me a big favor, Sebastian?"

"Anything, big sister," he said.

"If you're going to continue protesting today," I said.

Sebastian nodded.

"Take a walk across the Capitol and visit the Senate," I said.

He gave me a salute and the dynamic duo walked out the door.

Chapter Nine

I'd just sat down at my desk to check email when Meg sauntered over. "Any luck figuring out who killed Melinda Masters?"

"Not yet," I admitted. "But it was still a productive day." I recounted my conversation this morning with Representative Bridget Cartwright, my lunch with Trevor and Doug, and my fact-finding mission about the Architect of the Capitol.

After listening to my story, Meg pouted. "I can't believe you had lunch at the Library of Congress and didn't invite me."

"The only reason that happened was that I ran into Trevor and texted Doug to let him know where we'd decided to eat," I said.

"I suppose so," she said, apparently mollified by my explanation. "Do you think Bridget Cartwright could have murdered the Architect of the Capitol?"

I rubbed my chin while considering Meg's question. "Absolutely. There's rumors that

Cartwright could face a formidable challenger in the next election. A new statue of James Madison on the Capitol grounds would yield her terrific press in the local media."

"Exactly what you need when you have a tight race," said Meg.

"We should know," I said. Maeve Dixon had almost lost her seat in Congress last year. We'd solved a murder case in record time to ensure that the police allowed us to leave the Washington, D.C. area to campaign for our boss.

"Don't remind me," said Meg. "By the way, Cartwright has a reputation on the Hill for a short temper."

"The type of temper who might take advantage of a situation to eliminate a rival?" I thought of the strangling vine that was used to kill Masters. Had Cartwright found herself in a heated argument with the Architect and made good use of the botanical weapon?

"Kit, if it's one thing I've learned in the past couple of years, almost anyone is capable of murder," she said.

"Well, that might be a bit of an exaggeration. But I understand your point."

My computer pinged, signaling an email had arrived. I glanced at the screen. "It's from Trevor. Let me read this quickly." I turned my swivel chair to face the monitor. A few seconds later, smiling, I said, "Good news."

"What's good news?" asked Meg.

"Trevor knows Marty Buchman."

Meg frowned. "Who's that and why do we care who Trevor knows?"

I ignored the second part of her question. "He's the reporter who wrote the article about shenanigans within the Architect of the Capitol's office a few years ago. Something tells me we need to find out if those accusations were real."

Meg rubbed her forehead. "Do you think this Marty Buchanan might have killed Melinda Masters?"

"Buchman, Meg, not Buchanan. You're getting him confused with the President who served right before Abraham Lincoln," I teased.

Meg tugged at her stylish two-buttoned camel blazer. She'd paired it with a matching sleeveless sheath, which flaunted her perfectly portioned silhouette. I didn't look too bad today, especially for having to rush out of the house after chatting with Sebastian and Doug. I'd tossed on my standard black pantsuit but had donned a yellow satin Henley top to add some color to the ensemble. I was no Coco Chanel, yet all hope was not lost.

"Buchanan, Buchman. I can't keep it all straight," she said. "And then there's something about Garfield thrown in. I suppose I need a doctorate in history to keep track of all the details in this case."

"Hopefully not, or we'd better hope Doug is paying close attention," I said. "But to answer your question, I don't know if Marty Buchman is a suspect. I still think I'd better talk to him about what he discovered a few years ago concerning the Architect of the Capitol and its operations."

"When are you planning to do that?"

"Don't know, but hopefully Trevor can set it up. If he can get Marty to agree to drinks tonight, are you interested?" Meg rarely turned down a happy hour.

"Normally, I would," she said coyly. "But I think I'll head home and freshen up before our dinner tonight."

I spoke slowly. "You're going home before dinner. And why would you do that?"

"Well, you never know, Kit," she said in an airy voice. "It doesn't hurt to look your best."

I couldn't disagree with that. "Okay, got it. I'm going to check with Trevor. Anything else I should know before I check in with the boss?"

"There is one thing," said Meg. "Jess and Oliver can't agree on the theme for the picnic."

"Theme? Why do we need a theme? All we need is a park, grill, food, and beverages." People who worked on the Hill were so used to controversy and complications, sometimes it was hard for them to complete the simplest tasks without a major crisis.

Meg ticked off things using the fingers on her right hand. "We need music, decorations, and activities. All of this requires a theme, Kit."

I threw my hands up in the air. "I concede. What are the options for a theme?"

"Jess wants to do a baseball theme. Oliver hates that idea. He prefers a Mexican fiesta."

I stood up and placed my hands on Meg's shoulders. "You are in charge here. I trust your decision in the matter." Then I hurried off to Maeve's office, ignoring the expletives Meg was uttering.

"Patsy, is Maeve available? I'd like to give her an update about my meeting this morning with Representative Cartwright," I said.

Patsy scrunched her face as she studied Dixon's schedule on her computer monitor. "She's here, but has a committee hearing she wants to attend for a few questions.

You've got five minutes with her."

I expressed my appreciation and knocked on Maeve's door.

"Come in, please," said my boss.

I strode across the room and sat across from Dixon, who was working at her desk. She looked up and straightened her shoulders. "Kit, do you have information about your morning meeting?"

I smiled and gave her a synopsis of this morning and afternoon's activity. She sat back in her high-backed chair and rubbed her chin thoughtfully. "Do you think you might be able to talk to this reporter?"

"Trevor is on it, ma'am. I'm hopeful," I said. "You remember Trevor, right?"

Even though Trevor didn't work for Representative Dixon, he'd become a semi-permanent fixture in our office, particularly when murder was concerned. "I do, so I share your optimism. But what do you think you'll learn from the meeting?"

"It's impossible to say," I said. "But worth following up on. If nothing else, it's informative for your service on the House Administration Committee."

"Good point," said Maeve. "I'm keen on the statue angle, however."

I wrinkled my nose. "You think Cartwright might kill for it?"

Maeve touched her fingertips together, forming a steeple. She tapped her fingers together several times. "Absolutely. Don't you remember what it's like to be in a tight reelection race?"

"Yes, although it's something I'd rather not think about too often," I said. "The memory still scars me."

"Exactly!" exclaimed my boss triumphantly. "Members know that the chance of not being reelected is quite small. But everyone knows someone who has lost or barely survived a really close contest. And they don't want anything to do with it."

"You're saying that Representative Cartwright might have killed Melinda Masters to get reelected?"

"Sure. It might sound goofy, but it's not," said Maeve. "Masters didn't support swapping out Garfield for Madison. Bridget probably viewed that as a threat to her popularity at home in her district."

"Could be," I said. "Aren't there more important things than a statue?"

"Of course, there are," said Maeve. "But Bridget has really pushed the envelope with the voters in her district. She feels pressure from both the conservatives and the liberals."

"So, an easy win would be a statue of

James Madison on Capitol grounds," I said, nodding my head.

"Just imagine all the photos and media coverage she'd get from it. Plus, it would attract voters from across the political spectrum."

I smiled as I stood up to leave. "Thanks, boss. Lest I forget, there's a reason why you're the elected member of the House of Representatives."

"Don't sell yourself short, Kit," said Maeve. "You're a pretty sharp politico, too."

"I'll try to remember that." From time to time, I had a confidence problem. That is, I forgot to have any in myself. I'd improved a lot in the past couple of years. I wasn't the same self-doubting Kit who'd worked in the Senate. Maeve Dixon deserved a good deal of the credit for my transformation. Many platitudes about Washington were overrated. A solid female role model wasn't one of them.

"One more thing," said Maeve. "Did you check in with Detective O'Halloran?"

"Not yet," I admitted. "But I will make sure I catch up with him."

"You might do that," said Maeve. "Remember, Rhonda Jackson is expecting you to serve as a liaison between her and the Capitol Hill police on this matter."

"How could I forget?" I muttered. In a clearer voice, I said, "Don't worry, ma'am. I'll secure an update from the detective."

Maeve nodded and returned her gaze to the papers on her desk, a surefire sign that I was dismissed. I skedaddled back to my desk and picked up the phone. Before I forgot, I needed to touch base with O'Halloran. I punched his extension on the keypad and waited for the phone to ring. It was doubtful he'd pick up. He was probably crisscrossing the Capitol complex to try to solve the murder.

I was altogether surprised when the good detective answered my call.

"O'Halloran here. Is this Ms. Marshall?" he asked.

"Yes," I sputtered, caught off guard. "How'd you know it was me?"

"I would think an amateur sleuth like yourself could figure that out," said O'Halloran. "Obviously the police on Capitol Hill have caller I-D. We want to know who we're talking with."

"Oh, yeah," I said sheepishly. "Not the hardest deductive reasoning in the world."

"How can I help you, Ms. Marshall?" asked the detective crisply.

"Given Chairwoman Jackson's instructions last night, I felt like it was time for a check in. Do you have any leads on the case?"

I heard a muffled sound on the line and something that resembled the smacking of lips. I'd caught O'Halloran at his desk because he'd be in the middle of his afternoon snack. Fifteen minutes earlier and I could have caught him at the Dunkin' Donuts inside the Longworth Building. It was one of his favorite haunts.

"Making some progress, Ms. Marshall," he said. "Be sure to tell the congresswoman that message."

"Chairwoman," I said. "You don't want to make that mistake twice."

More sounds came over the line. This time it sounded like a straw straining to capture the last couple ounces of iced coffee. At least O'Halloran would have the energy to keep investigating.

The detective ignored my comment. "Interesting office politics over at the Botanic Gardens. You wouldn't think plants could be so controversial. But it turns out they are."

Now we were getting somewhere. "What do you mean by that?"

"Talked to a few staffers over there this morning," he said. "Including Grant Dawson. Quite a personality. Let's just put it

162

this way. I'm not so sure Mr. Dawson is broken up over the death of the esteemed Architect of the Capitol."

"I talked to Dawson last night," I said. "Then he arrived at the crime scene shortly after Meg found the body. He showed up with Doug after I yelled for help."

"He mentioned that," said O'Halloran. "Seems like he was nearby right after the murder was committed."

"I never thought of that. I didn't ask him how he heard my call for help."

"He said he came across your husband waiting outside the tropical exhibit. They both heard your screams and opened the door to find you," he said.

"It's certainly plausible," I said. "After all, it was a big event at the Botanic Garden last night with the corpse flower bloom. He was probably tidying up and making sure everything was set with the caterers."

"Or he'd just murdered his boss and was fleeing the scene," said O'Halloran. "He stopped to talk to your husband because you'd been so chatty with him earlier in the evening."

"I can't disagree with you there. But let me tell you about what I discovered today." Then I launched into a summary of my discussion with Representative Cartwright and the possibility of a past scandal inside the Architect of the Capitol's office.

"Not bad legwork," said O'Halloran. "But who cares about an alleged impropriety from a few years ago? That's a helluva long time ago in Congress years."

I giggled. "Like dog years?"

"Let's face it. On Capitol Hill, someone's enemy today could be his best friend tomorrow. This place doesn't operate on normal standards of time. It works the other way, too. People hold grudges for twenty years about the stupidest things."

I had to hand it to the detective. He'd absorbed the culture with impressive perception.

"I don't know the answer to your question," I said. "But it still seems like something that deserves investigation."

"Well, I can't believe I'm going to say this, but what the heck?" said O'Halloran. "You follow that angle, and we'll keep comparing notes. It seems esoteric, and I definitely don't understand all the complicated operations which make this place tick."

"You got it," I said, a little too eagerly. "Thanks for working with me."

"One caveat, Ms. Marshall."

There was always a catch. "Go ahead." But he didn't have to say it. I already knew what he was going to say.

"If there's even the hint of danger, I want you to stop snooping," he said. "Call or text me immediately."

"I understand," I said dully. I'd heard this all before.

"I'm serious, Ms. Marshall," said the detective. "Do you know what's worse than solving the murder of a high-ranking legislative branch official?"

"No, Detective," I said weakly. Although it was obvious where he was going with this.

"Solving the murder of *two* high-ranking legislative officials. Don't add to my body count, Ms. Marshall. And that's an order."

CHAPTER TEN

I hung up the phone and sighed deeply. The detective didn't need to remind me about the dangers of chasing a murderer. Almost reflexively, I rubbed my hip. A killer I'd encountered previously had gotten dangerously close to making me one of his victims. I didn't want a repeat performance with this case.

My email inbox pinged. A message had arrived from Trevor. Brilliant. I clicked on the message and read it.

Marty can meet tonight. 5pm. I will drop by office to pick you up.

Good news, yet quite unusual that Trevor would walk over to my office in the Cannon Building. Why not just tell me where to meet? I hit the reply button.

Where are we going? I can catch up

with you there.

I drummed my fingers on my desk, waiting for Trevor's reply. Finally, it showed up in my inbox.

Trust me on this, Kit. We need to go together. You'll never find it on your own.

How utterly annoying. Even worse, my inner Simone de Beauvoir told me it smacked of sexism. Women couldn't find their way around the big city. I was about give Trevor a piece of my mind when it dawned on me that I should wait until he had actually taken me to Marty Buchman. Trevor was a prickly character. My luck, he'd react badly to my scolding and call the whole thing off. I closed my email inbox to minimize temptation to fly off the handle.

I made a quick turn around the office, checking in with our legislative staff concerning their ongoing policy work. The pace had picked up. The next week would be a sprint to the finish before everyone left Washington for pleasant vacation locales. The staff in Maeve Dixon's office knew the drill. Everyone was preparing for the hard work immediately before us, albeit with visions of sandy beaches, poolside bars, and piña coladas dancing inside our heads.

The last two staff sat in the far corner of our crammed office space. Jess was our social media coordinator, and Oliver was a legislative correspondent. That meant Jess wrote tweets, responded to Facebook posts, and came up with creative pictures to feature on Maeve's Instagram feed while Oliver wrote responses to constituents who had emailed our boss. They were both in their mid-twenties, a few years out of college and trying to make their way in our nation's capital. Somewhere along the path, they'd fallen in and out of love with each other. No big deal, except this was the House of Representatives and that meant they still needed to sit next to each other every single day until one of them found another place to work. It was an ongoing office saga that ranged from highly entertaining to highly annoying. Their latest feud concerning the annual Maeve Dixon picnic had trended toward the latter instead of the former.

"Afternoon, Jess," I said with as much cheer as I could muster. I saw Oliver glance up, a scowl on his face. "You too, Oliver."

They both grunted nearly inaudible hellos.

"What are we hearing on social media

today?" I asked Jess. Then I turned to Oliver. "And how's the mailbag?"

They both gave me uninspired replies about the nasty messages they were dealing with from the public and a run-down of the issues they'd heard most about today. The dynamic duo was never thrilled with each other these days, but today they seemed particularly annoyed.

Since they were Meg's direct reports, it didn't seem like I had to probe to discover the cause of their displeasure. After all, there were some mysteries I preferred not to solve. "Okay. Thanks for the update." I started to back away in the direction of my office.

Before I could make my escape, Jess spoke. "One more thing, Kit." She cleared her throat.

"Yes," I said, with my voice rising. "What is it?"

"Given the immigration crisis we're dealing with in the United States today, do you think it's suitable for Congresswoman Dixon's picnic to double as a Mexican fiesta? With people in sombreros eating taco-themed burgers, swinging at piñatas shaped like donkeys?" she asked.

I narrowed my eyes. Before I could say anything, Oliver piped up. "Wait a second.

169

This one," he pointed directly at Jess, "wants a baseball theme. Maeve Dixon doesn't even like baseball!" In a pique of anger, he threw his pen across his cubicle. Due to the incredibly cramped space, it hit the fabric wall and bounced back directly, nearly hitting him in the face.

I shook my head and inhaled a deep breath, a feigned calming exercise. The rest of the staff were staring. There was no privacy in a congressional office. It's what made minor problems like this into major crises. There would be buzz about this so-called altercation for days to come. I looked for Meg, but her desk sat empty. No rest for the weary.

"How about neither?" I countered. "Let's focus on having an old-fashioned picnic with no themes or special games. Just a bunch of people in a park, eating as many hamburgers and hot dogs as they please."

Jess and Oliver were silent and stone-faced. I waited for them to respond. When they didn't, I spoke again. "Sound like a plan?"

They looked at each other. "We'll think of something," said Jess.

"Thank you." I turned on my heels and trotted back to my office. Soon Trevor would be arriving to take me to an undisclosed location for drinks. Knowing him, I wouldn't be totally surprised if it was Capitol Hill's version of the Batcave.

Doug needed to know my plans, so I picked up the phone and dialed his extension. Now that he worked at the Library of Congress, he was on the same phone system as congressional offices.

The line rang twice, and Doug picked up. "Hey, sexy Ms. Marple," he said playfully.

His greeting startled me. I was certainly more used to a muffled hello. Doug was often buried in a mountain of books when I called. It usually seemed like I interrupted right when he was on the brink of making some important historical discovery.

"You sound awfully chipper," I said.

"Any progress on the murder?"

Doug had definitely caught the mystery-solving bug. "Some developments. In fact, that's why I'm calling. I was able to identify the reporter who tried to expose the Architect of the Capitol a few years ago. Of course, Trevor ended up knowing him, and he arranged for drinks tonight."

Doug was silent for a moment. "Do you want me to come?"

"You see, that's the thing. Trevor won't even tell me where we're meeting. He's coming in a few minutes to take me to the location," I explained. "He's being super secretive. It's probably best if I go alone with him. I don't want the journalist to get spooked."

I could almost hear Doug's enthusiasm deflate over the phone. "I understand," he said in a clipped voice. "When should we expect you home tonight?"

"Maybe seven? Then we can go out to dinner with Sebastian. Meg invited herself, too."

"Sounds fine."

"Hey, I hope you're not angry with me. But this case needs to be solved, pronto. Congresswoman Dixon has already talked to me twice about it today. She's got the chair of her committee breathing down her neck to find Masters's killer."

"I'm sure we can talk about it tonight," he said. "Listen, I'd better get back to my work. I'm going to squeeze in another hour of reading before going home."

"Bye, Doug," I said softly, setting the phone back in its cradle. Guilt washed over me. Maybe I should have just told Doug to come with us. But my gut told me this hadn't been an easy meeting for Trevor to secure, and it was important to speak with Marty Buchman. Tomorrow I'd figure out a way to include Doug in our sleuthing so he'd feel like he was part of the gang. Before Doug worked nearby, it was easier to fill him in on the case in the evenings or mornings. Now that he was a fellow Capitol Hill denizen, he obviously felt more compelled to join our merry band of politicos-turned-detectives.

Suddenly, I felt like someone was looking at me. I swiveled my chair around to face the front of my office. Trevor was standing directly in front of my desk.

"When did you arrive?" I asked. "And how did you get in here?"

"Just a moment ago," he said calmly. "Your boss was leaving when I arrived. She graciously opened the door for me and said I should make my way to your office."

It was a perfectly acceptable explanation, although I privately wondered whether Trevor didn't possess some hidden superhero ability to apparate upon command.

"Are you going to tell me where we're going?" I asked while gathering up my purse and phone.

"You'll see soon enough," said Trevor. "Is your other half coming with us?"

"Doug? He wanted to come, but I thought you'd want to keep this pretty tight."

"Actually, I meant Meg. From experience, I naturally assume you've already invited her." Trevor adjusted his glasses.

"Nope, afraid not," I said. "She's decided to skip this happy hour."

"That's decidedly odd behavior," said Trevor, his brow furrowed.

"I wouldn't worry about her. She wants to go home and get beautiful for dinner tonight," I said.

"Dinner? I didn't know Meg was dating again." He had a puzzled look on his face.

"She's not," I said. "At least, not officially. She's just preoccupied with Sebastian."

"Your brother? The protest-obsessed techie?"

I laughed at Trevor's amusing, yet accurate, description. "That's the one."

"He doesn't seem like her usual type," said Trevor.

My forehead wrinkled. "I'm not sure Meg really has a type. Except she's terribly prejudiced toward guys who are soft on the eyes. And my brother would certainly qualify."

Trevor said nothing in return. "Shall we go?" I asked. "We shouldn't keep Marty waiting, since he agreed to meet on such short notice."

Trevor blinked his eyes several times, as if he was trying to focus on what I was saying. "Yes, we should go now."

Before he turned to leave my office, I touched my hand lightly on his arm. "Trevor, are you feeling alright? You seem distracted." Trevor was usually laser-focused on the task at hand. It was both one of his most admirable and annoying qualities.

"I'm fine," he said quickly. "Let's not be late."

Meg was at her desk when we passed by. She put her hand up to her ear, motioning for me to call her while she mouthed "Let me know about dinner." I kept moving but gave her a "thumbs up" sign to let her know I'd be in touch.

After we exited the building, Trevor pointed for me to follow him along Pennsylvania Avenue. We passed by the conventional happy hour establishments, like Sonoma, the Hawk & Dove, and even the Tune Inn. Then we entered Seward Square, and Trevor slowed his pace.

"Are we having a happy hour in the park with our guest?" I asked. "If so, there's a liquor store a few blocks away. I can purchase a bottle of wine."

Trevor smirked. "Very funny, Kit. I'm simply trying to remember the exact location of the establishment." He scanned the square and pointed to the northeast corner. "That's where we need to go. A few blocks on North Carolina Avenue."

"Are we going to Eastern Market?" I asked, not bothering to hide the excitement in my voice. Eastern Market was a neighborhood food and art market within Capitol Hill. The plans for it were included in the original conception of the city by Pierre L'Enfant. The North Hall of the market was built by the same architect who designed the original Smithsonian buildings. In 2007, a fire severely damaged Eastern Market, but it was rebuilt and served as the center for neighborhood life on the Hill. Even though Eastern Market was only a fifteen minute walk from the Capitol, I rarely had the opportunity these days to visit, which was quite a shame. The vendors, surrounding restaurants, and artists were amongst the best in the entire city.

My hopes deflated for a pleasant summer evening at Eastern Market when Trevor quickly replied, "No, we're not."

Now I was puzzled. We were headed in that precise direction, but if we weren't going to a bar in Eastern Market, what sort of plans did Trevor have in mind?

We took a sharp right down Seventh Street Southeast with the main market building now on our left. "Oh, we're going to Tunnicliff's Tavern," I said. The neighborhood watering hole had been around for years. It was a still a mystery why Trevor couldn't have just met me here. Everyone knew where Tunnicliff's was. It was one of the top places in D.C. to have a drink before noon, not that I made it a practice to imbibe alcoholic beverages in the morning hours.

Trevor just shook his head but remained silent. We walked up to an Italian restaurant next to Tunnicliff's. Every outdoor table was filled to capacity. I'd heard about the Florentine Acqua Al 2. It had a good reputation. But it seemed hardly the right place to meet discreetly with a journalist who wanted to keep a low profile. Dining at Acqua meant you wanted to see people and be seen.

Trevor blew past the terrace diners and strutted up to an unmarked door. I tugged at his sleeve. "Um, Trevor, the door to the restaurant is right there," I said, pointing to the main entrance. "If we want a table, I'm pretty sure we need to see the host inside."

Trevor ignored my comment and opened the door. He motioned me to enter. "Ladies first." His lips were sealed in a tight smile.

Sometimes you needed to take a leap of faith. I went inside the building and stared down a long, dimly lit hallway. This excursion was shaping up like a bad horror movie. I half expected an evil doll or deformed backwoods ogre to emerge out of the darkness and chase me down the street.

Trevor pushed ahead and bolted down the hallway. This was ludicrous. "Trevor, I demand to know where we're going," I said, half-panting as I jogged to keep up with him.

As we reached a flight of stairs, he turned around. "Have you ever heard of a speakeasy?"

"You mean like in the days of Prohibition?" I asked. "Last time I checked, it's legal to drink alcohol on Capitol Hill. More like required behavior, in fact."

"Fair point," said Trevor. "Speakeasies have made a comeback, even though they're not illegal establishments. Fancy cocktails in hidden locations have a certain cache."

"So, what's the name of this place?" I asked as we climbed the stairs.

"Harold Black," said Trevor. "Now do you see why I couldn't just give you the address? You'd still be standing outside, looking around like a lost puppy."

I resented Trevor's characterization, which seemed way too harsh. After all, I had solved several murders on Capitol Hill. Surely, I could have figured out the entryway for a hidden bar.

"Give me a little credit," I murmured. "I'm not an idiot." Sometimes I wondered why our quasi-friendship persisted. Although he had admirable qualities, Trevor could be a major punk-ass.

Trevor turned to face me abruptly as we reached the landing. "I don't think you're an idiot," he pronounced.

"Well, sometimes you treat me like one."

Even though the lighting was low, I could tell that Trevor's face had turned a shade of deep crimson. "That's not my intention, Kit."

"It may not be, but it comes off like it is."

Trevor grimaced. "I apologize. Tonight, I didn't want you to get lost. So that's why I insisted we walk over together."

"Fair point, but why not just say that, Trevor?" I asked. "It would make it a whole lot easier if you were honest instead of snarky."

Trevor wrinkled his nose. "I guess we're being completely truthful, then."

"Absolutely. After all, shouldn't friends level with each other?" Rhetorical questions sometimes needed to be asked. In this case, Trevor might benefit from a reminder about how friends typically interacted with each other.

Trevor bit his lip. "In that case, I'd like to

tell you something."

"Okay, but shouldn't we speed this up? We have a date with Marty Buchman, and I'm kind of eager to keep it."

Trevor half-suppressed a laugh. "Funny you should mention dating," he said. "Because I need your advice. I'd like to ask Meg out."

CHAPTER ELEVEN

There was no point trying to hide my reaction to Trevor's revelation. My mouth fell open as my fingers touched my parted lips. I would have had a similar reaction if someone had told me Maeve Dixon had been elected Speaker of the House.

Trevor appeared nonplussed. "Something the matter?"

"It's a bit of bombshell," I stammered. "You always seem so . . ." I searched to find the right word.

He smiled coyly. "Annoyed with Meg?"

"Yes," I said, relieved he understood my confusion. "You're not similar at all." I hadn't meant to sound so blunt, but it was the truth.

"You know what they say. Opposites attract," said Trevor. "Do you think she'll accept my offer?"

I swallowed hard. Should I tell Trevor his chances were slim or let fate take its course?

Ever the compromiser, I opted for something in between.

"It's hard to say. She's not really dating too much these days," I said, leaving out her recent obsession with my younger brother.

"It never hurts to ask." Trevor took a deep breath.

"True enough. But you're outside the profile of the typical guy she goes for. You do realize that, Trevor?"

"I know, I know," he said, his shoulders slumping. "She goes for the guys listed in the Fifty Most Beautiful People of Capitol Hill list."

"Quite literally." Meg had dated so many men on that list, I'd lost track.

"But she took a hiatus from dating, and I thought that might mean she was reconsidering her choices," said Trevor.

"Yes, because her last boyfriend turned out to be a major disappointment." That might be the understatement of the year.

"Well, no time like the present. Of course, I'll keep you posted. It's always important to keep the best friend in your corner." He winked clumsily.

I turned to face the door, which had a "Please Knock and Wait to Be Greeted" sign on it.

"The entrance to Harold Black, I presume."

"Be my guest." Trevor motioned that I should do the honors.

I knocked on the door, and a man answered. "Good evening, and welcome to Harold Black. Do you have a reservation?" I peeked around and noticed the bar was quite small and exceedingly dark. Candles augmented the otherwise dimly lit room. I half-expected Humphrey Bogart to emerge out of the shadows and remark, "Here's looking at you, kid!" with a glass raised.

Trevor spoke up. "We're meeting someone who has a standing reservation, as I understand it. Marty Buchman."

The host's eyebrows raised. "Ah, yes. Marty is a regular customer. Always here on Wednesday evenings. You'll find him in our corner booth." He motioned to the rear of the bar, which was even darker than the rest of the place.

"This is very cloak and dagger," I whispered to Trevor. "Are you sure you know what you're doing? We're not meeting a spy or some clandestine character, are we?"

"For goodness sake, Kit," Trevor hissed. "He's a reporter who likes to meet his sources in a place less public than the Hawk 'n' Dove. That's hardly a crime. In fact, it's an indicator of good taste. Try to enjoy it. This is what you might call a throwback."

I kept silent, even though I was annoyed Trevor had dissed one of my favorite Capitol Hill watering holes. If I was really honest, trendy spots in Washington exhausted me. It was impossible to keep up, and inevitably by the time I got around to patronizing a so-called hot spot, it wasn't so hot anymore.

We approached the table to find a man slumped in the corner seat, a straw fedora pulled low on his head. He was sipping on a drink and reading a folded-up newspaper, glasses sitting on the edge of his nose.

Thankfully, Trevor took the lead. "Marty?"

Our guy looked up immediately, seemingly startled to see us standing at the edge of his table. But his countenance changed almost instantly, breaking into a wide grin. "Trevor, it's been a long time." He extended his hand for Trevor to shake.

Now that Marty Buchman had looked up, I could see he was a bulky guy, probably in his mid-fifties. He had a pale face with a five o'clock shadow and dark circles underneath his eyes. No wonder he liked spending time in the furtive recesses of Harold Black. He didn't seem like someone who exactly thrived in the unrelenting sunlight of Washington, D.C. in late July.

"Marty, I'd like to introduce you to Kit Marshall, chief of staff for Congresswoman Maeve Dixon from North Carolina," said Trevor. "But even more importantly, she's assisting the police on the Architect of the Capitol murder."

Our guest turned his gaze to me. He looked me up and down. "Please sit," he said. "You certainly don't look like a detective."

We took our seats, and I spoke up. "I'm not a licensed detective. But I've helped solve several other murders on Capitol Hill. Congressional leadership wants this murder solved quickly."

Buchman took another sip of his dark-colored drink. I doubted it was Pepsi. "Well, whatever congressional leadership wants in this town, congressional leadership gets," he said in a mocking tone.

I bristled at his comment. Marty Buchman was a jaded journalist, likely a has-been. I hoped Trevor hadn't drug me out tonight on a fool's errand while Sebastian and Doug waited for my return.

Trevor must have sensed my unease. "That's neither here nor there, Marty. The reason why we're here is that Kit found out about an article you wrote a few years back about the Architect of the Capitol. We want to find out the backstory."

Marty laughed. "Good old Trevor. Always wanting to get down to business. Before we do that, don't you think you two Hill rats should have a drink? You could benefit from some loosening up. You're both wound tighter than a pickle jar." He picked up a menu and placed it between us.

Actually, a drink sounded appealing after my helter-skelter day. I scanned the menu, replete with high concept cocktails. "How's the Juan Appleseed?"

Marty rubbed his chin. "It's more of an autumn cocktail." He squinted his eyes. "How much of a risk taker are you?"

I hesitated before answering. "I have my moments."

"Not the most enthusiastic response, but it'll do," said Marty. "The bartender over there can make you a custom cocktail if you let the waiter know what you like."

"I'm game," I said. "You only live once."

Trevor wrinkled his nose. "Normally, I'm quite adventurous."

I worked hard to make sure my face remained neutral. I'd never thought of Trevor as the adventurous type.

"But today, I think I'll go with the Mule It Over," he finished.

Marty's face brightened. "Excellent

choice. A classic vodka concoction."

He called our waiter over and placed our order, adding a Harlem Stir for himself. I explained I preferred gin and liked sweet drinks over bitter.

"Anything more specific?" our waiter prodded.

"Nope," I said. "I'm more of a wine drinker. I don't drink much liquor."

The waiter nodded, obviously unimpressed, before he scuttled off.

I leaned forward in the booth. "Thank you, Mr. Buchman, for meeting with us on such short notice. I know you must be very busy."

"First off, let's go with Marty now. I'm not sure I'll ever answer to Mr. Buchman," he said. "Second, I'm not sure how busy I am these days, but I'm always willing to help someone who's trying to make sure justice prevails."

"That's certainly my motivation, *Marty*," I said, emphasizing his first name. "We want to find out who killed Melinda Masters. And that means figuring out what was going on inside the Architect of the Capitol's office."

The waiter arrived and served our drinks. He presented me with a tall glass with ice filled with a light pink liquid. "I think you'll like this," he said. "Top shelf gin, a strawberry lemon syrup, our specialty homemade tonic, and fresh strawberries to top. Perfect for a hot summer night."

My eyes must have lit up like a poolside Charlie Rose. Trevor said, "Go ahead, taste it and let us know what you think."

I stirred the drink and took a sip. "Just like a gin and tonic, only better."

"That's high praise coming from her," said Trevor. "She and her best friend are the reigning queens of Capitol Hill happy hours."

Marty straightened from his perennial slump. "You're becoming more interesting by the minute, Kit Marshall."

"I'm flattered," I said. "Can you tell us about the *Examiner* article you wrote about the Architect? Why did you write it, and who were your sources?" I took another big sip of my drink.

Marty backed up against the edge of the booth. "Whoa, that's a lot of questions. Just let me tell my story." He took a deep breath. "A few years ago, I got a call from a burner phone."

"How'd you know it was a burner?" asked Trevor.

Marty wrinkled his nose. "I don't trust calls if I can't identify the source. I have a service who traces them for me. And this one was a burner. Come on, Trevor, give me some credit. I'm an investigative reporter."

"Okay, so you got a call from a burner," I said, trying to move this along. "And then what happened?"

"The guy on the other end of the line wanted to give me a tip that something funny was happening with the contracts at the Architect of the Capitol," said Marty. "He'd just lost out on some big bid to rebuild the sidewalks around the Capitol. He got my attention. It's not every day you get a tip like that. After all, the Architect is big business, at least by Capitol Hill standards."

"Hundreds of millions of dollars flow through the A-O-C every year," I said. "I read it in the Congressional Research Service report."

Marty nodded. "Many of the contacts are multimillion-dollar initiatives. Believe me, I've been reporting on stuff like this for over twenty years. I know when someone is pulling my leg or if it's sour grapes. My gut told me this guy was telling the truth, at least from his perspective."

"So, you had a good lead," said Trevor. "What did you do after the call?"

"Well, there's a lot of procedures in place for federal contracting to make sure this type of funny business doesn't happen. Even though I believed my caller, I wasn't sure he had a legit case," said Marty, gulping down the last sip of his drink.

He motioned for the waiter to pour him another. I put my hand over the top of my glass, indicating I didn't need a second drink. The libations at Harold Black weren't the watered-down variety. To my surprise, Trevor ordered a refill. Maybe he was loosening up these days.

"How did you check up on his story?" I asked.

"I don't divulge my methods or my sources," said Marty cryptically. "But let's just say I did my homework. And my phantom caller provided me with several documents which verified his story."

"I take it your source thought he'd missed out on a big federal contract," said Trevor.

"More than one," said Marty. Our waiter returned with the two drinks. Marty didn't waste any time. He grabbed his and took a sip while giving Trevor a sideways glance. "You're buying tonight, right?"

Trevor nodded. "Of course, Marty. You're doing us a favor by talking."

Marty seemed satisfied with Trevor's

response. A tight smile spread across his face. "Music to my ears. Particularly since I'm in between jobs these days."

"I thought you wrote for the *Examiner*," I said.

"You may not have noticed given your cushy federal government job," said Marty. "The journalism industry has turned upside-down in the past decade. There are very few permanent reporter gigs anymore." Marty's eyes, which had sparkled a few minutes ago, looked flat and lifeless.

"I know what you're talking about," I said. "But I would have thought someone with your stature might have survived the downsizing."

Marty smacked his lips after another sip of his Harlem Stir. The man certainly could hold his bourbon. "Investigative journalism is a luxury these days. But I'm lucky. Given my name, I can cobble together a decent existence by freelancing."

"You don't write for any one publication?" asked Trevor.

"No allegiances and no ties," said Marty, shoulders back proudly. "It's actually better this way. I come up with good stories and sell them to the highest bidder."

I'd wondered why Marty Buchman had been so solicitous when Trevor had contacted him. Something was rotten in the state of Denmark, and it smelled like a Pulitzer Prize. Marty had been nominated once but had come up short. My Spidey sense told me he wanted to even that score.

"And are we fodder for your next big story?" I asked, tracing my finger around the rim of my now-empty glass.

Marty scowled. "Don't flatter yourself too much, Ms. Marshall. So far, you ain't told me crap. I always drink at Harold Black on Wednesday nights. I merely told Trevor where I'd be, in case he wanted to buy me a few." He lifted his glass and tilted it toward me. "Or maybe three."

Trevor leaned in. "Kit's working on the murder of Melinda Masters." He waved his hand impatiently. "I can tell you some other time why a congressional chief of staff is assisting the Capitol Hill police on these matters. Suffice to say, it's a long story. But she has reason to believe something fishy might still be going on at the Architect of the Capitol."

I quickly recounted the limited information I'd managed to gather earlier today. Marty appeared to listen intently, without interruption or questions. At the end of my short speech, he leaned back in the booth and rubbed his eyes.

"Bridget Cartwright is an intelligent and potentially ferocious Pitbull," pronounced Marty. "Let's put it this way. It's unlikely she's going to bark up a tree without due cause. It's a waste of her time to pursue leads without merit."

"You think she's right to believe that contracts aren't being awarded properly," I said.

He waved his hand dismissively. "It's too early to say. Hell, the guy I had as a confidential source turned out to be tenuous. But he put me in contact with others who corroborated his story. It didn't make a lot of sense who was winning some of these big dollar awards. They weren't low-cost and they weren't hitting all the required marks. It smelled. Big time."

"But Melinda Masters didn't even work for the Architect of the Capitol when this happened a few years ago," I said. "And we're trying to solve her murder. I'm not sure there's a connection, even if there were shenanigans under the previous Architect."

Marty and Trevor both sat silent. I'd made a good point. The former Architect of the Capitol was long gone. He'd retired to some tropical location, as I recalled. he'd benefited from kickbacks during his tenure, but he wasn't still in the game.

"Unless it was much more complicated than we imagined," said Marty slowly. "What if there was a desire to continue fixing contracts and Masters didn't approve?"

Trevor drained his glass. "That could make sense, I suppose. But then that means the culprit was internal. He or she had to bump off Melinda so the sting could continue."

I nodded. "That's a motive for murder." Then I snapped my fingers. "That guy Steve."

"Steve who?" asked Trevor. "There's probably about a million in Washington."

"The executive director of the Botanic Garden. Grant Dawson pointed him out to me last night before the murder," I explained. "He was the deputy but got passed over for the job when Melinda was appointed."

Marty rubbed his chin. "Plausible enough. He's the heir apparent. But when he doesn't get the full-time gig, he gets greedy. Maybe Masters won't play ball."

Trevor adjusted his glasses. "And he's got no choice but to murder her."

"It's a good theory, but we've got no real evidence." I glanced at my Fitbit. It was close to seven. "Look at the time! I have to run. My brother is in town, and I'm meeting him for dinner."

"Not just him," said Trevor, a hint of glumness in his voice.

"That's true," I said. "Meg and Doug are coming, as well." I turned to Marty. "That's my best friend and husband, respectively."

Marty extended his sizable hand, which reminded me of a bear paw. "Pleasure to meet you, Kit Marshall."

"Likewise," I said. "Can you continue to think about our discussion?"

Marty scrunched up his face, like he was trying to solve a complicated math equation. "I have to admit I'm intrigued. Right now, I'm in between gigs. So, I might be able to put some time into this."

"That's totally up to you," I said. "Unfortunately, Trevor and I don't have a budget to hire consultants on our murder cases. But that doesn't mean we're not eager to have help along the way. My boss is counting on me to help solve this murder. But I also really want to make sure the guilty person is brought to justice."

Marty tipped his hat in response. I turned to Trevor. "I'll be in touch."

"Please do," said Trevor. "Remember, my boss wants this murder solved just as much as yours."

I smiled tightly. "Thankfully, I don't

answer to your boss, but I understand." I waved goodbye and hustled out of the dark bar and into the July night.

The Eastern Market metro was nearby. Could I hop on it and meet everyone at the restaurant by half past seven? I texted Doug, Meg, and Sebastian on a single thread. They agreed to meet at Nam-Viet, a longstanding Arlington Vietnamese restaurant only two blocks from the Clarendon metro station. As long as there were no catastrophic delays, we could be seated and enjoying spring rolls in no time flat.

Thankfully, the evening rush on the Metro had passed and the ride was uneventful. The relative peace and quiet gave me an opportunity to think about Trevor's out of the blue revelation. Had I missed something? I wracked my brain. Now that I knew about Trevor's hidden feelings for Meg, a few details made more sense. It had surprised me that he was willing to meet us the night of the murder at Ted's Bulletin. Trevor didn't keep late hours. But he'd used it as an opportunity to see Meg. He'd obviously been surprised when I told him she might consider dating again, especially with Sebastian in the picture. Had Trevor wanted to ask Meg out for a while, since she declared her moratorium on romance after the election? If so, Trevor had been waiting a long time for his opportunity.

The biggest puzzle was Trevor's switch in opinion of Meg. When we worked in the Senate office together, he'd made it abundantly clear he thought both of us were intellectual lightweights. His opinion had softened over time, although this latest development represented a drastic shift. Meg was definitely a looker, so it shouldn't be too surprising Trevor found her alluring. Who knows? Maybe Trevor had always had a crush on Meg but never had the courage to act upon it. The origins of his affection were unknown, yet I wasn't entirely sure they would be reciprocated. While Meg's dating behavior had decidedly matured in the past couple of years, she'd always gravitated toward men who were pretty darn attractive. That being said, Trevor wasn't completely disadvantaged in that respect, although his appeal was likely an inside-the-Beltway phenomenon. He was successful, self-confident to a fault, and well-mannered. Dressed for success, Trevor always made an impressive appearance; he probably had a style guru on his speed dial. Like other Washington men, a tendency toward cockiness made him seem emotionally unavailable. Trevor aimed to lower his protective shield and take a risk by pursuing Meg.

Even if it didn't work out, I hoped she would let him down easy. Should I give her a heads up about it? My best friend intuition told me I should, but Trevor hadn't explicitly asked me to speak with Meg about it. As with everything in Washington, it was best to keep my mouth shut until I had more information to make a reasoned decision. I couldn't remember the last time that advice had failed.

Just as I was about to turn my thoughts to murder, the subway train arrived at the Clarendon station. Five minutes later, I spotted Doug, Meg, and Sebastian, their faces partially obscured behind menus.

"Good evening, everyone," I said cheerily.

Doug patted the chair next to him. "Have a seat. Don't worry. We already put in two orders of crispy spring rolls."

Sebastian rubbed his hands together in anticipation. "I'm looking forward to dinner. Vietnamese cuisine is one of my favorites."

"Nam-Viet is a special place. The food is delicious, but it's also historically significant," said Doug.

Meg grinned as she placed her napkin on her lap. "Tell us all about it."

I narrowed my eyes but kept quiet. Meg

was not a fan of Doug's historical musings, but she must have sensed Sebastian's interest.

Our plate of spring rolls arrived, and we each selected one. Doug and I wrapped them in leaves of lettuce, served alongside the rolls, and then dipped them in the light sweet and sour sauce. Fried with pork, vermicelli, and chicken, the rolls weren't exactly low-calorie, but a meal at Nam-Viet wasn't complete without them.

After a few bites, Doug spoke up. "Many Vietnamese immigrated to the United States after the war in the 1970s. Because of ties to the embassy, a high percentage ended up in the Washington area. They settled in Arlington because it was an economical alternative to the city. This was before the retail and residential development here. The cornerstone was in Clarendon, where many Vietnamese businesses thrived."

Sebastian tilted his head. "I walked here from your condo. I didn't see many Vietnamese owned establishments."

Doug finished off his roll and reached for another. "Very observant. The Vietnamese population has moved from Clarendon to several miles west in an area of Falls Church called Seven Corners. Eden Center is now the major hub of stores and restaurants. Nam-Viet is the only surviving Vietnamese restaurant from the days of Clarendon as Little Saigon."

Our waiter arrived to take our order, which was easy for me. I loved the Pho Ga, which was Vietnamese noodle soup with chicken. Doug preferred the Pho Bo, served with beef. Sebastian ordered the Hanoi grilled pork, and Meg opted for the popular Lemongrass Chicken.

"I'd love to talk more history," I said, squeezing Doug's arm. "But I've got other topics to discuss."

"What is it, sis?" asked Sebastian.

"Oh, that's an easy question," said Doug. "When there's a murder to solve, Kit has a one-track mind."

"Me, too," said Meg defensively. "I was just about to ask about the meeting with the journalist."

I recounted our conversation at Harold Black's speakeasy with Marty Buchman.

Sebastian pursed his lips. "Sounds a bit too film noir for my tastes. Are you sure it's safe to pursue criminal leads? These characters seem unsavory."

I helped myself to tea, served in small white pot with four small accompanying glasses. Despite the heat of the summer, I couldn't resist Nam-Viet's perfect blend of sweet and spicy fragrances. "Not any more intimidating than the other suspects we've dealt with," I said. "Besides, we're working with the police on this one."

"What does Detective O'Halloran think?" asked Doug.

"The police spent time at the Botanic Garden today," I said. "He mentioned there was intrigue there. Office politics and whatnot. I believe he spoke with Grant Dawson."

"Doesn't that support what you learned from your source today?" asked Sebastian.

Our waiter arrived with our food and set steaming plates and bowls before us. "Anything else I can get you?"

I wiggled my hand. "You know the type of sauce I like."

He nodded eagerly. "Coming right up."

Meg picked up her chopsticks and dove into her chicken. "What did you ask for, Kit? I didn't know the Marshall siblings were such fans of Vietnamese food." She touched Sebastian's arm lightly, which would have been fine except he'd just speared a sizable piece of grilled pork. It flew out of the grasp of his chopsticks and landed in the middle of the table.

"I'm so sorry," gushed Meg.

Sebastian blushed, Doug tittered, and I decided to ignore the faux pas altogether.

The waiter arrived with a big bottle of what I affectionately called "rooster sauce" but was properly known as sriracha. The nickname came from the big picture of a rooster on the bottle. Made from a paste of chili peppers, vinegar, garlic, sugar, and salt, sriracha wasn't for the faint hearted. Doug shuddered. "I don't know how you inhale that stuff, Kit. It gives me heartburn."

I turned the bottle upside down and squirted it into my big bowl of soup, not unlike a ten-year old adorning his hot dog with a healthy dose of ketchup. "To each his own," I said. "It clears my sinuses."

"Hear, hear." Sebastian grabbed the bottle from me and squirted a blob onto his plate. "Kit and I loved spicy food when we were growing up."

After stirring my soup, I took a sizable sip with the oversized spoon provided with it. "Heavenly," I murmured as the burn of the sriracha warmed my entire body. I'd forgotten Sebastian and I shared similar taste buds. The reminder of our family bond was comforting to me.

After taking a big gulp of water, I pointed my chopsticks in Sebastian's direction. "To answer your earlier question, I suppose you're right. If there was discord at the Botanic Garden, it could be tied to the bigger issues we heard about today."

"It sounds like a nightmare. Not like the management in our congressional office, which is top notch." Meg smiled slyly at Sebastian, who seemed to avoid her gaze. he was afraid he'd lose another yummy piece of pork if she touched him again.

"That's not the pot calling the kettle black or anything," said Doug, inhaling a long noodle from his Pho Bo.

"I happen to agree with Meg," I said. "But I'm not sure this was Melinda Masters's fault due to a lack of management skills. She was selected for the position because she brought an outsider's perspective to the office. And she'd been a successful leader in private industry."

"But maybe that was her problem." Sebastian rubbed his chin thoughtfully. "Outsiders often try to institute changes too quickly. The murderer decided to put a stop to it."

"It's a plausible motive," I said. "Now we just need to figure out who might have felt threatened enough to kill her."

Doug picked up the bottle of sriracha and squeezed a couple more squirts into my soup.

"What was that for?" I asked.

"Helping you clear your brain," he said. "You're going to need it to solve this murder."

CHAPTER TWELVE

After dropping Meg off at the Metro station, we strolled back to our condo building. At nine o'clock, the heat had finally broken, and a short evening walk became bearable.

"Sebastian, how are you enjoying your stay in the greater Washington area?" asked Doug in a friendly brother-in-law tone.

"I've always liked D.C.," said Sebastian. "I wonder if this is the right time for a move."

If dusk hadn't already fallen, Sebastian would have certainly seen the expression of shock on my face. "Permanently?"

As soon as I'd spoken, I regretted it. What a crappy big sister I was. I should have said, "What wonderful news!" But I'd been disconnected from Sebastian for years. The change was almost too sudden.

My brother turned to look at me. "There's plenty of opportunities for tech work in this area. And given the political climate, it seems as though the time for protesting is ripe."

"That makes sense," I said with no delay.

"Sounds like an exciting prospect," said Doug enthusiastically. "Here we are."

We'd arrived at our condo building. A minute later, we braced ourselves at the door. "We need to be careful. Clarence likes to escape into the hallway," I explained.

Sebastian nodded. "I know. We had an incident earlier today."

After a swift opening and closing of the door, we were inside in a flash. Clarence sat at our feet, tail wagging. To my surprise, he jumped up on Sebastian and ignored Doug and me.

"Traitor," I murmured, staring at my dog.

"What was the incident concerning Clarence?" asked Doug.

"It wasn't a big deal." Sebastian rubbed Clarence's ears. "We came home and fell asleep for a while. I guess we were exhausted."

"Taking over a congressional office can have that effect," I said, my lips pursed together.

Sebastian ignored my comment and continued with his story. "I woke up and realized I'd forgotten to eat lunch. I took a quick trip to your local deli and came back with a turkey sandwich. I guess Clarence got excited when he smelled the turkey. He tried to grab the sandwich from me as I opened the door. He must have figured out he could run down the hallway, so he sprinted to the other end before I could catch him and bring him back to the condo."

This was typical Clarence shenanigans. But I suspected Sebastian was holding back. "That was it?" I asked in a strained voice.

"One of your neighbors did open her door and yell at us," he said, his cheeks flushed.

"Undoubtedly, it was Mrs. Beauregard," said Doug. Our elderly neighbor preferred cats over dogs ("much more civilized animals") and detested Clarence's exuberance. His recent penchant for barking had pushed Mrs. Beauregard over the edge. She routinely reported Clarence to the oversight board, reciting chapter and verse from the sacrosanct condo covenant to bolster her claims.

"I believe that was her name," said Sebastian. "But don't worry. I talked with her and she seemed happy as a clam when I left."

"You charmed Mrs. Beauregard?" I asked, the pitch of my voice rising at the end of the question.

Sebastian ran his fingers through his hair.

"I think so. She invited me and Clarence over for tea later this week if we have time."

Doug and I exchanged a glance of pure wonderment. My brother could surely turn on the charm when necessary. He did have a future in Washington, D.C.

After we said our good nights and Clarence got a brief walk around the neighborhood, I fell into a deep slumber. In my dream, I was standing in the middle of the Botanic Garden greenhouse. Plants were all around me and it was perfectly quiet. Then, the corpse flower started opening and closing its petals rapidly, like it was morphing into a man-eating plant. I half-expected Rick Moranis to burst into song as the plant exclaimed "Feed me, Seymour." But no such luck. Instead, the plants began to rustle, and before I could move, their vines grew longer and wrapped themselves around me like a boa constrictor. I tried to grab the vines and pull them off, but they were too powerful. One wrapped itself around my neck and I opened my mouth to scream, but nothing came out.

The next thing I knew, I was sitting upright in bed, sweat pouring off my forehead and neck. Clarence woke up with a start and growled, probably annoyed his dream about chasing squirrels and eating unlimited milk-bones had been rudely interrupted. Snoring like there was no tomorrow, Doug didn't stir for a moment. I reached for a glass of water on my nightstand and took a long sip as I tried to shake my nightmare. It wasn't unusual for me to dream about work, but when my job intersected with murder, the results were less than auspicious.

When Clarence realized nothing was amiss, he settled down and fell back asleep. It wasn't quite as easy for me. Too much was rolling through my brain. My biggest problem was figuring out who killed Melinda Masters and why. Besides wanting to bring the murderer to justice, my boss was counting on me since Chairwoman Jackson wanted it solved pronto. Then, there was the bombshell Sebastian had dropped tonight after dinner. What would it be like if my little brother moved to Washington? After living on the west coast for so many years, why was he keen to relocate suddenly? Layered on top of Sebastian's reappearance was Meg's seeming obsession with him. If he moved here, would they become involved romantically? Although I knew Meg and my brother were grown adults and could pursue a relationship if it made them happy, it made me squeamish to think that my best friend might hook up with my brother. And if that wasn't enough, there was the added bonus of Trevor's admission that he secretly pined for Meg. I had no idea how that would evolve, but it could certainly make our future crime-solving endeavors much more complicated if Meg demonstratively rebuffed Trevor's advances. How did I get involved in all these dramas? Sometimes I felt like the eye of the storm, a relative space of calm with chaos spinning out of control around me.

Both Doug and Clarence snored in peaceful sync with each other. Evidently, neither was bothered by these troubles. Clarence had a good excuse: he was a dog. But Doug never suffered from the anxiety which came with solving the world's problems. I needed to take a page out of his playbook, but only after I solved this murder.

The chimes of our intelligent personal assistant woke me hours later. "Alexa," I barked. "Alarm off."

In a pleasant voice, she responded, "Okay."

How I wished all my daily interactions could be so civil.

Sebastian was still sleeping, and Doug said he had a breakfast at Georgetown to attend this morning. I really needed to get to work early, but I hadn't exercised in days. I remembered Sebastian's recommendation about burpees. Twenty burpees were better than nothing. At the end of it, I was panting, and my arms were sore from pushing my body from the ground. Maybe Sebastian knew what he was talking about.

With no additional delays to hinder my morning ritual, I arrived at work shortly after eight. Most congressional offices didn't get moving until much later in the morning, but Maeve Dixon believed in early starts. Sure enough, I saw the light on in her private office. Most likely, she'd already worked out at the House gym, read the major newspapers, and drank her breakfast protein shake. I was much less ambitious, but I did need some coffee. Before searching for some much-needed caffeine, I'd better give Maeve an update and make sure she still wanted me to devote time to the murder.

Our scheduler hadn't arrived yet, so I knocked on the door gently and cracked it open. "Congresswoman, it's Kit. Do you have a minute?"

Maeve was studying her iPhone with her reading glasses perched on the edge of her nose. She waved me in. "Good morning," she said crisply as she removed her cheat-

211

ers. "Do you have an update for me on the Masters investigation?"

I'd worked for Dixon for almost two years now, and we'd weathered through a tough reelection campaign together. Her all-business demeanor still caught me off guard. At least she'd wished me a good morning. Sometimes that didn't even happen.

"It was an eventful evening." Then I launched into a detailed description of our meeting with Marty Buchman at the secret speakeasy.

Dixon listened intently, her forehead crinkled in deep thought. "Did you ask him about Bridget Cartwright and a possible motive?"

"We didn't talk about the Garfield statue. But he did say that Cartwright was a tough legislator and she never focuses on problems that don't exist."

Dixon pushed her chair back from the desk and stared out the window. After several moments of silence, she asked, "Did you tell the detective about this development?"

"Not yet, but I did speak with him on the phone yesterday. He spent several hours at the Botanic Garden, talking to employees who might have known Melinda Masters or seen something suspicious at the reception."

"You'd better touch base with him again," said Dixon. "It's fine for you to pursue different leads, but you should both share information. That's the only way to ensure this case will be solved quickly. And I can also tell Rhonda Jackson that her idea for a liaison was a good one." Maeve smiled mischievously.

"Understood, ma'am. I'll get on it." I turned to exit her office.

"Kit, wait a second. What's your next move, by the way?" she asked.

"I might touch base with Grant Dawson at the Botanic Garden," I said. "My brother pointed out last night that Dawson might know something about this alleged malfeasance."

Dixon nodded. "Well, at least you're still getting to spend some time with him, even if the discussion revolves around murder."

I decided to let sleeping dogs lie. My boss didn't need to know that Sebastian had led the impromptu protest inside her congressional office yesterday. I had a feeling her encouragement to spend more time with my only sibling might evaporate if she knew the complete truth about his extracurricular activities.

I rushed back to my desk and picked up

the phone. Before forgetting, I'd better touch base with O'Halloran. This time, I wasn't so lucky. His phone rang, but no one picked up. Same thing with his cell number. "Drat."

"What's the matter?" I turned and spotted Meg right outside my office.

"Come in." I replaced the phone on its cradle. "I was trying to reach Detective O'Halloran to give him an update."

Meg wore a pretty red wrap-around dress with tan high heels. "Is that new?" I asked, pointing to her frock.

"This?" she answered innocently. "I picked it up on sale. I'm not sure if I've worn it before."

That was a prevarication if I ever heard one. Meg knew exactly when she last wore every single item in her closet. She might even keep an Excel file, for all I knew. She was very keen on not repeating outfits based upon her social calendar.

I narrowed my eyes but decided for the second time this morning it was better to move on rather than engage.

"Do you want some coffee?" I asked. "I'm headed over to Longworth to grab a cup."

"Sure. Just let me get my purse. I'll see you in the front," she said.

I glanced at my email inbox. It was full of

214

unread messages, undoubtedly other chiefs or committee staff directors asking for Maeve Dixon's support on amendments, bills, or co-signed letters. Normally, I'd go over the most relevant prospects with Meg and then we'd present our boss with options. But it was clear that Dixon wanted my attention focused on the Melinda Masters case.

Meg was waiting for me in our small lobby, engrossed in conversation with our newly minted staff assistant who'd survived yesterday's office occupation. "Ready to go?" I asked.

"Sure, boss." She followed me out of the office.

I inwardly groaned. Meg liked to call me "boss" around the other staff members. She thought it mitigated allegations of favoritism since we were best friends in addition to work colleagues.

"What was that all about?" I asked. "Is there a problem?" Sometimes, new hires didn't work out. If that was the case, I needed to know pronto. The staff assistant was the most junior person in a congressional office but served a critical function as the first line of friendly defense as constituents or other important people entered our office suite.

"Burt was giving me an update concerning our ongoing picnic saga," said Meg.

"I spoke with Jess and Oliver yesterday," I said. "Everything seemed like it was moving in the right direction."

Meg hit the elevator's down button. "Well, of course they acted that way in front of you. You're the boss, Kit. They're not going to air dirty laundry when you're around."

Frowning, I said, "There's an open-door policy in the Dixon office. Staff know they can speak honestly."

We stepped onto the elevator and went down to the basement. Meg placed her hand on my arm. "The boss is still the boss. Anyways, Burt told me the latest dispute is about dessert. Jess wants to order a cake and Oliver wants brownies and cookies. We don't have enough money for both."

I rubbed my temples. "Please tell me you're going to sort this out. If I'd known it was going to be so difficult to organize an office picnic, I would have told Maeve to forget it and take everyone out for pizza instead."

"Don't worry. I'm on it," said Meg. We walked through the basement of the Cannon Building, the crossroads for Capitol Hill. "More importantly, what did you think of last night?"

216

I looked at Meg quizzically as we walked past the Longworth Building post office. "Last night? What do you mean?"

"Our dinner, silly," she said. "Did Sebastian say anything?"

I knew what Meg was hinting at, but I wasn't going to take the bait. "He liked the restaurant," I said blandly.

We walked inside the rear of the large Longworth cafeteria and stopped in front of Dunkin' Donuts. "Not about the food, Kit," said Meg impatiently. "About me."

"Oh," I said meekly. "It didn't come up."

Meg's forehead wrinkled in anger. "Really?" she asked, the incredulity dripping from her voice. "And you didn't ask?"

"In case you didn't notice, I have a lot on my mind these days," I said.

Behind us in the queue, a deep voice interrupted our conversation. "Hopefully not too much on your mind that you're not sharing with me, Ms. Marshall."

We swiveled around to find Detective O'Halloran standing behind us.

"Oh, it's you," I said excitedly. "I called you a few minutes ago, but you weren't at your desk."

"The detective's location at this time in the morning is no mystery," said Meg.

O'Halloran's face turned red. "I do like a

chocolate frosted with my coffee." By the sizable paunch beneath his belt, he was certainly guilty as charged.

We approached the counter. "Detective, this one's on me." I ordered our coffee and added a donut for our friend. I reached in my purse to take out my wallet when Meg spoke up.

"Add a Boston Kreme to the order," she said. I raised my eyebrows. How Meg fit into a size four was the biggest unsolved mystery of all time.

I grabbed our food and joined Meg and Detective O'Halloran at one of the small nearby tables. He smiled eagerly when I put the donut and coffee in front of him. "I know it's silly, but I can't really concentrate until I've had my morning sugar fix."

"I'm the same way with caffeine," I admitted.

Meg took a big bite of her Boston Kreme. "So good," she said dreamily. She looked at the Detective, who was wiping a remnant of chocolate from the corner of his mouth. "What's new with the case, Detective?"

"We got a preliminary report back from the coroner late yesterday," he said.

I perked up. "And what did you learn?"

"Asphyxiation was the cause of death," he said. "No big surprise there. Those strangler fig vines are damn strong. We're keeping the gory details out of the papers, of course. Don't want anyone else weaponizing plants at the Botanic Garden."

"Anything else illuminating?" I asked. O'Halloran knew he was supposed to share information per Chairwoman Jackson's instructions, but I doubted he'd offer too much unless pressed. Police and politics don't make for good bedfellows.

O'Halloran hesitated. The sugar must have heightened Meg's observational acuity, too. She shot the detective a suspicious glance. "Are you holding back on something?"

O'Halloran sighed. "Melinda Masters was killed shortly before you found the body. We already suspected that was the case, but the coroner confirmed it."

"We saw her at the reception, but on the early side of it," I said. "Meg spotted her across the room."

"It seems as though the murder occurred near the end of the evening," said O'Halloran. "I checked with the Botanic Garden yesterday. They tightly controlled attendance for the event since it was a V-I-P congressional viewing of the corpse flower."

"That means our killer attended the reception," I said. "An outsider would have

219

been noticed, particularly near the end of the event when the crowd had thinned."

The detective polished off the last of his donut before answering. "That's a logical conclusion. We can't rule anything out at this point, but I agree that our resources should be focused on those people who were inside the Botanic Garden on the evening of the murder."

It wasn't much, but it did provide much needed focus to the investigation. "Thanks for sharing that information, Detective." I stood up to leave.

"Do you mind telling me where you're headed next, Ms. Marshall?" he asked. "After all, this new protocol involves both of us sharing information."

"That's a fair point," I said. "The person who knows the guest list the best is Grant Dawson, the executive director of the Botanic Garden. I figured I'd speak to him."

O'Halloran shrugged. "I talked to him yesterday. I guess it can't hurt. Remember, he's on our suspect list. He had the opportunity and means to kill Masters. He knows all the plants inside the exhibits like the back of his hand. He could have planned the murder weeks in advance, waiting for the opportunity to strangle the Architect with those fig vines."

I shuddered. The thought of Grant Dawson or anyone else stalking Melinda Masters and waiting for the opportunity to strangle her with a plant growing inside the Botanic Garden was a nasty thought. All murderers were deranged, but this killer seemed diabolical.

"I'll be careful," I said. "Meg can come with me. Safety in numbers, right?"

To my surprise, Meg shook her head. "I'm afraid I can't, Kit. With you out of pocket, someone needs to attend to the legislative work for the voters of North Carolina. I have several meetings this morning with staffers from other offices."

I swallowed hard. Nothing was more exciting than solving mysteries, yet my involvement came at a heavy price. "You're right, Meg. Congressional business comes first. We can't both be distracted by this murder."

Meg patted my hand. "Don't shortchange yourself. The head of an important legislative branch agency was murdered. Capitol Hill won't be the same until the killer is caught."

Detective O'Halloran cleared his throat. "Of course, the Capitol Hill police have this situation under control. Please feel free to negotiate political deals and draft legislation. Or whatever Hill staff do."

"I'd like nothing more than to concentrate on my day job, Detective. But remember I'm working on this case at Chairwoman Jackson's direct request," I said.

"So it's congressional business after all." Meg wagged her manicured fingers in my direction. "See you back at the office. And Kit, don't forget to ask Sebastian if he enjoyed dinner last night." She flashed a knowing smile and dashed off.

"If your gal pal can't join you at the Botanic Garden, are you planning to go over there alone?" asked O'Halloran. "If you ask me, that place is spooky. All kinds of creepy and crawly things overshadowing narrow labyrinths. I don't know how those people work there."

"Well, they are botanists, Detective. Presumably, they like plants," I said.

O'Halloran sighed. "I suppose so. To each his own. Apart from my lack of a green thumb, I'd still rather you didn't head over there alone. For all we know, the killer might get unnerved by all the questions and decide to orchestrate a repeat performance."

The detective had a point. There were a lot of nooks and crannies at the Botanic Garden. I wouldn't want to find myself in a dark corner with a murderer who felt like I knew too much.

"What if I ask Doug if he can join me?" I asked. "He's on a fellowship at the Library of Congress. It shouldn't be a problem for him to meet me at the Botanic Garden."

O'Halloran's face relaxed. "Good idea, Ms. Marshall. It's much harder to kill two people than just one."

I suppressed a giggle. "I suppose that's one way of looking at it. Hopefully, there will be no more dead bodies at the Botanic Garden."

The detective pulled out his handkerchief and wiped it across his moist forehead. It was next to impossible to escape the torrid summer heat in Washington, even inside the air-conditioned halls of Congress.

"Amen to that," he said, giving me a two-fingered salute. "I trust you will let me know if you uncover anything noteworthy."

I nodded my head, and O'Halloran ambled off. As he walked away, I realized I'd neglected to ask him what he was doing today on the case. The collaborative approach to solving mysteries was new territory for me. At least he'd shared the information about the time of death, which pinpointed our suspects to those who attended the reception.

I pulled out my phone and texted Doug.

Free for sleuthing?

Three dots appeared.

Finishing up with curators. Free at 11.

I glanced at the time. That was perfect timing. I could answer emails while finishing my coffee and then meet Doug at the Botanic Garden.

Perfect. Meet @ Botanic Garden.

It was a short jaunt from the Library of Congress to the Botanic Garden. Of course, during ninety-degree weather in the middle of the summer, a brief walk might turn into the equivalent of a sauna bath.

I turned attention for the next thirty minutes to my oversized Styrofoam cup of java and the numerous bolded messages on my iPhone. Thankfully, many of them could be ignored because they were about issues Maeve Dixon didn't care much about or wouldn't support. The small number of important messages were triaged and sent to Meg for further dissection.

With my emails answered and a large quantity of caffeine ingested, I took off down Independence Avenue for the Botanic

Garden. I'd just pulled out my phone to text Doug when I spotted him approaching. His wavy hair had become downright bushy, and beads of sweat glistened on his forehead. I fished around my purse for a clean tissue and handed it to him.

Doug shook his head in revulsion. A Boston native, he'd never really adjusted to the torrid heat of the D.C. summer. After removing his glasses, he mopped his face and threw the Kleenex in the nearby trash can.

"Disgusting," he remarked.

"Just think of the weight you shed on your walk," I said. "You're five pounds lighter."

"Not worth it." Then his face brightened. "But I'm glad you texted and asked me to join the investigation."

I didn't dare tell him he was second banana to Meg. Instead, I gave him a peck on the cheek. "You'll be helpful. The timing strongly suggests the murderer attended the reception. Melinda Masters was killed shortly before Meg found the body."

"Got it," he said. "What's our plan?"

"We'll interrogate Grant Dawson," I said. "I want to figure out if he knows anything about the alleged malfeasance within the Architect of the Capitol's office. And figure out who on the guest list he might finger as our killer."

"Good strategy. Anything else?" he asked.

"Well, Grant Dawson is a suspect, too. Detective O'Halloran mentioned that he didn't exactly see eye to eye with Melinda Masters. We need to get to the bottom of that. After all, he showed up immediately on the scene."

"Almost too convenient," said Doug.

"That's what O'Halloran thinks," I said. "He definitely knows the plants inside the conservatory really well. He would have been aware that the strangler fig is strong enough to serve as a murder weapon."

"That's an important point. Let's go inside and see if we can have a heart-to-heart with Mr. Dawson."

We entered the building and told the volunteer at the information desk we'd like to see Grant Dawson. An older gentleman, he frowned and shuffled papers.

"Do you have an appointment to see him?" he asked.

A perfectly good question, but the answer was no. I'd thought about calling ahead for an appointment but didn't want to give Dawson advance notice about our visit. Better off we caught him in the moment without an opportunity to prepare for our conversation.

"We don't," I admitted. "But I'm sure he'll see us if you give him our names. We're helping with the murder investigation of Melinda Masters." We plunked down our business cards on the desk. The volunteer held them an inch from his eyes, trying to read the small print.

"You're not police officers," he said.

"Correct," said Doug. "But Kit has been asked by the chairman of your congressional oversight committee to assist with the Masters case."

Even our volunteer understood he couldn't argue with Doug's explanation. Without another word of protest, he picked up the phone and called Grant Dawson's office. He lowered his voice and turned away so we couldn't hear the conversation.

"I'd love to know what he's saying about us," said Doug.

"I don't really care, as long as he gets the message to Grant that we're here," I said.

The volunteer swung around to face us. "Mr. Dawson is happy to meet with you. He asked to meet you by the *titan arum*."

He must have noticed the puzzled looks on our faces. "The corpse plant."

"Of course," I said, wrinkling my nose. "Does it still smell like . . ."

"Rotting flesh?" asked the volunteer. "The

answer is no. The *titan arum* has passed its bloom peak. It has now collapsed. Mr. Dawson thought you might want to see its full cycle."

"Oh yes, thank you," said Doug. "That's very thoughtful of him. We'll head there now. Appreciate your help."

Doug gently grabbed my arm and guided me toward the entrance of the conservatory. He whispered, "Best get out of his way. I think he was tiring of us."

I giggled. "Can you blame him? We tend to exhaust people with our endless questions and demands."

We found Grant Dawson standing in front of the corpse flower, which looked as though it had seen better days. The tall rod in the middle of the flower had collapsed with the bloom closed around it.

"What happened?" I asked, pointing to it.

"The bloom only lasts for a day," said Grant. "The energy required for it is so massive, the flower can only sustain it for a short period of time. After pollination, the spathe collapses and the bloom finishes. That's why we organized the congressional reception on Tuesday evening. It was timed perfectly to see the *titan arum* in its full glory."

"Unfortunately, whomever murdered

Melinda Masters used the timing for nefarious reasons," I said. "That's why we're here."

Dawson eyed me suspiciously. "The detective who was here yesterday mentioned that Jackson had put you in charge."

"Chairwoman Jackson asked me to collaborate with Detective O'Halloran and provide my boss with periodic reports," I clarified.

Dawson shrugged. "It's all above my pay grade, darling. What do I know? I just grow plants for people to enjoy." He motioned with his right hand as visitors meandered around us.

"It's quite impressive," said Doug sincerely. "Do you have a place in which we can speak to you privately?"

"Of course," said Dawson. "Follow me."

We weaved through the throng of tourists, who, despite the corpse flower's condition, had decided it was still worthy of a selfie. Grant buzzed us through an inconspicuous door marked "STAFF ONLY." We were led into a spacious office with a view of the street. Unsurprisingly, the office was decorated with both actual plants and paintings of plants.

He sat behind his desk and showed us to seats opposite him. "Normally, I offer visitors a glass of sherry," he said in his southern drawl. "But it's a bit early for it, even by my standards."

"We try not to drink before noon," I said lightly. "Especially on government work days."

"Sugar, those are words to live by," said Dawson, his eyes sparkling.

"Mr. Dawson, I know you must still be upset about Melinda Masters's death," I said. "Have you had a chance to think further about the events leading up to the murder on Tuesday evening? Something you overheard or noticed?"

Dawson ran his hand over his designer tie, which matched his light pink dress shirt perfectly. He had on a seersucker suit, a classic Washington summer favorite. Some men looked horribly out of place in them. With his southern gentility, Dawson might have been born in the thin, puckered fabric. Even though he had a slight stomach paunch, doubtless the result of too many afternoon glasses of sherry, he still managed to carry off the look flawlessly.

"I told the police everything I know. No great revelations since yesterday, missy," he said.

It was impossible to miss the biting tone that had crept into his voice. Doug leaned forward in his chair. "Had you heard anything about unfair contracting practices in the Architect's office?"

Grant tittered. "Let me tell you something about the A-O-C. The Botanic Garden employs about seventy people. That's out of two thousand total staff who work for the Architect. We're small potatoes. Our entire operating budget is smaller than the bigger contracts the A-O-C handles. So why would I know anything about bad contracts?"

I wasn't about to let Dawson off so easily. His "aw shucks" routine didn't convince me he was completely in the dark.

"You're one of the agency's senior employees, Mr. Dawson. I'd imagine you attend meetings and have regular interaction with the Architect and her office," I said. "Are you telling me someone as observant as you wouldn't have picked up some valuable intelligence over the years?"

Dawson sighed and rubbed his bald head. "I don't know why you're barking up this tree. No pun intended."

"We're trying to figure out if Melinda Masters was involved in financial wrongdoing that could have led to her death," said Doug. "It seems like a plausible motive."

"Well, that's where you're wrong," said Dawson. "Melinda and I didn't always see

231

eye to eye on things. But she was as straight as an arrow."

"You don't think she might have been involved in steering funds to certain companies and then benefiting from the favors?" I asked.

"Hell, no." Dawson's face turned a dark shade of pink that clashed with his shirt. "Why would you believe something like that?"

I didn't want to name Marty Buchman as my source. Something told me that Marty valued discretion and if I wanted to keep getting leads from him, I'd better zip it.

"We've been doing our homework," I said quickly. "It might mean that Melinda Masters crossed paths with a few shady characters."

"Honey, that's for sure," said Dawson. "Hundreds of millions of dollars flow through the Architect's office. There's gotta be a few bad eggs in the bunch."

"What about the Deputy Architect?" asked Doug. "You pointed him out to us on Tuesday night."

"Steve Song." Dawson leaned back in his yellow leather high-backed office chair. It was far posher than the cheap fabric swivel chairs we had in our congressional suite. Grant Dawson didn't strike me as someone who settled for bargain basement quality.

"Didn't he have a motive for killing Melinda?" I asked. "He got passed over for the top job. Now he'll have another chance to serve as the Acting Architect."

"That's true," said Dawson, with noticeable hesitancy in his voice.

"But you don't think he murdered her?" I asked.

"I wouldn't discount him," said Dawson slowly. "But Steve is a right nice guy. A real peach. Doesn't seem to fit."

Pretty much all the murderers we'd dealt with in the past couple of years matched that sanguine description. We couldn't let personality get in the way of seriously considering a suspect.

"You mentioned earlier that you and Melinda didn't always see eye to eye," I said. "What types of disagreements did you have with her?"

Grant sighed. "Typical work considerations. As you know, the Architect serves as the titular head of the Botanic Garden. As the executive director, I'm responsible for the daily operations. We needed to agree on big items."

"Such as?" I asked. Were plants really that controversial?

Grant ticked off a list of items using the

fingers on his right hand. "Major exhibits, public programming, services for Congress, budgeting," he said. "You're a chief of staff who works for an important person. Need I say more?"

"And Masters didn't like your ideas?" asked Doug.

Dawson pursed his lips. "I've spent my career working in horticulture and public gardens. I know the science behind what everyone else takes for granted. Let's just say Melinda was more interested in increasing our attendance numbers at the lowest cost possible. I had to speak for those who can't."

I raised my eyebrows. "Your junior staff?"

"Bless your heart," said Dawson. "Hell, the staff have mouths. I'm talking about the plants!"

This conversation was getting weirder by the moment, yet something told me Dawson hadn't told us everything he knew.

"Anyone else we should consider?" I asked.

"You already know about Congresswoman Cartwright," said Dawson. "She'd given Melinda a run for her money in the oversight hearings. She was dead set on replacing the Garfield statue on the Capitol grounds with James Madison." Dawson scoffed. "Nepotism in its worst form, even if Madison was a southerner."

"You didn't approve of the suggested replacement?" I asked innocently.

"Approve? You need to make sure you learn your history. Garfield was an admirable man and his assassination was a terrible ordeal for the country. Take a page from your husband here, the fancy historian." He huffed and puffed, beads of sweat now glistening on his forehead.

"I didn't realize it was such a sore point," I said.

"Budgets are tight around here," said Dawson. "We exist on a shoestring at the Botanic Garden. And then some ambitious congresswoman wants to replace a perfectly fine statue on Capitol grounds, just because her constituents want more homage paid to a historical figure who happened to reside inside the boundaries of her congressional district. It really dills my pickle!"

I had to admit that I'd learned more southern slang from Grant Dawson than all my combined trips to Dixon's North Carolina district.

"Did you happen to notice the Congresswoman around the time the body was discovered?" asked Doug.

Dawson shook his head. "How in the hell

would I know where she was? It's not like I can keep tabs on all the politicians who troop through here."

"What about you?" I asked.

Dawson raised his eyebrow. "Just what are you asking, darling?"

"It's understandable you didn't keep track of others' whereabouts during the reception," I said. "But we know now that Melinda Masters was killed shortly before Meg found her body. As I recall, you were on the scene immediately."

Doug piped up. "You were. In fact, you were right behind me."

Dawson's nostrils flared. "Now I know what this is about. You think I killed Melinda Masters!"

"We never said that." I smiled calmly at Dawson.

"You didn't have to say it. You're a typical Yankee. Always mistaking a southerner for a fool," he said.

"That's completely irrational," said Doug, adjusting his glasses.

Dawson scoffed. "You're damn right. I'm madder than a puffed toad right now."

I had no idea why a puffed toad might be angry, but I got the gist of Dawson's statement. "If you can just tell us where you were before the murder, we'll get out of your way."

Of course, if it turns out you killed Melinda Masters, not even the threat of an enraged puffed toad will save you.

Dawson shot me a sidelong glance, obviously weighing whether answering our question was worth getting us to leave him alone. Finally, he relented. "I was headed back to my office to retrieve my briefcase when I heard the ruckus. I changed course when I spotted your husband rushing through the double doors toward the garden court," he said. "You know the rest."

"Can anyone verify your whereabouts?" asked Doug.

"Several of the catering staff might have noticed me. They were dismantling the bar and the food stations when I walked through the last time," he said. "A number of people were leaving the reception at that time, as you know. I'm almost certain I saw Cartwright walk out the door. And Gordon Romano."

"The Comptroller General?" I asked. That was the fancy title for the head of the GAO, the Government Accountability Office, which served as Congress's watchdog on issues related to performance, waste, and fraud.

"The one and only," said Dawson. "I assume you've spoke with him already."

I leaned forward, sliding my chair closer to his desk. "No, we haven't. I remember he was a guest on Tuesday night, but we haven't spoken to everyone who attended. We're focusing on the people who had a connection to Melinda."

Dawson snorted. "Then you don't want to skip over Gordon Romano, sunshine."

CHAPTER THIRTEEN

I said nothing while considering Dawson's words. Romano ran a big legislative branch agency, but otherwise, there was no obvious association between GAO and the Architect of the Capitol. In fact, GAO wasn't even located on Capitol Hill.

"And why might that be?" asked Doug, a blank expression on his face. He looked as confused as I felt.

Dawson proffered a cocky smile, relishing that he knew something we did not. "Not everything has to do with politics and government," he drawled. "Romano and Masters were lovers."

I blinked rapidly. He had us there. In our rush to discover a plot involving millions of dollars, kickbacks, and nefarious accounting practices, we'd missed an obvious motive for murder: romance gone wrong.

"I didn't realize Melinda was single," I

said. "Or Gordon Romano, for that matter."

"Typical of a married person," said Dawson bitterly, staring at my ring finger. "The District of Columbia has the lowest marriage rate in the entire country. It's safer to assume someone is single rather than hitched."

I ignored Dawson's editorializing and pondered his revelation before asking an obvious question. "Were there any problems in their relationship?"

"In polite society, you don't exactly ask your boss about her love life," said Dawson. "They'd been dating for several months."

"The relationship began after she became the Architect of the Capitol?" asked Doug.

Dawson thought for a moment before answering. "Yes, I think so. I'm almost positive they met at a congressional reception soon after she was named to the position."

The existence of a love interest certainly threw us a curveball. Even so, paramours didn't go around murdering each other unless there was a good motive. Romano found out Masters had cheated on him? Or more plausibly, Masters might have wanted to end the relationship and Romano took the news badly.

I moved to stand. "Thank you for this

information. You've been helpful." *Despite the feigned charm of southern insults.*

"You be sure to tell your boss about how accommodating I've been," said Dawson. "And the esteemed Chairwoman, too."

I offered my hand for a shake, but instead Dawson took it and gave me a light kiss. "Southerners are true gentlemen."

"So charming," I muttered as I motioned for Doug to follow me out of the office.

When we reached the public area of the gardens, Doug whistled softly. "That guy is a real piece of work. I couldn't tell if he wanted to become your new best friend or your worst enemy."

"A chameleon," I pronounced. "Hard to discern because they are always changing their colors."

"At least he gave you valuable information at the end of the conversation." Doug motioned toward the exit. "Care to join me for lunch at the Native American Museum?"

I hesitated. The Smithsonian's National Museum of the American Indian was right around the corner. The museum was legendary for the delicious food served at its cafeteria. We were so close, I could practically taste the buffalo chili and traditional fry bread. But duty called, and I wasn't done at our current location quite yet.

"Don't you think we should take a look at the murder scene again?" I asked.

"I'm sure it's roped off, but I bet we can talk our way into getting a glimpse," said Doug. "By now, the police will have scoured the site and removed all physical evidence. Are you sure it's worth it?"

"No, I'm not," I admitted. "But I'm not sure when we'll have an excuse again to take a look. Let's go." I pulled Doug's arm toward the double doors leading to the tropical plants area of the conservatory.

Sure enough, there was yellow crime tape surrounding the entire area where Melinda's body was found. A bored-looking police officer stood at the edge of the barrier.

"Let's walk around it and see if anything comes to mind," I said.

We carefully circled the perimeter. Doug was right. There were no physical signs that a murder had taken place here less than forty-eight hours ago. The long vine of the strangler fig which had served as the murder weapon was gone, surely clipped off the larger plant and kept for evidence. We stopped near the small stream which ran through the exhibit.

I lowered my voice to make sure the police officer wouldn't hear our conversation. We didn't need to draw any suspicion on ourselves.

"Something did pop into my brain as we walked around the crime scene," I whispered.

Doug leaned closer. "Did you solve the mystery?"

I giggled. Doug was an enthusiastic sleuth and a little preemptory. "Not yet. However, how did our killer know about the strangler fig?"

"What do you mean, Kit?"

"Well, if I wanted to kill someone at the Botanic Gardens, I wouldn't automatically think *ficus aurea,* would you? There wasn't tight security at the congressional reception. A murderer could have brought in a knife or even a gun with a silencer if he or she planned to kill Melinda Masters."

"And that means the murder wasn't premeditated?" asked Doug.

I frowned. "I'm not sure yet. It might mean it was a crime of opportunity. If that's the case, our perp knew something about the Botanic Garden. Enough to realize the vines of the strangler fig were the perfect weapon."

Doug snapped his fingers. "Grant Dawson! No one knows the plants in this place better than him."

I nodded. "You're certainly right. But what was his motive?"

The police officer glanced in our direction. He probably wondered why two professionally dressed thirty-somethings were hovering near a crime scene, whispering like high schoolers sharing secrets in study hall.

Doug must have noticed, too. "Let's get out of here."

As we hustled toward the door, I felt my phone buzz. It was a text from Meg.

Pls head back. Crisis brewing.

So much for a juicy bison burger with homemade chips. I typed my response.

Back in 15.

I put away my phone and gave Doug the bad news. In my best southern accent, I said, "Sorry, darling, but duty calls. I'll have to take a raincheck on the cafeteria."

He sighed. "Now you're talking like Grant Dawson, missy."

"I could finger him as our prime suspect since he had the means and opportunity, but we need to figure out why he'd want Masters dead," I said. "I can't believe he'd kill someone over a disagreement about flower arrangements."

"That's oversimplifying it. Artistic vision can be a major point of contention," said Doug. "Think about all the spats I've had with my editor over the years."

"You don't need to remind me," I said, smiling. "Every time you finish a book, my blood pressure rises at least ten points."

Doug chuckled and gave me a kiss on the cheek. "Good luck solving whatever crisis is pulling you back to your real job."

I crossed Independence Avenue and entered the Rayburn Building. With the heat and humidity, it made more sense to weave through the hallways and underground tunnels to reach our Cannon office rather than try to trudge up a sidewalk that could easily fry an egg.

I opened the door to our office suite and immediately knew something was amiss. Instead of one assistant manning the entrance, three junior staffers surrounded the front desk. With frantic looks on their faces, they took turns grabbing at phones and shouting at each other.

"No, don't transfer that guy. He's not even a constituent," barked Jess, one-half of the infamous picnic duo.

"Don't we need to log the call, even if it's not from the district?" asked Oliver, her former boyfriend.

"It's too confusing for me to think straight," wailed our staff assistant, whose desk had been overtaken.

They were so busy arguing with each other, no one had even noticed I'd walked into the office. I marched to the desk and pounded my hand on top of it.

"Team Dixon! What is going on here?" I demanded.

Three pairs of eyes followed my voice. The staff assistant gulped. It was his job to keep order in our anteroom, and he knew the melee I'd walked into was verboten.

"Sorry for the disturbance, Kit. But we're in the midst of a crisis here," said Oliver. Even as he spoke, the phones continued to ring off the hook.

"I certainly concur," I murmured.

After running her fingers through her long blonde hair, Jess started to explain, but I cut her off. "Where's Meg?"

Collectively, they pointed to our office area. "She's back there."

"Continue answering these calls, but please stop arguing," I said, pointing to the door. "You never knew who might pay us a visit."

The junior staffers nodded their heads solemnly. As I headed to our staff area, I heard Jess whisper, "Nice job, Oliver. You're going to get us all fired."

The private area of our congressional suite was in similar disarray. At least no constituent or important visitor could see this pandemonium. Meg was hunched over her desk, barking out orders. Her blonde bob, which rarely included a strand of hair out of place, looked like she'd been through a hurricane. The neatly tied bow on her red wrap-around dress sagged, giving her a lopsided appearance. Even her flawlessly applied makeup couldn't hide the red flush that had overtaken her porcelain face.

"Meg, what is going on here?" I asked.

"Oh, Kit, thank goodness you're finally here," she said. "Our office is getting bombarded by a group concerned with corporate hegemony. They've been tying up our phone lines for over thirty minutes!"

"Transfer one of the calls to me," I said, heading for my office.

My phone buzzed immediately. A woman's voice was on the line. "Hello, I'm Margaret Smith, and I want to fight back against the corrosive power of multinational banks and large corporations. We are the ninety-nine percent who will not accept the greed of the one percent." She took a pause to breathe. "Will you pass my message along to . . ."

I heard a shuffling of papers before she continued. "Um, Representative Maeve Dixon of North Carolina."

"Listen, I know you don't live in Representative Dixon's district. Which group is organizing these calls? You're bombarding our phone lines, and it's causing a real problem for our office," I said.

More shuffling of papers. "Um, could I speak to someone in charge, like the chief of staff?"

"I am the chief of staff. And tell whomever is in charge of the phone bank that my next step is tracing these calls to the source." I slammed down the phone.

Meg cracked open my door. "Any luck?"

"Not really, but at least I gave the caller a piece of my mind," I said, rubbing my temples. The Calgon "take me away" vintage 1970s commercial immediately sprung to mind.

"It's really strange," said Meg, frowning. "We haven't had phone calls about big business in a while."

"Since when?" I asked, a heavy dose of suspicion in my voice.

Meg considered my question for a moment before answering. "Since the Occupy

Wall Street movement fizzled out, I guess."

I looked Meg square in the eye. "I don't believe in coincidences. Meg, can you give me some privacy for a few minutes."

"Sure, boss," she said, hurrying away. My best friend knew from the tone in my voice when it was best to clear out.

I wasn't going to waste time texting. This situation demanded a phone call. A few seconds later, Sebastian picked up. "Hey, Kit Kat. How's your day going?"

"I was making some progress on the murder investigation and had planned to have lunch with Doug," I said. "Instead, I had to hustle back to the office because my phone lines are being flooded by calls about corporate greed. You wouldn't happen to know anything about that, would you?"

There was silence on the other end of the line.

I waited several seconds before I spoke again. "Sebastian, you're avoiding my question. Are you responsible for this?"

"I guess so," he said. Then he added quickly, "But only indirectly. I have no control over which politicians get called. I swear I didn't know Dixon had been targeted."

"Sebastian, for God's sake. She's on every political hit list. Democrats don't think she's

249

liberal enough, and Republicans want to defeat her every election." I sighed. "Can you get them to stop?"

"Sure thing. I'll tell the guy in charge here to lay off Dixon," he said. "A personal favor."

I rolled my eyes. How did I end up being indebted to Sebastian?

"Things are wrapping up here," he said. "Since you couldn't go to lunch with Doug, do you want to join us for some food?"

"Us?" I asked warily.

"Clarence and me, of course," said Sebastian.

"He's making phone calls with you?"

"Sure," said Sebastian. "He's very popular, Kit. A big morale boost to the entire cause."

My dog had become a critic of capitalism. Until he realized where Milk Bones came from. Then I strongly doubted he'd support the cause. Clarence was a true believer, unless his stomach got in the way.

"Why don't we meet at Mr. Henry's Restaurant?" I said. "They have an outdoor patio so it won't be a problem with Clarence."

"I'm writing it down. See you there in a half hour."

I cleared my throat. "One more thing

before you hang up, Sebastian."

"Anything, Kit."

"Before I leave to meet you at Mr. Henry's, the phone calls better have stopped. Understand?"

"Your wish is my command, big sister." Sebastian clicked off the call.

I imagined Sebastian rubbing a golden lamp, muttering "abracadabra." And then magically, the telephones would fall silent. Just like Aladdin, surely my wish was too good to be true.

I opened my office door slowly and listened. To my astonishment, the legislative staff area had fallen silent.

"Meg," I whispered. "What happened to the phones?"

She shrugged. "A minute ago, they just stopped," she said in a low voice. "Why are we whispering?"

"I have no idea," I admitted. "But I'd rather not jinx it. I think my brother fixed it."

Meg broke out in a huge grin. "Oh, Sebastian," she swooned.

"Let's not get too carried away. He was behind the phone banking today, although he didn't know Congresswoman Dixon had been targeted."

"Oh, of course he didn't," said Meg,

smoothing her hair. "He'd never deliberately do something like that."

"Except for yesterday, when he led a protest inside our office," I said warily.

"Another rookie mistake," said Meg. "It's hard adjusting to life in Washington. Don't be too hard on him."

I pressed my lips together in a slight grimace. "I'm going to have lunch, right after I send an email about the Masters case. Are you able to hold down the fort when I'm gone this afternoon?"

Meg answered in the affirmative and proceeded to brief me on the most pressing policy matters confronting Representative Dixon. After a short exchange, I retreated to my office and messaged the staff director for the House Administration committee. Chairwoman Jackson needed to get me an appointment this afternoon with Gordon Romano. While Grant Dawson was certainly a credible suspect, it wouldn't hurt to speak with Melinda's supposed love interest.

As the head of a big agency like GAO, Romano would never take a spur of the moment meeting with me. But if the committee which had oversight over his agency contacted him, he'd have no choice. Since we were dealing with a loose murderer on Capitol Hill, targeted arm-twisting seemed appropriate.

I hustled out of the office, heading down Pennsylvania Avenue toward Seward Square. Instead of peeling off toward Eastern Market like last night, this time I continued to walk due east. Mr. Henry's was a block beyond the square, right on the corner of Sixth Street Southeast. There was no way to miss it with the distinctive sign pronouncing its name to all those thirsty patrons who made their way from Capitol Hill to enjoy a libation. Over fifty years in existence, Mr. Henry's qualified as a veritable neighborhood landmark. During happy hour one night, a crusty bartender told me the pub had launched the career of Roberta Flack. Now Mr. Henry's hosted jazz dinners and notable local singers as an integral and vibrant component of the D.C. music scene.

Sebastian was sitting underneath a blue umbrella on the patio. One hand held a frothy beer. The other clenched a black leash, which was attached, of course, to Clarence. As I approached the table, Clarence emerged from underneath the table, and I noticed he was sporting a shirt.

"What is he wearing?" I asked, barely audible. In truth, I was afraid to learn the answer to my question.

I bent down to give Clarence a chin rub and that's when I saw the writing on his white jersey. Blazoned on his doggie chemise was the phrase "FIGHT THE POWER." Had Clarence met Flavor Flav this morning and struck up an unlikely friendship?

"Oh, that's just an anti-corporatist slogan we promote," said Sebastian absently. "We had some canine souvenirs printed up so our most dedicated supporters could wear matching outfits with their pets. Isn't it cute?"

I narrowed the gaze directed at my younger brother. "I'm not sure cute is the right word. Crazy is more appropriate."

Sebastian looked up from the menu he was studying. "Why the animosity, Kit? Big business is ruining democracy. The corporations line the pockets of those who we elect. Including your boss."

I was well aware that Maeve Dixon accepted political contributions from certain industry representatives and corporations. But that didn't mean she was for sale — or that she'd been successfully bought.

"It's more complicated than what you describe, Sebastian. It can be hard for outsiders to comprehend, but this place isn't exactly black and white. Choices aren't always wholly good or bad."

Sebastian thought about my statement for a moment. "If you take money from big business and then don't vote the preferred way, aren't they going to stop giving money?"

"They might," I explained. "It really depends. Sometimes, it's not about votes. And quite frankly, if a donation gets rescinded during the next election cycle, it's not the end of the world. There's almost a limitless supply of campaign dollars available from a whole host of organizations and interests."

"Ah, so you do admit there's a connection between the decisions politicians make and the money they raise," he said. "Corruption should be the middle name around here."

"You assume there's always a *quid pro quo*," I said, using the Latin for this for that. "And I'm telling you that in my experience, it rarely happens. Lobbyists can use donations for influence. But it doesn't always translate into a preferred action."

Sebastian sighed and placed his menu on the table. "This is all so complicated. I don't know if I can really live here permanently, Kit."

Clarence growled softly, most likely to remind us to order our lunches. I glanced at my iPhone. "We should flag down a waiter.

I might have an important meeting this afternoon."

Sebastian did as he was told, and we placed our order a minute later. "So now you don't want to stay in Washington?" I asked softly.

Sebastian's remark hinting that he might relocate had surprised me last night. Notwithstanding the pop-up protests he'd managed to orchestrate in the past forty-eight hours, I'd grown warmer to the idea of having my little brother nearby. Our parents were free spirits who enjoyed the freedom of retirement. Despite the heavy concentration of wineries in nearby Virginia and Maryland, I seriously doubted they'd ever move to Washington. Of course, Doug was my present and future. Nonetheless, I found comfort that someone from my past, like Sebastian, could become part of my everyday life.

Sebastian answered my question with one of his own. "Do you even want me to move here? It seems like I'm causing you headaches you don't need. Just like the old days. You were always the fixer in our family."

I smiled. Sebastian's recollection was accurate. When problems arose, I was always the one who figured out a solution. This is what solving murders was about, too. "You can't possibly maintain the pace of disruption you've set since arriving. Besides, Meg had a good point. It takes time to adjust to life here."

Sebastian straightened in his chair. "Speaking of your friend Meg," he started.

I cut him off. "What you don't need is a romantic entanglement to complicate matters. You can tell me to bugger off, but I really don't think hooking up with Meg is a smart idea."

Sebastian ran his fingers through his sandy blond hair. "You're absolutely right, big sister."

I was so shocked at his answer, I almost fell off my chair. Before I could respond, the waiter delivered our food, a chicken taco salad for me and a turkey burger for Sebastian.

"You're not interested in Meg?" I asked.

He grinned coyly. "I wouldn't put it that way. But as you said, it's not a great time. Quite frankly, she seems eager for a stable relationship. And that's not something I'm in a position to offer right now."

"Funny you mentioned that," I said. "Trevor told me recently he's carrying a torch for Meg."

Sebastian wrinkled his nose. "That guy seems weird." He took a big bite of his burger and swallowed. "Then again, he's definitely got his act together. Might be exactly what your friend needs."

I pushed some guacamole around on my plate. "I'd like to answer your question, though," I said. "I hope you do consider moving here, Sebastian. I know we haven't been close in the recent past, but that doesn't mean it always has to be that way."

I might have been imagining, but I thought I saw a tiny tear form in the corner of his eye. "Thanks, Kit. That means a lot to me. I'll think about it."

I reached out and patted Sebastian's hand. Clarence misinterpreted my gesture as an overture to share my lunch with him. He growled, followed by a staccato bark.

"Clarence, hush!" I exclaimed. "You know the etiquette when we're eating outside at a restaurant. People don't appreciate it when a dog disrupts their meal."

He cocked his head to the side and stared at me with a puzzled look on his face.

"Sit down, and I'll give you a treat," I said. Clarence obliged, and I fed him a small piece of chicken.

"He likes to bark," said Sebastian. "You might need to take him to obedience training."

"We've been there and done that," I said,

sighing. "Last fall, he had an unfortunate experience at agility training. So, we can't go back."

Sebastian chuckled and patted his head. "Well, I guess no one's perfect, even a mutt as cute as Clarence."

I put my fork down and took a long sip of water. My neck stiffened with tension, and I rubbed the back of it. When this investigation was over, I made a mental note to book myself a therapeutic massage.

Sebastian must have picked up on my unease. "What's the matter?"

In my best Tommy Wiseau impersonation, I clenched my fists in front of me. "You're tearing me apart, Melinda Masters!"

Sebastian almost spit out a chunk of turkey burger. "It can't be so bad that you're quoting famously bad scenes from *The Room.*" He looked at me skeptically. "Is it really that dire?"

I tilted my head. "I'm spinning in circles with this one. Maybe I'll catch a break soon." I stuffed a forkful of chicken, sour cream, and beans in my mouth. "By the way, I'm a sucker for kitschy movie quotes."

Sebastian raised his eyebrows. "Thanks for the warning." He finished his last bite of the burger and washed it down with the remainder of his beer.

I threw down my credit card. Sebastian made a move to grab the check, but I stopped him. "Sorry, not this time. Lunch is on me."

He pulled back his hand. "Alright, but how about some free advice instead?"

"Go for it," I said. "I'm all ears." As if on cue, Clarence wiggled his butt, and I gave him a kiss on his nose.

"Maybe you should forget this murder business," said Sebastian.

We both stood up and walked toward the patio's exit. "You think I should give up?"

"Same old Kit. Never wanting to admit defeat and always solving the problem. But listen to reason. You're not giving up," said Sebastian, his face tightening. "It's not your responsibility to find out who killed Melinda Masters. As I'm beginning to understand, you already have a pretty important job. Leave the police work to the detective."

"You're forgetting that my boss wants me to investigate. Per the chairwoman's orders," I said.

"Just tell Maeve Dixon you're out of the homicide business and you'll relay any information from the police to her," said Sebastian, the volume of his voice rising. "It's too dangerous. You've been lucky in the past with these other killers. Don't push it."

I crossed my arms over my chest. "How do you know about the other cases?"

He turned to face me. "There's a thing called the internet out there, Kit. I'm a technology professional. I know how to use it."

"Then you know that I caught the killer each time before," I said. "I've told Doug this a hundred times. I'll be careful."

"Famous last words." He gave me a half hug. "I'll see you tonight at the condo."

When Clarence realized we were separating, he issued a protest growl. I crouched down to pet him. "Behave, Clarence. I don't want any more barking, even if you're now friends with Mrs. Beauregard." Clarence listened solemnly to my words, and then happily trotted behind Sebastian down Pennsylvania Avenue with his "FIGHT THE POWER" emblem proudly blazing the path ahead.

CHAPTER FOURTEEN

Before returning to the office, I needed to check if the committee staff director had managed to secure an appointment with Gordon Romano. Scrolling through my growing list of unread messages, I finally spotted the email. For the first time today, I'd caught a break. Not only had she gotten me an audience with Romano, but he was actually on Capitol Hill this afternoon for other meetings. He'd squeeze in thirty minutes with me at two-thirty. I had just enough time to beat it back to the office and meet him inside the committee's suite.

Should I text Doug and ask him to join the meeting? Fingers wrapped around my iPhone, yet I restrained myself from typing a message to my husband. Gordon Romano was a middle-aged muckety-muck bachelor. Since he'd been dating Melinda, he obviously had a thing for attractive, powerful women. Masters had been the total package: a looker with a resume as lengthy as Michelle Obama's memoirs. Doug was eager to stay involved in the case, but this wasn't an appropriate assignment. Instead, I punched out the time and location of the meeting and sent it to Meg. She was the right sleuth for the job.

Twenty minutes later and at least a pound of sweat lighter, I breezed through security at the Longworth Office Building and took the elevator to the third floor. I turned the corner and spotted Meg down the long corridor, waiting outside the committee suite. She motioned frantically for me to hurry.

"Kit," she hissed. "Can you give me background? All I got from you was an obscure text about a meeting here in Longworth to interrogate G-A-O. That's not how it works."

Meg was referring to the fact that GAO serves as the investigative arm of Congress. They were the ones who typically asked the hard questions. Today would be a departure from normal practice. Indeed, our guest of honor was in for a complete role reversal.

"We're here to talk with Gordon Romano, the Comptroller General," I said. "Because of the deluge of phone calls at the office this morning, I didn't have a chance to tell you what I learned from Grant Dawson.

Romano and Masters were romantically involved."

Meg's eyes widened. "Maybe she wanted to break up with him, and he got angry."

"Certainly possible," I said. "Although I don't think they'd been dating that long. It seems a bit of a stretch he'd be violently upset about ending a brief relationship."

Meg pulled out her compact, checked her makeup, and carefully applied powder to her nose. "Powerful men are obsessive. They don't like it when they can't have what they want."

"Fair point. I also want to ask Romano about these allegations of malfeasance within the Architect of the Capitol. Congresswoman Cartwright told me she informed the Comptroller about her suspicions, but she didn't get any traction from him on the issue."

"How can I help?" asked Meg.

My best friend had refreshed her appearance since I saw her before lunch. Her wraparound dress clung to her figure, and her cute blonde bob was neatly tucked behind both of her ears. Meg was self-aware about her physical allure, yet I often wondered if she grew tired of using her bombshell status as a strategic advantage.

I spoke carefully. "I think you can just . . ."

I searched for the right words. "Be you."

Meg blinked several times, her black mascara accentuating her already long lashes. "Well, that's easy." She gave me a nudge. "If he's such a ladies' man, I'll have him eating out of the palm of my hand."

So much for my feminist musings. Part of me heard the inward groan of Gloria Steinem loud and clear. The other half cheered the possibility of squeezing an important clue out of Gordon Romano if we played our cards right.

"Let's go inside and tell the committee staff we're here. The meeting was arranged through them," I explained.

Luckily, the front desk assistant knew about the appointment and escorted us to the conference room. The Comptroller sat at the end of the table, his face buried in his iPhone. When we walked in, he stood up immediately and extended his hand.

"Ladies, it's a pleasure to meet you," he said, smiling. "Although I wish it was under better circumstances. My name is Gordon Romano."

We accepted his hand politely and introduced ourselves. I'd seen Romano at hearings but hadn't paid him much attention. His greying hair, reading glasses, and frown lines put him around fifty years old. Although Romano wouldn't give Brad Pitt a run for his money in the looks department, he had an affable, inviting manner about him. His strong posture and firm handshake conveyed a confident aura, no minor matter when it came to dealing with lawmakers on Capitol Hill. The romantic tie to Melinda Masters made sense; they would have easily become a prominent D.C. power couple if she hadn't suffered an untimely death.

Meg and I sat opposite Romano. "Thank you for meeting with us, Mr. Romano. As you know, we work for Congresswoman Maeve Dixon and have been instructed by the chair of this committee to follow the investigation concerning the murder of Architect of the Capitol Melinda Masters."

He nodded his head, a grave expression on his face. "Yes, the staff director explained the facts when she called me earlier today. It's been a terrible tragedy."

Meg piped up. "You were at the reception at the Botanic Garden on Tuesday evening, correct?"

"Yes, I was. I've given my account of that evening to the police, of course," he said.

"We understand that," said Meg sweetly. "We wanted to ask you about your romantic connection to the victim." She gave Romano her best "come hither" look.

Romano shifted uncomfortably in his seat. "We'd been dating for a few months. A limited number of people knew about it. Melinda didn't want to make it public until we thought it was serious."

"You were okay with keeping it casual?" I asked. It seemed important to establish the nature of their relationship. A couple dates hardly established a motive for murder, unless Romano wanted more from it.

Romano paused, in an effort to choose his words carefully. "I enjoyed Melinda's company very much." He stared at his hands. "I was willing to take it slow. We were both high-ranking government officials. This approach made sense."

"Did you spend any time with Melinda the night she was killed?" asked Meg.

A pensive expression on his face, Romano stared directly at Meg. "Not as much as I wished I had. We saw each other at the reception briefly and had only a moment to chat."

"What did you discuss?" Meg leaned forward in her seat.

"Nothing consequential, I'm afraid," said Romano. "She did mention an altercation before the event with Representative Cartwright."

"An altercation? Is that how Masters

described it?" I asked. Cartwright had admitted to meeting with Masters and disagreeing about the statue but hadn't depicted it as acrimonious.

Romano removed his glasses and chewed on the earpiece. "It was clearly contentious. You must know, Ms. Marshall, dealings with Bridget Cartwright are more often adversarial than not."

He'd given me a big opening and I intended to use it. "Speaking of Congresswoman Cartwright, she told me how concerned she was about reports of malfeasance within the Architect of the Capitol's office. Do you know anything about that?"

Romano squinted. "Malfeasance is a loaded term. What do you mean by it?"

"A problem with the contracting. As you know, the A-O-C deals with hundreds of millions of dollars in government contracts each year. If certain companies or firms had the inside track, it would be a huge scandal."

Romano leaned back in his chair. "Ms. Marshall, those are heavy accusations." He sighed heavily. "Do you know what city planner Pierre L'Enfant called Capitol Hill when he chose it as the location of Congress?"

Meg and I both shook our heads. History wasn't my finest subject, which often proved problematic since I was married to a historian.

"L'Enfant said it was a pedestal waiting for a monument," said Romano. "In the 1870s, Frederick Law Olmsted designed the green space surrounding the Capitol Building. Now, the Architect of the Capitol is in charge of hundreds of acres, filled with trees, installations, and plants for public enjoyment."

The Comptroller paused to take a deep breath and Meg seized the opening. "That's very inspirational, Mr. Romano, but what does that have to do with alleged fraud in the Architect's office?" She tapped the table impatiently with a manicured red nail.

"What I'm trying to say is there's a long history of responsibility and pride for the maintenance of Capitol grounds. It's a serious matter if there are accusations of so-called malfeasance," he said.

Romano was a tough cookie. He wasn't bending one inch, even under some tough tag team interrogation. "So, you didn't believe Bridget Cartwright's claims?" I asked.

"It's not my job to believe or not believe claims, Ms. Marshall. She's a rank-and-file member on a committee. We prioritize our work at the Government Accountability Office. Unfortunately, we have more requests for our work than staff to perform investigations," he said.

"So, it's a question of resources and nothing else?" Meg smiled seductively and edged her chair closer to the table. "Don't worry. You can tell us the real reason."

But Gordon Romano remained stoic, seemingly unfazed by Meg's allure. "Sorry to disappoint, ma'am. We simply can't keep up with all the requests for work."

Meg slumped backward. She said nothing, yet I had no problem reading her mind. The "ma'am" comment had offended her. At the very least, Meg expected a "miss."

"Can you tell us about the night of the murder?" I asked. "You chatted briefly with Melinda. Then what did you do?"

"I schmoozed with several members of Congress. That's why I attend these events. You have to keep the politicians happy," he said, his eyes sparkling. "Before the tragedy, that night wasn't a memorable one, I'm afraid."

"You didn't make plans to leave with Melinda?" asked Meg. "That would seem to make sense if you two were dating."

"I'd asked about it, but Melinda didn't want anyone to know we were an item," he said. "She knew there were select reporters attending the event, covering the bloom of the corpse flower. She didn't want to risk it. After I talked to the important people, I used the facilities and left the reception."

"Since you spent time with Melinda outside work, do you have any idea about who might want to kill her?" I asked.

Romano clenched his jaw. "It's hard for me to say. I don't like to speculate. As the head of the Government Accountability Office, you must realize my job is to evaluate the facts, plain and simple."

"We completely understand," said Meg in a soothing voice. Meg the seductress had magically changed into Meg the comforter-in-chief. She reached across the table and patted his hand. "It must be a difficult time for you. Any insights you can give us will help the police solve Melinda's murder quicker."

"And we don't want a killer running around the grounds of Capitol Hill," I added.

Romano stared at me with an unnatural stillness. "No, we don't. And certainly not someone who strangles a woman inside the Botanic Garden with a vine."

Meg shuddered. No doubt, the image conjured up the unpleasant memory of discovering Melinda's corpse.

I nodded slowly, urging Romano to divulge the names of any suspects who might have wanted Melinda dead.

Romano swallowed hard. "I'm hesitant to accuse people in this fashion, but after all, this is Melinda we're talking about. Even though it was a casual relationship, I cared for her." He took a deep breath. "She did mention Steve Song gave her trouble from time to time."

"That was her deputy at the Architect's office," I said. "Mr. Romano, you shouldn't feel guilty about mentioning him. His name has come up in other conversations."

"I was afraid that might be the case," said Romano. "I knew Steve when he served as the Acting Architect of the Capitol before Melinda's appointment. He was always a pleasure to work with. He provided me with the information I requested for audits and other routine investigations. That's why I don't like mentioning his name as a potential murder suspect."

"Yet, you just did." Meg tapped her long fingernail to her perfectly matched red lip. "There must be a reason you think he could have murdered Melinda Masters."

Romano adjusted his tie, which was already perfectly straight. "I mentioned him for a reason. On a few of our dates, Melinda talked about his harsh demeanor toward her."

"Can you tell us more about it?" Why did I feel like I was pulling teeth during this interview?

"The usual stuff," said Romano. "Denigrating comments, undermining her, criticizing her openly when other senior staff were around."

"Usual?" said Meg. "That sounds awful."

"Government bureaucracy can be a nasty business," said Romano. "It's not for the faint at heart."

Being a chief of staff had its significant challenges, but I also worked with terrific people. Even if two of them were currently at war over our upcoming Saturday picnic.

"Enough to threaten her life?" I asked. After all, difficult people were a dime a dozen and murders weren't an everyday occurrence in the workplace. Although I had to admit there had been quite a few homicides on Capitol Hill since I started solving them.

Romano shrugged. "Melinda didn't like to talk about it much. But I do know she was consulting with her legal counsel to figure out if she could fire him."

Now we were getting somewhere. "Did Steve know Melinda might let him go?"

"I'm not positive since I don't talk with him regularly," he said. "But Steve has been around Washington for a long time. I think he'd know if he was about to get canned."

Particularly if he was acting the way Romano described it. Harassing the boss seemed like a surefire one-way ticket to the unemployment line.

Meg smiled broadly. "That certainly gives us a motive to consider. Doesn't it, Kit?"

I nodded slowly. "It could be the break we've been searching for. We haven't spoken to Steve Song yet. Now he'll go to the top of my list."

"Anyone else we should prioritize?" asked Meg in her most business-like tone. Once it was clear Romano wasn't buying, Meg had lost interest in the seductress approach.

Romano furrowed his brow. "There was another guy who gave her trouble at work." He snapped his fingers. "The head of the Botanic Garden. Isn't Dawson his name?"

"Grant Dawson," I said. "I spoke to him earlier today. Funny you should mention him."

"Why is that?" asked Romano, his hands folded neatly on the table.

"Because he's the one who urged us to talk with you," I said. "You seem to be pointing fingers at each other."

Gordon Romano leaned back in his chair and laughed heartily. "Dawson is a character. I've never seen anyone so passionate about plants. He has a particular vision for the Botanic Garden and doesn't take kindly to those who question it. I suppose he told you about my romantic involvement with Melinda and implied that could have given me a motive to murder her."

"Something like that," I said. "He wasn't specific."

"And that's because there's no basis to it, Ms. Marshall," he said. "I know our esteemed elected representatives have a penchant for playing loose with the facts. But even you know it's impossible to build a case if nothing supports it. My relationship with Melinda was completely innocent. We were romantically involved, but not serious enough to cause heartache for either of us if it didn't work out. Certainly not a motive for murder."

I glanced at Meg, who nodded. It was our sign to end the interview. We both stood up, and Romano followed suit. We shook hands again, exchanged goodbyes, and found ourselves in the hallway outside the committee suite.

After pulling out her phone, Meg studied it and sighed. "Too much to catch up on.

Can we walk and talk at the same time?"

"Of course. I wouldn't have it any other way," I said.

We huddled close so no one else in the crowded hallways could hear our conversation. "Besides the tip about Steve Song, that was a big bust," said Meg.

"I'm not quite as negative about it," I said. "We also confirmed that Romano and Masters were romantically involved. And we know Representative Cartwright and Melinda really got into it over the Garfield statue right before the murder."

Meg nodded. "Don't forget Grant Dawson, either."

"He definitely had opportunity and means, and Gordon Romano suggested he disagreed with Masters about how to run the Botanic Garden. For someone as passionate as Dawson, it could be a credible motive."

Meg was just about to respond when we heard a man's booming voice from across the hallway. "Meg Peters!"

We stopped in our tracks outside the House of Representatives basement post office. A well-dressed, attractive man in his mid-forties jogged up to us.

Meg cleared her throat. "Clay Donovan, you may not have met Kit Marshall. She's chief of staff for Maeve Dixon." Then she turned to me. "Clay has worked on and off on Capitol Hill for several years. But now he's Bridget Cartwright's chief of staff."

"Nice to meet you," I said. He pumped my hand several times, a wide grin spread across his face.

"Great to bump into you, Meg. I've been thinking about looking you up since I returned." He looked directly at my best friend, his gray eyes glowing. I had a feeling the professional connection was secondary to an opportunity of a more personal nature. Bracing myself for Meg's typical brush-off, I leaned backward and scanned the hallway for a polite yet plausible escape. If all else failed, I could always claim a pressing need to purchase postage stamps.

Much to my surprise, Meg moved closer to Clay, her lips parted. "Well, I guess it was destiny." She laughed and smoothed her hair into place.

I wasn't sure what Meg was up to, but this conversation was getting a little too *Young and the Restless* for my taste. Actually, Clay didn't seem quite so young, which made it sketchier.

"I'm sorry I didn't meet you the other day," I said. "I had a brief meeting with your boss because the Chairwoman of House

277

Administration asked us to keep tabs on the Melinda Masters murder investigation."

"Yes, Bridget did mention she had a meeting about it," he said. "I hope there's progress on solving it."

"We're getting there," said Meg. "We just had a meeting with Gordon Romano, the Comptroller General."

Running into Clay had been fortuitous. "Your boss had an interest in the Architect of the Capitol. In fact, she asked Romano to begin an investigation. She's concerned about improprieties surrounding big dollar contracts," I said.

Clay nodded gravely. "Bridget talked to me about this issue. As you know, she's quite passionate about eliminating corruption in government."

"And equally passionate about eliminating the Garfield statue on Capitol grounds and replacing it with James Madison," I said. "Something your constituents would certainly appreciate."

My accusation didn't throw Clay off kilter. He waved his hand and laughed. "That Garfield nonsense. She knows it's not going anywhere. You think Congress will actually pass a law to swap out one dead white guy with another? Come on."

"That's not what we heard," said Meg.

"Gordon Romano told us that Representative Cartwright was lobbying Melinda Masters hard on it."

Clay's crow's feet appeared when he smiled. "Bridget did that so she could tell people in her district she tried to make it happen. But she was really using it as an excuse to get to know Melinda Masters better."

I blinked. "So she could figure out what was going on inside the Architect's office?"

"You could say that," said Clay. "She wanted to figure out if Masters was covering up something. Or if she was putting an end to the problems inside the Architect's office."

"It's a roundabout way of doing business," I remarked, my eyebrows raised.

"It might be, but as you probably know, Bridget Cartwright has her own way of getting things done," said Clay. "I'm just along for the ride."

Meg beamed and touched his arm lightly. "You're too modest. Representative Cartwright is lucky to have such an experienced chief of staff join her team."

Clay straightened up, clearly enjoying the vote of confidence. "Ladies, it was a pleasure to chat with you. I need to get back to the office." He leaned closer to Meg and spoke in a lower voice. "I'll drop you a line later today, if that's okay with you."

Meg winked and turned on her heels to head up the short incline connecting Longworth to the Cannon Building. "And what was *that* all about, Meg?" I asked when I caught up with her.

"Clay Donovan," she said dreamily. "I've had my eye on him for some time. It's perfect timing."

I thought of a way to say it tactfully, but instead I just blurted it out. "Isn't he a little, you know, old for you?"

Meg turned to face me. "If you must know, I'm starting to think maturity might not be a bad quality in a man."

"No offense, Meg, but you're all over the map," I said. "First, you're obsessed with my younger brother. Now you're hitting on some guy ten years older than you. What gives?"

Meg sighed and glanced at her phone. "Let's talk about this later. I've got a ton of work before I can even think about calling it quits for the day."

I studied my best friend. Normally, I wouldn't take no for an answer. I'd hound her until she told me what was going on with her. But she had a point. It was nothing that couldn't wait.

I exhaled loudly. "You win. After all, tomorrow is another day."

If I'd known about the chaos which was about to descend, I might not have been so optimistically blasé about the future.

CHAPTER FIFTEEN

The next several hours were a swirl of brief meetings, emails, and phone calls. Despite Maeve Dixon's desire that I reprise my role as Capitol Hill amateur sleuth extraordinaire, I still had a day job. Even murder didn't stop political deals, press interviews, and inquiries from lobbyists. My phone pinged, and when I checked it, only then did I realize it was almost seven o'clock. Undoubtedly, Doug was wondering when I would arrive home.

I'm home w/ your brother. Are you joining???

That was Doug-speak for "please get your butt home now, Kit." I typed a reply.

Leaving in 5. Pick up dinner?

Neither of us really cooked. But we were masters of local takeout and delivery.

282

Italian Store?

Doug knew my weakness. The Arlington eatery had the best pizza in the Washington, D.C. metropolitan area. We tried to limit our intake to avoid expanding waistlines. Today seemed like a good day for a treat. Besides, Sebastian would enjoy Italian Store pizza, which imitated New York rather than California style pies.

Phone in the order & I will pick up.

Even if I hadn't identified Melinda Masters's killer today, at least the mystery of what we were eating for dinner had been solved. I was the last person in the office this evening, so no good night pleasantries were necessary. Post rush hour and with traffic lighter than usual due to summer vacations, I stood outside our condo door a mere thirty minutes later, balancing an enormous pizza box while fishing my key out of my purse.

I heard a soft growl on the other side of the door. No doubt Clarence was poised to attack. With his keen beagle mutt scent, he'd certainly figured out what we were having for dinner. Clarence wasn't picky in the food department, but Italian Store pizza was his all-time favorite.

Just as I was in danger of dropping our prized pie, the door swung open. Sebastian appeared with a big smile on his face, holding a glass of wine in one hand and Clarence's collar in the other.

"Smells delicious," he said. Clarence immediately barked in agreement.

An open bottle of Virginia's Three Foxes Riesling sat on the coffee table. Doug was ensconced in his iPad, undoubtedly checking up on the day's news. He also had a glass of wine in his hand.

"Looks like I missed out on happy hour," I said, the disappointment evident in my voice.

Doug looked up from his online browsing. "Yes, but the good news is we saved you a glass. By the way, there's no shortage of wine inside this condo."

I put the pizza on the counter and carefully slid it as far away as possible from the edge. We'd learned a few years ago that when it came to pizza, Clarence did not always play by the rules of doggie decorum.

"Shall we eat?" I grabbed three plates from the cabinet. "Personally, I'm famished."

Sebastian had thoughtfully poured me a glass of vino and handed it to me. "It looks like you need a drink, Kit."

"Unfortunately, Washington has that effect on people," I said. "It has one of the highest rates of alcohol consumption per capita in the country."

Sebastian raised his glass. "Quite frankly, that doesn't bother me one bit."

We served ourselves huge slices of pepperoni pizza and took seats at our dining room table. Most of the time, Doug and I ate in our living room while we watched television. Sitting down at the table was a nice change.

After several bites and a few more sips of wine, Doug asked, "Did you make any more progress on the case today?"

I summarized our brief conversations with Gordon Romano and Clay Donovan. After picking off the pepperoni, I fed a slice to Clarence, who licked his lips repeatedly. It was a toss-up whether he liked the gooey cheese, crust, or pepperoni the best. If I had to bet, I'd put my money on the latter.

"So, what's your next move?" asked Doug.

"I really need to talk to Steve Song," I said. "All roads seem to point to him. Melinda Masters told Romano that Song was harassing her."

"Sounds like he might be trouble," said Sebastian, his brow furrowed. "Should you talk to this guy alone? If he's hothead, he might turn on you."

Doug grabbed another slice and took a big bite. He put up his finger to indicate he had something to say on the matter, just as soon as he wiped the sauce from the side of his mouth.

Finally, he spoke. "Sebastian is right. Even if Song isn't the murderer, he sounds like he's a real piece of work. You don't want to poke the bear."

As if on cue, Clarence growled softly. I snuck him another slice of pepperoni and his butt wiggled in delight.

"Don't worry. I'll figure something out," I mumbled. I was used to Doug's persistent concern for my welfare. With Sebastian in the mix, now I had to fend off another circumspect family member.

"Too many people have pointed their fingers to the Architect's office," said Doug. "Something must have been going on, but what?"

"Even more importantly, how is it related to Melinda Masters's murder?" I asked.

"Maybe not at all," said Sebastian. Clarence had shifted positions and was now resting his head on my brother's knee. Sebastian snuck him a small bite of crust. It hadn't taken very long for Clarence to figure out Sebastian was a sucker.

"It's a possibility," I admitted. "Bridget Cartwright might have gotten frustrated at Melinda and killed her in a moment of anger. Cartwright must have attended other functions at the Botanic Garden. She knew what types of plants were inside the conservatory."

"If that's the case, she might have planned it," said Sebastian. "She knew Melinda would be there for the corpse flower reception."

"True enough," said Doug. "But didn't you say Cartwright's chief of staff downplayed the removal of the Garfield statue?"

I nodded. "I only met Clay Donovan this afternoon. It's impossible to judge whether he was telling the truth or selling us a bill of goods."

"If Cartwright did kill Masters, she might have told Donovan about it. He could be covering up the motive by talking to you and Meg," said Doug.

"It was curious that we coincidentally happened to run into him in the hallway and he was overly eager to speak to us," I said. "Well, he was mostly interested in Meg."

The edges of Sebastian's mouth tweaked upward. "That's not farfetched. I'm glad Meg has a potential suitor on the horizon."

"She has more than one," I murmured, thinking about Trevor. I'd have to find a way to tell Trevor the threat of younger Sebastian had been replaced by the mature Clay Donovan.

Before popping the last bite of pizza in his mouth, Doug said, "Don't forget Grant Dawson, either. That guy is as high strung as they come."

"Romano said he disagreed with Masters about the operations of the Botanic Garden," I said.

"That's definitely a motive for murder," said Doug. "Remember how passionately he spoke about it to us? If Masters was getting in his way, he might have cooked up this scheme to murder her. And he was right behind us after Meg discovered the body."

I smiled at Doug. He brought up good points. No doubt he was embracing his role as an amateur sleuth assistant.

His comments reminded me this case had more theories than explanations. Without hard evidence or an eyewitness, finding the killer seemed as elusive as fixing the American health care system. There were a number of credible solutions, but nothing seemed like the right fit.

I got up to wrap the leftover pizza. Clarence eyed me suspiciously. He viewed leftovers as wasted opportunity. On the other hand, neither of us needed another bite. I tugged at my waistline. With the exception of the burpees this morning, I'd ignored my workout regimen. Of course, it was nothing a jog tomorrow wouldn't remedy. I grabbed my phone and texted Meg. I could kill two birds with one stone. I wanted to catch up with my best friend, and I needed to burn some calories. I rubbed Clarence's belly, which seemed bigger than it was a few weeks ago. No doubt he was likewise feeling the effects of Sebastian's visit, too.

"If Meg wants to go for a jog tomorrow, you can join us," I said to Clarence. "You're looking a little chubby."

Clarence cocked his head and continued with his dubious stare. He probably wasn't too pleased with the chubby comment, but he loved the promise of a morning sojourn. Thankfully, Meg responded affirmatively, and we agreed to meet at seven o'clock for our exercise.

Sebastian was sitting in our guest room on the bed, studying his phone. I knocked on the door before I entered, and he looked up. "Come on in."

I stepped just inside the door. "What do you have planned tomorrow? I know you've enjoyed including Clarence in your activities, but I'd like to take him with me. It's Friday and after we're done with our morning jog, he can spend it at our office." Maeve Dixon loved dogs and welcomed Clarence on days when it wasn't too busy. Fridays were usually a safe bet.

Sebastian smiled. "I'll miss him, but it's probably best if he's with you tomorrow. My meetings won't be so . . ." He paused to search for the right word. "Freewheeling."

That didn't sound like Sebastian's normal Washington, D.C. repertoire. "Really? What's up?"

"I have job interviews scheduled," he said evenly.

"In Washington?" I asked. Why hadn't Sebastian told me?

"The surrounding area. As you know, the Dulles corridor was once known as the Silicon Valley of the East. It's cooled down, but it's still a top place for technology."

Dulles wasn't exactly next door, but it was still a lot closer than California. "So, you are serious about moving here." It was somewhere between a statement of fact and a question.

He nodded. "Of course. Otherwise, I wouldn't have set up these interviews. To be perfectly honest, I wanted to make sure it made sense for me to move here. I wasn't sure if you'd want it."

I swallowed hard. "Of course, I want you to move here. Why would you think otherwise?"

"You've built a whole life for yourself." He swept his arms around the room. "Adding a protesting little brother to the mix might not be in the cards. And as I know well, you like your independence. I wouldn't want to cramp your style, Kit."

I walked over to the bed and sat down next to Sebastian. "Nonsense. I'm not sure I have a style to cramp. I'm thrilled you've come back into my life."

"Ditto, Kit Kat," he said, his face softening.

I reached over and gave him a hug. "Try hard in those interviews tomorrow. Don't screw it up."

He let go and crossed his heart with his finger. "I promise." Then he reached across the bed and grabbed a skinny felt box. "I bought you something."

I opened it up, and inside was a fancy silver pen. "This is really nice, Sebastian. You didn't have to get me anything."

"You've put me up for the past several days and introduced me to your friends," he said. "But take a look. I had it engraved."

I read the striped inscription on the side of the pen aloud. "Politics can be murder."

I gave Sebastian a hug. "I love it. I'll take it to work and smile every time I use it."

"It seemed appropriate, given your job and your extracurricular activities," he said, smiling.

"I'm looking forward to you becoming a more permanent part of our lives here, Sebastian." I fought back the tears welling up in my eyes.

"Me, too. After spending a few days here, I think Doug needs some help making sure you don't get yourself in trouble." He smiled. "Don't forget to warm up for your jog tomorrow with a few burpees."

As a self-confirmed tech geek, Sebastian prided himself on his forecasting. Who knew his talent for accurate predictions extended to crime solving and murder?

CHAPTER SIXTEEN

Friday is the only day of the week I instruct my intelligent personal assistant to snooze. Frequently, the House of Representatives had adjourned the night before and with Maeve Dixon safely back in North Carolina, a few precious minutes of sleep are often a small reward for making it to the end of the work week.

However, this morning, Clarence and I had an early morning date with Meg for exercise. After throwing off the covers, I dressed quickly, picked up the gym bag I'd responsibly packed the night before, and grabbed Clarence's leash.

"Let's go buddy," I said. "We're burning calories before work today."

Clarence's floppy ears perked up, and he licked his lips. Unfortunately, Clarence often thought excitement meant food was forthcoming. He was in for a rude awakening. The temperature would surely hit ninety degrees today, but the weather would be manageable for one or two hours after sunrise. The only time to exercise in Washington during the summer was the early morning. The heat clung to the city in the evening, making nighttime jogs miserable. Besides, who had the energy to run five miles after the day's battles had already taken their toll?

Doug hadn't gotten up by the time we were ready to leave. "See you later this evening," I said. "By the way, I'm taking the car today since I have Clarence in tow. Enjoy the Metro."

My husband murmured an indistinguishable reply that even our top World War II codebreakers couldn't interpret.

"Is something wrong? I need to meet Meg for our jog," I said, trying to hide the exasperation in my voice.

Doug ran his fingers through his bushy hair. He muttered something again. This time, I could make out the words "drive," "home," and "together."

I snapped my fingers. "Oh, you want us to drive home together tonight after work. Sure thing. I'll be in touch to let you know how my day is going." Then I called over my shoulder, "If I need you on the case, I'll text you."

This time, there was no response except a snore. Twenty minutes later, Clarence and I parked inside the underground congressional office complex garage. We cleared security through our building and emerged from the north side exit, then jogged across Independence Avenue to meet Meg at our designated rendezvous on Southeast Drive. The apex of Capitol Hill, this particular spot was a good place to begin a run. The first quarter mile was a breezy downhill warm-up.

Sure enough, Meg was stretching out as we arrived. Previously, my best friend had been allergic to exercise. But during her hiatus from the opposite sex, she'd taken up jogging and seemed to make it a habit. This included a new-found love for expensive athletic gear. Today she sported a pair of fuchsia running shorts, a matching cotton headband, and a fitted ribbed white tank. On the other hand, I had on an old "Dixon for Congress" T-shirt from last year's campaign. It still had the barbecue stains from the North Carolina state fair. Luckily, it no longer smelled like brisket.

Meg bent down and patted Clarence on the head. "I hope you're ready for a big workout this morning." Clarence once again licked his lips, undoubtedly confusing "workout" with "breakfast."

I stretched my legs and arms and then handed Meg Clarence's leash. "Time for my warm-up," I said. "Burpees."

Before she could say anything, I hit the deck and knocked out fifteen in a row. Meg applauded when I finished. "Sebastian is having a good influence on you."

After a few more stretching exercises, we began our jog at an easy pace. As we passed the United States Capitol to our right, Meg pointed to the statue on the west lawn. "I wonder what President Garfield would think if he knew his likeness might have caused a murder."

"I want to ask you about that." I was now huffing and puffing as we leveled out and headed for the pedestrian path on the National Mall. "Did you believe Clay Donovan when he said Congresswoman Cartwright didn't really care about replacing Garfield with James Madison?"

Meg didn't respond immediately, although it was impossible to know whether she was trying to catch her breath or thinking about my question. We paused at an intersection to allow traffic to pass, and she took the break as an opportunity to speak. "Not really. Clay is a smooth operator and a Hill veteran. He seemed too eager to separate

Cartwright from the statue issue."

We resumed our run, now heading up the short hill leading to the Washington Monument. Several years ago, a significant earthquake damaged the monument's structure. After generous donations from wealthy benefactors supported the required repairs, it was open again for business. Tourists had already started to queue around the flags which surrounded the obelisk. Visitors often remarked that Washington's skyline wasn't as impressive as New York, London, or Paris. Per federal law, most didn't know that no other building within the District of Columbia could surpass the height of the Washington Monument. It guaranteed that D.C. would never have the same grandiose appearance of a cosmopolitan world capital. But it did ensure that no one missed the splendor of the Washington Monument.

"I had a similar impression," I said as we descended the other side of the hill. "You're the one who's known him for years."

Meg shrugged. We slowed down as we approached the World War II memorial and another busy intersection. Clarence took advantage of the pause in running to turn around and pull in the other direction.

"What are you doing, Clarence?" I asked. "We're headed toward the Reflecting Pool so you can chase the ducks."

Clarence was undeterred. Although I'd read scientists hoped technology would enable dogs to speak in the next decade, that day wasn't here yet. In his clumsy beagle mutt fashion, he pointed his nose in the direction from which we'd come. Then, in an instant, his body was perfectly still with his tail pointed parallel to the ground. His snout twitched as his floppy ears moved forward.

"What's wrong with him?" asked Meg. "I've never seen Clarence so discombobulated."

He was my dog, who I'd raised from puppyhood, and quite frankly, I'd never seen Clarence vexed, except if there was a fox in the vicinity. As widespread as the pesky suckers had become, I seriously doubted his arch nemesis had invaded the crowded grounds of the National Mall.

"Don't know," I confessed. "He seems agitated."

The "walk" sign illuminated so we jogged across the street. Clarence reluctantly followed. After we'd reached the memorial, he turned around again. This time, he snarled. I could see the edges of his white incisors peak through his parted lips.

Meg's mouth fell open. "Am I delusional,

or did Clarence just growl?"

"He did." Clarence's hackles were now raised, the fur covering his neck and back lifted. His canine non-verbal communication couldn't be clearer. A threat was nearby.

We trotted to the other side of the memorial and stood underneath the Pacific theatre arch. Constructed in 2004, the semi-circle structure included fifty-six pillars and two towering archways, centered by an impressive fountain. With the Lincoln Memorial to our back, we scanned the entire area.

Clarence sat down and looked at me, his tail beating back and forth with the precision of a metronome. His big, brown eyes were trying to tell me something.

Meg broke the silence. "Clarence is definitely concerned. I have a feeling we're being watched."

The sun had begun to rise, its brightness complicating any attempt to discover the source of Clarence's unease. "I don't see anyone but joggers and the normal early bird tourist crowd," I said.

Meg put her hand over her eyes to shield the light. After another minute of scanning the crowd, she admitted defeat. "Me, neither."

Clarence's hair went back down. I petted his head, and he licked my hand. "He seems to have calmed down."

Meg wiped the sweat off her face. "Whatever it was, Clarence didn't like it."

I tightened my grip on his leash. "And dogs don't hide their feelings. I know we were going to circle the Reflecting Pool, but I think we'd better head back to the office."

"I second that," said Meg. "I've had enough exercise and excitement for one morning."

We returned to a comfortable jogging pace. Clarence appeared no worse for the wear. He focused on the multitude of squirrels and dogs who crossed his path but didn't show any more signs of distress.

We had just passed the National Museum for Modern Art when I remembered I hadn't yet broached the subject of Meg's love life.

"Have you reconnected with Clay Donovan?" I asked.

"He texted me last night," she said.

"You're going to start dating again?"

Meg shrugged as she tucked a stray piece of blonde hair underneath her headband. "Seems like it's time." The words came in between increasingly short breaths.

This was as good a time as any to tell her about Sebastian. "My brother might try to find a job and relocate to Washington."

We stopped at a traffic light near the Smithsonian Air and Space Museum. "That's really good news, Kit."

"It is," I said slowly. "But I'm not sure he's ready for a serious relationship."

Meg exhaled before speaking. "Neither am I."

"Are you sure?" I asked. "It seems like you are."

"My last relationship ended really badly. I needed time off to recover. Now I'm ready to date again, but I don't think I should restrict myself to one guy," she said.

"Not even Clay Donovan?" I asked slyly.

Meg slowed down. "Let's walk for a minute." We approached the Botanic Garden. The day had begun on Capitol Hill. Independence Avenue was filled with cars and taxis, revving up their engines as they proceeded up the steep climb to the United States Capitol.

"I've learned my lesson," huffed Meg as she gestured toward the Botanic Garden. "I'll answer Clay's text after we solve Melinda Masters's murder."

"Good idea," I said. "And who knows? Maybe a potential suitor will materialize out of nowhere and surprise you." Trevor would have to find the right time to tell Meg about his feelings. In the meantime, I could at least try to pave the way for the unorthodox match.

"A year ago, I wouldn't have been open to that possibility. But now I am," said Meg.

We'd reached the base of the steep hill. "Ready to do this?" I asked. We had a pact. No matter how tired we were at the end of our run, we always ran up Capitol Hill.

"I was born ready!" Meg took off like a shot up the incline.

"What are you doing?" I yelled, already twenty feet behind her. "That's not fair!"

Meg looked over her shoulder without slowing down. "Loser has to pick up the next happy hour tab!"

Clarence licked his lips and as we settled into a slow, steady trot, I remembered another valuable political axiom. Sometimes, accepting defeat gracefully was the only way forward.

CHAPTER SEVENTEEN

We arrived at the Cannon Building sweaty and drained. Exercising before work was exhausting. Why had I insisted on such torture? Then I remembered the slices of pizza scarfed down the night before and felt gratified I'd hauled myself out of bed. Political success might occur infrequently these days, but at least tenacious joggers could still conquer Capitol Hill.

After grabbing my gym bag from the car, Clarence and I made our way to the office. There was an infrequently used women's shower in our building basement, near the tunnel that led to the Library of Congress. Far from lavish, it served its purpose on the days I chose to exercise before work.

Clarence and I walked into our office suite with the front desk staff assistant. "As soon as you're settled, can you watch Clarence while I clean up?"

"Sure enough. I just love Clarence." He

reached down to pet him, and Clarence licked his fingers.

"I'll get him some water and breakfast and then deliver him to you," I said.

Clarence and I trotted to my office. A frequent enough visitor, Clarence knew the routine. He sat on his comfy cushion in the corner and waited patiently while I poured doggie food into his bowl and filled another container with fresh water. Thirty seconds later, the kibble was gone and drips of water were spilling from the outer edges of his mouth.

"You're a very messy drinker, Clarence. We'd never be able to take you to a fancy reception."

"That's why Clarence can't come to work every day," said Meg, appearing at the door. "We all know you'd talk to him and forget about the rest of us."

"Well, Clarence rarely disagrees with my opinions. It's hard to compete with that," I said.

"Fair enough," said Meg. "If you want to shower first, I'll get us breakfast. Coffee and a bagel?"

I hesitated. Yogurt would be better than a bagel. On the other hand, I had just run several miles. Surely that justified the carbohydrates.

"Sounds good," I said. "But make sure it's light cream cheese."

Meg rolled her eyes and said nothing before walking out of my office. Clarence licked his lips, no doubt reacting favorably to the mention of a bagel.

"Don't get your hopes up," I said to him. "You're going outside with Sam, and he doesn't have any food."

Clarence happily followed me to the outer lobby area and sat down next to the staff assistant behind his desk.

I handed him Clarence's leash. "I'd keep him close to you, even though we're unlikely to get visitors this early in the morning. We had an unfortunate incidence once before." I was referring to Clarence's impressive ability to steal ice cream from small children. We managed to fix the situation, but no one wanted a repeat performance.

"Got it," said Sam. "The phone calls don't usually heat up until ten or so. It won't be a problem to keep an eye on Clarence."

I hurried downstairs and had just turned the corner down the hallway when I skidded to an abrupt stop. I'd almost crashed into Trevor.

He wrinkled his nose. "Dressing down for work these days, Ms. Marshall?"

"Actually, Meg and I went for a run this

morning on the Mall," I said.

His face softened at the mention of Meg's name. "A pleasant start to the day, I trust?"

"Mostly. Something strange did happen." I told Trevor about Clarence's odd behavior. Trevor wasn't a dog lover, but he was familiar with Clarence's typical happy-go-lucky demeanor.

He wrinkled his brow. "That sounds highly suspicious." He glanced at his watch. "I've got a meeting in five minutes. Do you have time at ten o'clock for coffee?"

I nodded. "Cafeteria?"

He shook his head. "Too many people eavesdrop in these buildings."

"Le Bon Cafe?" The French cafe was a short walk away from House offices.

"See you there." He looked me up and down. "I hope your attire will have improved."

Typical Trevor. Of course, he'd never have to worry about Meg looking slovenly. She was a walking advertisement for *Cosmopolitan.*

I showered as fast as I could and threw on a black cotton dress with tan polka dots, the perfect casual outfit for a Friday on Capitol Hill. The stretchy fabric allowed me to move freely, a godsend in the sticky summer months of Washington, D.C. I checked my reflection in the mirror. Ponytails were perfectly fine on days in which no formal meetings were scheduled. I applied a light dusting of makeup with a splash of lip gloss for color. Black mule sandals finished off the look. In my book, any day in which I didn't have to squish my feet into heels was a blessing.

I pulled open our office door and instantly knew something was terribly amiss. Meg and Sam were bent over Clarence, examining him. Clarence was sitting in the middle of our lobby, enjoying the attention.

Meg looked up. "Kit, thank goodness you're back."

"What's wrong?" I asked, my voice filled with alarm.

"You're not going to like this," said Meg. "Sam, show her what you found."

Sam stood and handed me a piece of paper which had been folded several times. Despite the crinkles, the large block writing on the note was easy to read:

NEXT TIME, I WON'T JUST WATCH.

I shook my hand holding the note. "How was this delivered?"

Meg and Sam glanced at each other. Sam's hands trembled, and he averted his gaze toward the floor.

It wasn't fair to put our least senior staff

member on the spot. "Meg, can you tell me what happened?" I asked.

She swallowed hard. "Since it's getting close to the end of our summer legislative session, Sam got a few more telephone calls this morning than usual," she said. "He left Clarence alone in the lobby momentarily to ask if anyone could join him on the phones."

"I was gone for two minutes, tops," said Sam, his voice quaking. "When I came back, Clarence was sitting in front of my desk and he had the note wrapped around his collar. I unfastened it and opened up the note."

Meg interrupted. "Then he screamed and I ran out to see what was wrong."

I sighed. Obviously, the same person who had followed us on our run this morning had lurked near our office and waited for an opportunity to send a foreboding message.

"Clarence hasn't been hurt," said Sam. "We looked him over from head to tail."

At the mention of his name, Clarence's ears perked up. He was no worse for the wear. Interestingly enough, someone knew the identity of Melinda Masters's killer. Unfortunately, that someone was a dog.

Meg's eyes narrowed. "Why not put the note on the desk or tape it to the door? Why bother with Clarence?"

I bit my lip. "It was a brazen move, like killing the Architect of the Capitol with a plant inside the Botanic Garden. The murderer wants us to know he or she can get to us anytime, anyplace."

Beads of sweat appeared on Sam's forehead. "There's a murderer here in Congress?"

I'd forgotten that as a junior staffer, Sam had no idea we'd been investigating the Masters murder. I put my hand on his shoulder. "Don't worry about it. Go back to your desk and make sure to let us know if anything else suspicious happens." I motioned for Meg to return to the office suite with me.

"Sure," said Sam shakily and then added quickly. "I'm glad nothing happened to Clarence."

"Me, too," I said, under my breath.

Meg and I bolted for my office and closed the door. "Are you going to let the Congresswoman know about this?" she asked.

Maeve Dixon had taken off for North Carolina last night to march in a town parade later today. She'd fly back to D.C. tomorrow morning to attend the staff picnic.

"No sense in alarming her. She's not going to leave the district, and there's nothing she can do today about it," I said. "We can tell her tomorrow."

Meg inhaled. "Okay, that's your call. What about Detective O'Halloran?"

I picked up my iPhone to check the time. "I've got to meet Trevor for coffee in a few minutes. I need his connections to get to Steve Song in the Architect's Office. Can you take care of calling O'Halloran and letting him know about the note?"

"I can do it," she said. "But he's not going to like it. This is a clear threat. He's going to want you to stop investigating."

"That's why you're the messenger and not me. If he can't speak with me, he can't order me off the case."

Meg took a deep breath. "What about Doug? Shouldn't you call him?"

Meg was right. I *should* call Doug. But he'd ask a million questions and Trevor was waiting. My penchant for independence frequently superseded my better judgment.

"I'll touch base with him in a bit," I said. "Don't worry. I'll tell him what happened."

"Be careful, Kit," said Meg. "This killer is deliberate and has a lot of patience. He or she waited for Melinda to be alone and in the right spot after the reception at the Botanic Garden. And then stalked us today during our run, waiting for the right opportunity to deliver that threat."

"You're right. It also means we must be getting close to the truth. Or the killer wouldn't be so threatened." I grabbed my purse. "I have to go now or I'll be late for coffee with Trevor. You know how he hates tardiness."

"Good luck," she said. "Wait. What should I tell Detective O'Halloran if he wants to speak with you?"

"Tell him I'm tied up in meetings all day," I said. "And I'll call him when I have a moment." Did white lies really count during a murder investigation? I had a feeling we were on the brink of a big break in the case, and I couldn't slow down for Detective O'Halloran.

The walk to meet Trevor was a short one. I considered weaving my way through the tunnels through the Library of Congress. However, I'd had bad luck in the tunnels once before during a murder investigation, so instead I opted for the above-ground route. Exiting the northeast door of the Cannon Building, our meeting spot was exactly one block due east. Fortunately, the concrete esplanade of the Library's Madison Building was teeming with Capitol Hill police officers, who kept careful watch over open spaces near the United States Capitol. Five minutes later, I opened the door to Le

Bon Cafe and inhaled deeply. Murder investigation or not, the smell of freshly baked cookies, muffins, and other savory breakfast items was downright intoxicating. Meg had retrieved breakfast for both of us, but in the flurry of activity concerning the note on Clarence's collar, there hadn't been a chance for a bite. I glanced around the small restaurant. Trevor hadn't arrived, so I had time to place an order and find a seat.

"Good morning," chirped the counter assistant. "What can I get for you?"

I studied the plastic covered menu intently, although there was no need to do so. I ate here at least once a week and had all the options memorized. There were many tempting options, including the Belgian waffle, French toast, and the baked egg strata. My stomach grumbled in hunger, encouraging a caloric splurge.

"Steel cut oatmeal," I said firmly. With cranberries, cinnamon, and toasted apples, it was both savory and healthy. "And a large coffee."

"For here or to go?" she asked pleasantly.

"For here," I said in unison with a familiar voice. My breakfast companion had arrived. "Hello, Trevor," I said. "Would you like something for breakfast?"

He sniffed, half appreciatively and half

dismissively. With Trevor, it was hard, if not impossible, to ascertain motives. "Smells quite good, but I'd better not. Don't want to put on any extra pounds." He looked at me knowingly.

"I haven't had breakfast," I said quickly. We sat down at the empty table by the front window.

Trevor studied me closely. "Did something happen since I saw you in the hallway of Cannon? You look flustered, even by Kit Marshall standards."

I ignored the sideways dig and told Trevor about the threatening note delivered via Clarence. Trevor leaned back in his chair and rubbed his forehead as the counter assistant delivered a steaming bowl of hot oatmeal to our table.

"Thank you," I murmured, picking up the spoon and stirring the delightful concoction. The sautéed apples and cinnamon really made the dish a healthier alternative to pie.

Trevor clenched his hands into fists. "You're not taking this threat seriously."

"Of course, I am. Why would you say that?" I asked between bites of oatmeal.

Trevor glared. "It certainly hasn't affected your appetite. What's your next move, Nancy Drew?"

As much as I loved the most famous amateur female detective of all time, when Trevor invoked her name, it was a sign of derision instead of affection.

I wiped my mouth and took a sip of coffee. "Steve Song. I need to speak with him. Can you help?"

Trevor adjusted his glasses. "Most likely. The Architect of the Capitol works closely with my boss, as you know."

"Yes. Spare me the lecture about how you need Melinda's murder solved so the search for a new Architect can begin."

"I'm glad you're paying attention, Kit. But yes, we are concerned about several long-standing projects, particularly the Cannon Building renovation," he said. "And that necessitates permanent leadership in the Architect's office."

"Steve Song doesn't make the grade?"

Trevor waved his hand dismissively. "He'll do the job in the interim, like he did previously. But it's not the same as having someone permanently committed to the work that needs to be done inside the Capitol complex."

"Well, I've heard through the grapevine that Steve Song might have wanted the big job, and he wasn't too pleased working for Melinda." I took the last bite of my oatmeal

314

and pushed my empty bowl to the edge of the table.

"I've heard those rumors, too." Trevor then lowered his voice. "Steve has a reputation."

"For what? At this point, I need specifics." A conversation with Trevor often left me exhausted, the mental equivalent of playing three sets at Wimbledon against Serena Williams.

"Normally mild-mannered, but he's got a temper that flares," said Trevor. "Sometimes he says things he shouldn't."

"That seems quite relevant, given the circumstances." I rubbed my temples. Dealing with a loquacious hothead wasn't my preferred Friday morning activity. On the other hand, Steve Song had zipped to the top of my suspect list. A convo with him would break the case wide open.

"You shouldn't meet with him alone in the dark recesses of the Capitol building," said Trevor.

I got his drift. Been there, done that, and suffered the consequences. "Can't you get me a meeting inside his office?"

"Which is in the basement of the Capitol," said Trevor tersely.

"Still, I don't think he's going to try to kill me in the middle of an office suite. Is he *that* dangerous?"

"I don't know, Kit." He inhaled quickly. "I'm not sure of anything anymore."

I raised my eyebrow. How could the most rational person since Descartes claim serious doubt concerning his ability to know?

I clapped my hands in front of his face, drawing the attention of the genteel cafe patrons surrounding us. "Trevor, snap out of it. What's wrong with you?" I scrutinized his face. "Are you ill? A fever that's making you delusional?"

Trevor sighed. "No, I'm afraid it's much worse than that."

I swallowed hard. "You're dying?"

He crossed his arms. "That is a ridiculous proposition."

Thank goodness the Trevor I knew was back. "What could be so bad, then?"

He lowered his head and rubbed his forehead. "It's Meg. I don't know what to do. And I've hopelessly fallen for her."

CHAPTER EIGHTEEN

I flopped back in my chair and covered my mouth. I was partially relieved, partially aghast. At least Trevor wasn't headed for a premature death. On the other hand, he was infatuated with my best friend, whose tumultuous track record in the romance department rivaled Liz Taylor.

I reached across the table and patted Trevor's hand in an attempt to comfort him. Speaking softly, I said, "Trevor, you know Meg is a bit of a crapshoot. Don't get too smitten."

He didn't pull away, as I'd imagined he would. "Understood. But I need to figure this out, Kit. Or move on."

I nodded while taking the last sip of my coffee. "Meg isn't the same person you knew years ago in Senator Langsford's office. She's been through a lot. I think she's open to new possibilities. But I have no idea if she's interested romantically in you."

Trevor didn't bristle. Despite his emotional vulnerability, I knew he'd appreciate frankness. "I'll have to take my chances, Kit."

"One thing is for certain," I said. "It doesn't look like it's going to work out with Sebastian right now. So, you don't have to worry about him."

"Is your brother returning to California?"

I tilted my head. "I hope not. He's interviewing for tech jobs today in the area."

"You'd like him to stick around?"

"Yes, I would. I've enjoyed having someone from my family nearby."

Trevor had a forlorn look on his face. "Everyone is busy in this city, bustling around with meetings, appointments, and happy hours. But it can also be lonely."

Meg had expressed a similar sentiment. It offered a glimmer of possibility that she wouldn't blow Trevor off? I'd better keep quiet. No need to raise Trevor's expectations about Meg, who had been mercurial in the past. She hadn't seemed quite so hot to trot, pun intended, about Clay Donovan this morning. It was because she thought he could somehow be involved with the murder of Melinda Masters through his boss, Representative Cartwright.

"Don't worry Trevor," I said with a heavy

dose of sympathy. "You'll find someone, whether it's Meg or another worthy woman."

Trevor pushed up his wire-framed glasses higher on his nose. "Well, enough of that business." He folded his hands on the table. "Back to more important matters. You need a meeting with Steve Song, correct?"

I straightened up, assuming a business-like posture to mirror Trevor. "Definitely. I understand your concern. Even if Steve is guilty, I don't think he'll try to hurt me if we meet at the Architect's main office inside the Capitol."

Trevor scrunched his face, apparently in deep thought. "I wish I could join you. But the Chief Administrative Officer needs me in a meeting at noon that might last for a while."

I waved my hand. "Don't worry about it. After all, I've been in tight situations before."

"Kit, that's exactly what I'm worried about," he said. "You've managed to survive, but it hasn't been pretty."

I considered my most recent escapades. Trevor had a legitimate point.

"What if I asked Doug to make a surprise appearance?" I asked.

"Why would Doug have business with the

Architect of the Capitol?" Trevor countered.

"Oh, I'm sure we can concoct a reason. That way, he wouldn't arrive with me, which would generate even more suspicion. But if something went wrong, he'd be there to help."

Trevor considered my proposition for a moment before answering. "It's not Ocean's Eleven, but at least it's something."

"Well, I'm not George Clooney, either," I said, laughing. "Or even Julia Roberts, for that matter."

Even the normally somber Trevor chuckled at that one. "Nor am I Brad Pitt. But who's keeping track?"

I smiled, satisfied that the outlook of my nemesis-turned-friend had brightened considerably. Adding Doug to the sleuthing mix was a good idea. This morning's threatening note had made me feel vulnerable, and Doug's presence would lessen my uneasiness. "Do you think you can get me an appointment soon with Steve?"

Trevor stood and grabbed his briefcase from the chair. "Absolutely. I'll email him on the walk back to the office. Stand by for a confirmation on the time."

I chugged the remainder of my coffee. "Thanks, Trevor. Oh, and by the way, you should come to our Maeve Dixon picnic tomorrow. It's at a park in Arlington. Meg is supervising the organization of it. I'll have her send you the details."

"Thank you for the invitation. I suppose that depends how my conversation goes with her later today," he said.

Oh dear. He's going to pop the question, so to speak.

I took a deep breath. "Trevor, I wish you the best of luck."

"Ditto, Kit Marshall." And then Trevor disappeared out the door of Le Bon Cafe in a flash.

"If Meg ends up dating him," I muttered. "Maybe she'll figure out how he's able to vanish without a trace."

I returned my bowl to the counter and headed out into the warm July sun. It was close to eleven o'clock. I'd better check back with the office and make sure everything, including the picnic, was on track.

Meg greeted me upon my return. "Any luck?"

"Trevor will get me a meeting with Steve," I said. "Are we all set for tomorrow's barbecue?"

She sighed. "It will work out, I'm sure."

"What's the problem, Meg? Don't hold out." As the chief of staff, the buck stopped with me.

"They can't decide which discount store to shop at tomorrow," said Meg. "Oliver and Jess have memberships at competing wholesalers. And they're currently at war about which one to use for the picnic."

I grabbed my purse and fished through it to find my wallet. "We're going to solve this right now."

Meg followed me out of my office into the legislative staff cubicle area. "Everyone gather, please!" I said in my loudest indoor voice.

The policy staff looked at each other quizzically but did as they were told.

"Here ye, here ye," I said. "We will now decide where the food for the picnic will be purchased. Heads goes to Oliver's choice, and tails to Jess."

I grabbed a quarter and tossed it into the air. After grabbing it, I smacked the coin on the back of my hand.

"Well, look at that, everyone," I said. "The coin says tails. So, wherever Jess wants to buy the food, it shall be done."

My small staff stared at each other with dazed expressions. I could tell what they thought. *Kit's gone crazy. The job has finally gotten to her.*

"Now everyone can get back to work," I said. Meg followed me back to my office.

"Are you okay?" she asked, her face scrunched up. "That coin toss was a bit unorthodox, even for you."

"I'm perfectly fine," I said, not hiding the annoyance in my voice. "The stupid picnic controversy needed solving, and I solved it. Now I can move onto the next problem, notably Melinda Masters's murder."

"Well, I don't think that can be resolved by flipping a coin, Kit," said Meg.

"Unfortunately, you're right. Trevor is worried about Steve Song. He thinks he's unpredictable with anger management issues."

Meg shuddered. "Sounds familiar. You'd better be careful. You can't solve every problem on your own. Do you want me to go with you?"

"I need a wing man, but this time, a diversion might be in order. And an element of surprise will work best. Doug should be able to help," I said. "I must tell him about this morning, too."

Meg nodded. "I'm sure we could come up with a story, but two people from the same office going to interrogate Song might raise his hackles."

"If he lives up to his reputation, we certainly don't want to poke the beast. I think I have an idea for Doug, but I'll need to call him to see if he can do it."

"I'll get out of your way, then." As Meg left the office, she turned around. "And thanks for solving the picnic problem. You're the boss around here for a reason."

I grinned widely at my best friend. "Thanks, Meg. That means a lot to me."

Meg closed the door behind her, and I sat down in my chair. I swiveled back and forth nervously as I considered what story I could devise to legitimate Doug's appearance at the Architect of the Capitol.

When I had it, I picked up the phone and dialed his Library of Congress extension. He picked up on the first ring.

"Hello, sweetheart. Did you solve the case yet?"

"Not yet, but that's why I'm calling. Are you up for sleuthing?"

Doug laughed. "I thought you'd never ask."

CHAPTER NINETEEN

We went over the plan until Doug seemed comfortable with it. My husband was relatively new to the mystery business and even though he was strikingly intelligent, I wasn't sure his street smarts always matched his intellectual bona fides. Time would tell, and there was no time like the present.

As we hatched our plan, an email arrived from Trevor, stating that I had an appointment with Steve Song at half past noon.

"Are you okay with everything, Doug?" I asked for the last time. "Trevor just contacted me, and I need to be over at the Architect of the Capitol's office in fifteen minutes."

"Don't worry, I can handle it," said Doug, with a heavy dose of confidence in his intonation. "You know, I've talked myself into a historical archive or two in my day."

I rubbed my forehead. "Is that really similar to catching a killer?"

Doug didn't acknowledge the sarcasm, intentionally or not. "Yes, I remember the time when I wanted to see a rare manuscript at the New York Historical Society. They were being stingy with access to the John Jay papers, which I needed to examine . . ."

"Fascinating, darling." I cut him off as politely as possible. "I'm sure you really did a number on them. But back to the task at hand."

"I'll be there ready for action," said Doug. "You can count on me."

"Don't forget our secret password. If either of us say *Clarence* then it's a signal that we're in trouble or can't stall for more time."

"No way I can forget that," said Doug. "See you soon, dear."

With that, he hung up the phone, and I bit my lip. Without a further thought, I casted my worries aside. Doug's head might reside in the clouds, but he was reliable and quick-witted. I'd never seen him take the stage before, so to speak, yet he'd never let me down. It was time to give Doug a chance to prove himself in the world of homicide and intrigue.

I grabbed my purse, said goodbye to Meg, and sped out of the office yet again. Did I really need to squeeze in a jog before work when my job required so much hustle? Five minutes later, I power-walked through the Cannon Tunnel in the direction of the United States Capitol. The entire complex, including the Library of Congress, was connected through underground tunnels. This enabled Members of Congress and staff to move quickly between committee hearings, office meetings, and votes without exposure to the elements. Newcomers to Washington thought the tunnels were most utilized during the winter months. Those of us who had been around for a few years knew the real value came in the summertime. Shelter from the heat and tourists was worth every penny spent on constructing and maintaining the subterranean labyrinth.

I wove through the maze of narrow hallways leading to the Senate side of the Capitol. Finally, I came upon an unassuming basement office with an "Architect of the Capitol" brass plate placed to the right of the door. I took a deep breath and walked inside.

A middle-aged woman looked up from her computer. "Can I help you?" she asked in an uninspired voice.

"I'm here to see Steve Song," I said cheerfully. "I suppose he's now the Acting Architect of the Capitol."

"Yes. Yet again." She might as well have been reading the class roll call in *Ferris Bueller's Day Off.*

I waited for instruction. In these situations, it was best not to engage.

Her hands danced across the keyboard. A few moments later, she finally spoke. "Please have a seat."

I sat in a government office chair and shifted nervously. Was I preparing to talk to a murderer? I'd certainly encountered my share of criminals on Capitol Hill. It was never a pleasant experience, and twice I'd fought for my life. The Architect of the Capitol office suite seemed normal enough. If I screamed loudly, one of the diligent federal government workers would surely come to my rescue, unless saving a congressional staffer from being strangled to death wasn't in their official job description.

A deep voice interrupted my daydream. "Ms. Marshall?"

Steve Song was standing in front of me. I stood up quickly. "Yes, that's me. Pleased to meet you." I stuck my hand out for a shake.

He gripped my hand firmly and pumped it three times. "Steve Song. Acting Architect of the Capitol."

He certainly didn't shy away from the title. I couldn't resist a dig. "What unfortunate circumstances."

Song took a step back. "Of course. I didn't mean to imply otherwise." He motioned with his hand for me to follow him. "Please come inside my office."

I walked down the hallway and noticed the plate outside the door had his name on it with "Deputy Architect of the Capitol" written underneath. At least he hadn't taken over Melinda's office. Yet.

"Have a seat," he said. "Would you like a glass of water or other refreshment?"

"No, I'm fine. I just walked over from the House. Thank goodness for the underground tunnels this time of year."

He smiled as he reclined in his high-backed swivel chair. "The A-O-C is happy to maintain them for congressional staff and the visiting public." He ran his fingers through his greying hair. He wasn't much taller than me, five foot eight. The cut of his dark blue suit indicated he was in good physical shape. Steve Song probably worked out, and I bet there were some well-defined muscles underneath his couture. Even though he wasn't a hulk of a guy, Steve could have easily overpowered Melinda Masters inside the Botanic Garden, especially if he caught her by surprise.

"I appreciate that you made time for me

to visit." While making small talk, I glanced around his office. His desk was messier than most high-ranking Capitol Hill officials. A coffee mug and half-eaten apple sat next to a stack of papers and several binders. Framed family photographs surrounded his huge computer monitor. Several yellow post-it notes were pasted onto different surfaces of his desk, scattered between random folders and other office paperwork.

He must have caught my inquiring stare. "Sorry about everything." He waved his hand indeterminately. "As you can see, the work is piling up. I'm not quite used to it yet."

"I apologize if I've been misinformed, but didn't you serve as Acting Architect of the Capitol before Melinda Masters was appointed?" I asked.

Steve clenched his jaw. "Of course. I suppose I just need to get back into groove."

"My boss was just getting to know Melinda," I said. "She didn't have much time as Architect of the Capitol. Can you tell me more about her?"

Steve sat back in his chair, his hands pressed together to form a steeple. "What do you want to know, Ms. Marshall?"

Suspects who answered questions with a question infuriated me. It either meant the suspect didn't know the answer or wanted to evade answering it. Since Steve had worked alongside Melinda, it was likely the latter scenario rather than the former.

"Basic stuff," I said. "Was she easy to work with? What were her big goals for the office? Are you planning to follow in her footsteps?"

"I wouldn't call those basic questions, but no worries." Steve picked up a pen from his desk and fiddled with it. "Listen, Melinda was as demanding as they come, and I've had a number of bosses since I started my career in Washington."

"What was she working on before she died? Anything in particular?"

Steve paused for a moment and then spoke slowly. "She was still getting her feet wet and learning the job. Melinda took the job seriously and thought a great deal about the funding Congress provides us. Our budget is a big one, and she wanted to know where every dollar was spent."

"Are you also concerned about the money? Not whether there's enough in the budget, but how it's spent." I remembered Marty Buchman and his obsession with chasing down the money. A common thread had presented itself, and I intended to follow the breadcrumbs.

Steve pursed his lips. "Ms. Marshall, this

office has close to eight hundred million dollars to spend each year. If I was concerned with the allocation of every last penny, I might as well chain myself to my desk. I'd never leave this place." He waved his arm in a circular motion around the office.

I tapped my fingers on the desk and glanced at my Fitbit. Doug was scheduled to arrive any minute. If I wanted to push Steve's buttons to get a reaction about Melinda's murder, this was the time. It's do or die. Too appropriate, given the situation.

"There's been allegations of financial malfeasance in the Architect's Office," I said. "What do you know about it?"

"Who's the source of these so-called allegations?" he countered. Again with answering a question with a question. I half-expected Alex Trebek would appear any moment, humming the *Jeopardy!* theme song.

"Several people, including a prominent journalist and a sitting member of Congress," I said, unwavering.

"Bridget Cartwright," he said bitterly. "That woman would kill her own flesh and blood if it meant securing more votes in the next election."

"Are you telling me that Representative

Cartwright might have murdered Melinda Masters?"

"How should I know?" he seethed. "If contracting money was spent improperly, then how come no one blew it wide open? Sounds like just the type of story that would have earned someone a big promotion."

Gotcha.

"Contracting?" I said quietly. "No one said anything about contracting. Except you, of course."

Steve's mouth slackened. It took him a moment to come up with an explanation for his slip. "That's what Cartwright said. She's been the only one making accusations." He glared menacingly. "Until now."

The temper I'd heard so much about had reared its ugly head. Where was Doug? He should have made his grand entrance by now. I'd have to try to calm Steve down on my own.

"Don't jump to conclusions," I said calmly. "No one is accusing you of anything."

His body was so rigid, I could have cracked an egg on it and he wouldn't have flinched. "It certainly sounds like you are," he said.

There was a knock on the door. "Steve, I hate to interrupt, but I need to speak with you." It was the woman who greeted me when I entered the office.

Steve rolled his eyes. "Now what?" he muttered under his breath. He got up from behind his desk and opened the door. "Can I help you, Margaret?"

The woman glanced at me and leaned in closer to Steve. I could hear the words "Library of Congress" and "irate" and "demands to see you." Perfect timing. Doug had arrived.

Steve turned toward me. "I apologize, Ms. Marshall. It seems as though there is an emergency leak at the historic Jefferson Building, and I need to make sure it's fixed. This should only take a minute." He sped out of the office, with his assistant trailing behind.

Now was my opportunity. I couldn't hear the histrionics, but Doug had promised he'd keep Steve occupied with his tale of woe for at least five minutes. The diversion either gave me an excuse to bolt or a chance to snoop. I was opting for the latter. Despite Steve's annoyance, there was no way he was going to harm me inside his office suite. If Doug could just keep him occupied, maybe I could spot something incriminating.

I got up and walked around Steve's desk. With so much clutter, it would be hard to find anything, let alone a clue. The good news was that he'd never notice if I moved things around.

I checked the computer. Too bad. It was locked, and there was no way I was going to figure out his password. Next to his computer screen, a huge three-ring binder was filled with budget documents. I flipped through it quickly. There might be something important inside, but it would take me a month of Sundays to figure it out. I picked up a notebook and examined it. Steve kept handwritten notes from his meetings, but again, I didn't have enough time to decipher his chicken scrawl.

Then I spotted a printed Outlook calendar. I was in luck. Steve was old-fashioned, like my previous (and dead) boss in the Senate. Even though his schedule was kept online, he preferred to print it out instead of reading it on his phone or computer. Sure enough, Tuesday's lineup had the reception at the Botanic Garden on it. What else had Steve Song been up to this week?

Nothing seemed unusual on Wednesday, although that day must have been thrown into a tizzy after Melinda was found dead on Tuesday night. I turned the page to yesterday's schedule. Immediately, I noticed a handwritten entry written into a block for five o'clock in the evening. Despite less than desirable penmanship, I could easily decipher two words: "Romano — Taft C."

How odd. Romano had to refer to Gordon Romano, the GAO Comptroller. But what did he have to do with Taft? I only knew two things about William Howard Taft. He was the only president to serve on the Supreme Court. And, he was so fat that he once got stuck inside a White House bathtub. Neither of those facts seemed remotely pertinent here. I grabbed my iPhone and took a photo of the entry so I could figure it out later.

The sound of Doug's voice brought me to attention. Uh-oh. Something was amiss. I moved from behind Steve's desk to the doorway.

"I don't have time to wait for repairmen today," said Doug. "I have an important appointment with my dog. His name is *Clarence.*"

Real smooth, Doug. At least he'd managed to find a way to give me a head's up that he couldn't keep Steve occupied for much longer.

I glanced back at Steve's office. If there was any evidence that Steve had murdered Melinda, it would remain undiscovered, at least for now.

I hustled down the hallway toward the reception area of the suite. Doug, now red-faced, had his hands on his hips. I stared at my husband with admiration. He'd managed to work himself up over a fake water leak. Maybe he could act his way out of a paper bag.

Doug glanced in my direction but did nothing to acknowledge my presence. After all, we weren't supposed to know each other. He continued with his tirade. "I'm returning to my office now, and I hope this matter will be resolved immediately." His eyes protruded from behind his glasses. "We simply cannot have scholars working in these conditions."

Steve was not to be outdone. "Dr. Hollingsworth, as I said five minutes ago, this matter now has our utmost attention. My assistant will make sure it's solved."

Margaret nodded her head and sat in her chair. From the look on her face, she'd do anything if Doug would just shut up and go away.

Doug sniffed. "Thank you." Then he turned to me. "Pardon my interruption, madam."

The "madam" was over the top. I had to stifle a giggle. Steve and Margaret were so relieved Doug had agreed to leave, they didn't notice my amusement.

I still wanted to ask Steve a few more questions. Doug and I had agreed that he'd linger outside in the hallway and we'd regroup over lunch, so I didn't have much time.

Steve turned to me. "Sorry for the interruption." He rubbed his chin. "What a difficult man. If he called our hotline, we would have made sure someone addressed the situation. I'm not sure why he felt the need to walk over here."

"I suppose some people want service immediately," I said, yet again suppressing a grin.

"Shall we finish our conversation?" Steve got up to lead me back to his office.

"I only have a few more minutes before my next appointment," I said. "Before I leave, I did want to ask you about your whereabouts the night Melinda died."

Steve's face reddened. "And why do you want to know about that?"

This guy never answered a question directly. He either had something to hide or was just plain annoying.

"I'm helping with the investigation," I said casually. "Chairwoman Jackson asked me to run point on it."

In a halting, high-pitched voice, Steve

asked, "Rhonda Jackson?"

"The one and the only," I said. Bringing up the Chairwoman's involvement was my trump card, no pun intended. Steve was the acting Architect of the Capitol, and Jackson was the head of AOC's oversight committee.

"How interesting." From the tone in his voice, it was evident he found this latest factoid anything but interesting.

"If you could share with me your whereabouts, I'm sure Chairwoman Jackson would appreciate it." After a moment's pause, I added, "She relies on me to provide her updates about the investigation." No doubt Jackson could get a briefing from the police at any moment concerning the murder, but why not press when I had Steve painted in a corner?

"I already told the detective in charge my story. I guess it can't hurt to tell you," he said. "I was at the reception that night. When the corpse flower is in bloom, it's all hands on deck. Everyone, including members of Congress, want to see it." He took a deep breath.

"When did you leave?" I asked.

"Near the end. As you know, the Architect of the Capitol was the host for the event," he said. "We had to stay for the entire reception."

"Did you talk to Melinda at all? Anything out of the ordinary?" I pressed.

"She seemed agitated," said Steve. "I assumed it was because she'd had another argument with Cartwright about the Garfield statue. The Congresswoman told me about it the next day. Now it's my problem to clean up."

"But you're not sure if it was Cartwright? Did you ask Melinda what was bothering her?"

"Didn't have time," said Steve. "Remember, we were at a reception with a lot of politicians. It's not an appropriate venue to talk openly. Even if other members of Congress can't stand Bridget Cartwright, they wouldn't take kindly to lowly public servants like us talking negatively about one of their own."

I had to give Steve that one. He wasn't a novice in the game of Washington, D.C. etiquette.

"Anything out of the ordinary at the reception? Something you saw might be a clue and you wouldn't necessarily know it."

Steve thought for several seconds, a somber expression on his face. "Not that I can think of. I'm sorry I can't be more helpful,

Ms. Marshall."

"Thanks for your time," I said, turning to leave. "I have one more question. Do you know the Comptroller General?"

Steve blinked. "You mean Gordon Romano?"

"Last time I checked, he was the head of the G-A-O," I said.

Steve nodded. "Of course, I know him."

"He was involved with Melinda Masters," I said. "Did you know about their relationship?"

"Melinda mentioned they were dating," said Steve. "I didn't think much of it. Typical Washington power couple, I guess."

"You aren't friends with Romano?" I asked.

"You can't lead an agency the size of the A-O-C and not become familiar with the Government Accountability Office. I wouldn't characterize our relationship as a friendship, though." Steve didn't hide the exasperation in his voice.

"Did you talk to him at the reception at the Botanic Garden?" I inched closer to the door.

"We exchanged pleasantries," said Steve. "Nothing important."

I opened the door to leave and then turned around quickly. "I'm sorry, but I have a final question."

Steve sighed. "I thought the question about Romano was the last one." Then he must have remembered my connection to Chairwoman Jackson. "Go ahead and ask it."

In my most innocent voice, I asked "Are you working on a project that concerns Taft?"

Steve's eyebrows furrowed. "Taft? As in William Howard Taft?"

"I would suppose so," I said.

"Not that I know of," he said. "But I'm not aware of all our projects, as you might imagine."

I extended my hand, and Steve accepted it. "Thank you again for your time."

Steve nodded politely. "Good day, Ms. Marshall."

I shut the door behind me and hustled down the hallway, where I found Doug hiding around a corner.

"About time!" he said. "I thought I might need to create another excuse to rescue you."

"What were you going to do? Pretend that Clarence had run away or something?"

Doug turned a deep shade of pink. "We had a code word, and I used it. I couldn't keep Steve occupied much longer."

I linked my arm underneath his. "Doug, I'm teasing."

His face relaxed. "I know. I mean, I was pretty sure you were pulling my leg."

At times, Doug and Meg were at odds with each other, often vying for my free time or attention. Distinct personalities as they were, both shared a strong tendency to view the world literally. Hyperbole, irony, and euphemisms did not come naturally to my husband or best friend. Since I often communicated using one of these feats of verbal wizardry, we occasionally got our wires crossed.

"Would you like to go somewhere for lunch and talk about everything?" I asked breezily. Even though Doug had a fellowship on Capitol Hill, the truth was I rarely saw him during the day. He was busy perusing the stacks and bugging curators for access to rare books and early American manuscripts. Lunch alone together would be a treat.

Doug glanced at his wrist. He was one of the few people who wore a watch that did nothing else but tell time.

"I can squeeze it in." He looked around the dismal, beige tunnel surrounding us. "How do we get out of here?"

I grinned and pulled him in the right

direction. Five minutes later, we were standing outside the Cannon Building, facing Independence Avenue. "Where should we go?"

Doug hesitated. "I don't have a ton of time. Any suggestions?"

I thought for a moment and snapped my fingers. "It's such a nice day with low humidity. Why don't we grab sandwiches at Gandel's and sit outside the Madison Building to eat them?"

"That sounds perfect," said Doug. "When we're done, I'll only have a short walk back to my office."

We took off to the intersection of Second Street and veered onto Pennsylvania Avenue. The picnic tables outside the Madison Building were empty. There would be plenty of seats available after we bought our sandwiches.

"This place is a ghost town on Fridays," I said.

"It's very quiet," Doug agreed. "That's because everyone selects Friday as a telework day."

I'd never considered it. There was no teleworking on Capitol Hill. Members of Congress expected their staff to be present and accounted for each and every day. Who would deal with the problems if congressional staff were teleworking? We reached Gandel's, and I motioned for us to go inside.

Doug stopped and pointed to the sign above us. "Wait a second. This is a liquor store?"

I laughed. "Don't worry. I'm not trying to pull a fast one. It's a liquor store and a deli."

Doug shook his head. "Not a bad combination, I have to admit."

We walked up to the counter, placed our order, and received slips of paper. As Doug stared at his, I guided him toward the cash register. "That's where we pay."

"This place is as retro as it comes." He pulled out his wallet and tossed down a credit card.

The lady behind the counter shook her head. "No credit card under twenty dollars, sir."

Doug wrinkled his brow. "Uh oh. I don't have any cash."

I smiled and tossed two bags of chips and a bottle of soda on top of our sandwiches. "Does that help?"

She rang up our additional purchases and nodded. "Over twenty dollars now. Good job."

I suppressed a giggle. We grabbed our lunches and headed into the warm sunshine.

A slight breeze made the day unusually pleasant. A few minutes later, we were enjoying our sandwiches on the Madison Building plaza with a view of the Capitol directly before us.

Doug bit into his "Gandel's Special" which was stuffed full of salami, ham, bologna, provolone cheese, and all the fixings. I'd opted for the equally huge but slightly tamer turkey, bacon, and Swiss. Doug swallowed and took a sip of our drink.

"I'm dying to know whether our escapade was worthwhile," he said. "Especially since I'll never be able to show my face at the Architect of the Capitol's office again."

"Well, at least not when Steve Song is in charge," I said. "I did find a clue. Or at least I think it's could be a clue." I told Doug about the calendar entry for yesterday that read "Romano — Taft C" and showed him the photo on my phone.

Doug pursed his lips. "Was Song working on a project with Gordon Romano concerning Taft?"

I snapped my fingers. "That's exactly what I thought. I asked Steve before I left about it, and he denied working on anything related to it."

Doug shook his head. "Maybe it's a location. Calendars usually include the meeting place. Do you think they were meeting at Taft's grave? Like Taft Cemetery? The letter C needs to stand for something."

"It's possible," I said slowly. "He's buried at Arlington National Cemetery. It seems like an odd place. And really out of the way for a five o'clock meeting for both the acting Architect of the Capitol and the Comptroller General."

"Also, too public. A number of tourists pass by Taft's grave. Besides John Kennedy, he's the only other president buried at Arlington. It's on all the maps highlighting the important monuments inside the cemetery."

"Well, that doesn't sound like a good place for a surreptitious meeting," I said. "I'm not sure how to crack this puzzle. But it seems awfully coincidental. And when I mentioned Romano's name, Song didn't reveal that he'd seen him yesterday."

"That does sound peculiar," said Doug, chomping his Gandel's Special. "By the way, this sandwich is delicious. I think I have a new place for lunch."

"Now you're a Capitol Hill insider," I said. "Not many people know about the secret deli inside the liquor store."

"What's your next move?" asked Doug.

"I feel like we're on the right track," I said. "By the way, Clarence knows who did it."

Doug's eyes bulged. "How would Clarence know who killed Melinda Masters?"

I recapped the eventful morning, including Clarence's suspicious behavior during our run and the note placed around his collar after we returned to the office.

"And you're only now telling me about this, Kit!" Doug's face contorted with concern.

"We didn't have a lot of time on the phone this morning," I said calmly.

"You must be on the right track if the killer is threatening you," he said. "And Clarence. Thank goodness he wasn't hurt."

I looked down at my sandwich. My appetite had suddenly vanished. If anything had happened to Clarence, I would never forgive myself.

"Maybe I should just let sleeping dogs lie, so to speak," I said.

"What do you mean?" asked Doug. "Are you giving up?"

"Things have changed. My brother is in the picture, you're working on Capitol Hill. Before today, I never imagined anyone could get hurt. It could be time to let the police do their job and get out of the way."

Doug crumpled up his sandwich wrapper, his appetite apparently not affected one bit by our conversation. "You might need some help. Don't give up so easily."

"What do you suggest?" I asked.

"Marty Buchman. You said he was a clever guy. Why not reach out to him? He might have found something important since you spoke to him."

"That's a good idea," I said slowly. "It also reminds me that Steve Song might have slipped up during our conversation. We were discussing the accusations about financial shenanigans in the Architect of the Capitol's office. Without prodding, he specifically mentioned contracts."

"Like he knew more than what he was letting on," said Doug.

"You got it. I have no idea if Steven Song is our killer, but I think he might be covering something up. Or covering for someone."

"Would he have been able to sneak inside your office and put that note on Clarence's collar?" asked Doug.

"I assume so. In his capacity, he knows where all congressional office suites are located. Given his length of tenure in the A-O-C, he must be familiar with all the buildings under his purview."

"Call Marty Buchman," said Doug firmly. "If he can't help you, then you can meet with Detective O'Halloran and tell him you're finished assisting with this one."

We got up and started to walk across the concrete esplanade. "I haven't even told you about Trevor. He's going to tell Meg he has a crush on her."

Doug rolled his eyes. "For heaven's sake. Timing is everything in life. Can't it wait until this mess is cleared up?"

I giggled. "Trevor's in love. He's not thinking rationally."

"I find this development the most baffling mystery of all." Doug leaned in and gave me a kiss on the cheek. "I'll walk over to your building after work so we can drive home together."

"Sounds like a plan," I said. "I'll let you know if I can get hold of Marty."

As I walked back to the Cannon Building, enjoying the pleasant afternoon sun, I searched my iPhone for Buchman's contact information. I found it in an email Trevor had sent a few days ago.

With any luck, Marty could help me wrap up the case quickly. Old axioms often ring true. Namely, be careful what you wish for.

CHAPTER TWENTY

By the time I returned to my office and settled in, Marty Buchman had already written back. He asked that I call him as soon as possible.

"Auspicious," I muttered. It never seemed like people you needed to speak with immediately returned your message, and yet those you wanted to avoid always replied pronto. My luck was turning around.

I dialed the number and a low, gravelly voice answered. "Who is this?"

"How about good afternoon or something more appropriate?" I countered.

"Identify yourself," insisted the voice.

"Kit Marshall," I said defiantly. "And I hope this is Marty Buchman."

The voice on the line sighed. "It's Marty. I needed to make sure this line hadn't been compromised."

"Compromised? May I ask by whom?" Here we go with the cloak and dagger routine again.

"Ms. Marshall, one high-ranking government official is already dead. Do you think the killer would hesitate eliminating a washed up investigative journalist or a congressional staffer?"

"I guess being cautious makes sense," I said. "Thanks for taking my call. I think it's time for us to compare notes again. I'm at the end of my rope and if I don't see a break soon, I'm bowing out of this investigation." I told Marty about the threatening note from this morning and the possibility we'd been followed during our jog around the National Mall.

"We definitely need to meet," said Marty, again speaking in a hushed voice. "Can't do this over the phone."

"Fine." I checked my calendar quickly on my computer. "Can you come to my office to chat? Let's say four o'clock today?"

Marty snorted. "I'm not coming to a congressional office to discuss a murder. We might as well exchange information on Twitter."

"Okay," I said slowly. "Where do you suggest we meet?"

"The summerhouse on Capitol grounds," he said quickly. "Six o'clock. There won't be tourists that late in the day. No one will notice us there."

I was thoroughly confused. "The summerhouse? I have no idea what you're talking about."

Marty chuckled. "I thought you were a sleuth, Ms. Marshall. I'm sure you'll figure it out." The phone clicked and the line went dead.

"Marty? Are you there?"

No response.

I slammed the phone onto the receiver. Maybe contacting Marty Buchman had been a fool's errand. What was a summerhouse? It sounded like a changing area for a swimming pool. There might be a pool inside the Senate gym, but I wasn't sure. How was I going to get access? I needed another mystery to solve like Joe Biden needed another internet meme.

As I was pondering my latest conundrum, Meg appeared. "Do you have time to meet with the staff briefly about the picnic? It's our final prep session."

"Absolutely," I said. At least there was nothing mysterious about a picnic.

"We're going to use Maeve's office," she said. "By the way, Trevor texted me."

I tried to maintain a poker face, which was oftentimes difficult. "Oh, really? What did he want?"

Meg narrowed her eyes. "He asked to speak with me later this afternoon. It seemed odd, but I told him to come to the office around six."

"Good idea. Maybe he'll have something interesting to say." Thank goodness, I would already be gone, desperately in search of the elusive Capitol Hill summerhouse or whatever it was.

Meg pursed her lips. "I feel like you're not telling me something."

I said nothing, trying my best to keep the expression on my face as neutral as Switzerland. Instead, I changed the subject. "Let's discuss the picnic!" I said a little too enthusiastically.

Meg gave me a funny look but said nothing. I followed her into the boss's office, where Jess and Oliver were already seated on the small chaise couch.

"All ready for the big shindig tomorrow afternoon?" I asked.

They both nodded their heads. Oliver wiped his forehead, and Jess fidgeted nervously.

"Is there another argument I need to know about?" Something didn't seem quite right.

Meg looked at her two employees. "Not to my knowledge."

"No, ma'am," said Oliver, his gaze averted.

"Terrific. The congresswoman flies in early tomorrow morning. She'll arrive around noon at the park. I'm sure she'll want to commandeer the grill. So, let's make sure the food is ready for her to cook when she gets there."

"We have a set up crew and a cleanup crew," said Jess. "We'll make sure we leave the picnic site exactly the way we found it."

"That's good to hear," I said. "Add another person to our list. My brother Sebastian will likely attend."

"And don't forget that Maeve said Chairwoman Jackson might stop by," said Meg. "She decided to remain in town this weekend."

"Anything else to add, team?" I asked. "Thanks again for working together on planning this."

I got up to head back to my office, but not before Oliver spoke. "Do you mind if Jess and I talk to you for a minute?" He added, "Privately."

"Sure," I said, sitting back down. Meg took her cue and left, a worried look on her face. Were Jess and Oliver going to lodge a complaint against Meg? Hopefully she hadn't strong armed them too much about the picnic.

"We wanted to give you an update," he said.

"An update on what?" Hadn't we just met about the picnic? Now I was confused, which seemed typical lately.

"The status of our relationship," said Jess demonstratively. "Working together on this picnic has brought us closer, and now we're back together."

"Oh," I said. "I wouldn't have guessed, given you argued like cats and dogs during the entire planning process."

Oliver turned red. "Some of that fighting was just an excuse for us to spend more time together on it, I guess."

"Love does manifest itself in strange ways," I said. "You're telling me in order to mitigate office politics?"

Oliver shook his head. "We agree on one thing. We can't work together and be together as a couple. We learned that last time around. I'm going to resign after the picnic. I've been thinking about getting a graduate degree." He put his arm around Jess, who blushed and curled up next to him.

"I'd appreciate at least two weeks' notice, Oliver," I said. Then I smiled. "All's well that ends well, I suppose."

"We think so," said Jess dreamily, as she stared into Oliver's eyes.

"Now if I could just figure out where the summerhouse is, I'd be home free," I muttered.

Jess snapped out of her reverie. "Did you say the summerhouse? The one by the Capitol?"

"Do you know where it is?" I asked. "Even better, do you know what it is?"

"Sure," said Jess. "Remember, I did social media for the Capitol Visitors Center before I applied for the job in Dixon's office. I know everything about the Capitol and its grounds."

My face brightened. "It's your lucky day. Can you tell me about it?" I pulled her off the couch and edged her toward the exit.

As I was shepherding Jess inside my office, Congresswoman Dixon's scheduler Patsy called after me. "Kit, Detective O'Halloran wants to talk to you this afternoon. Please give him a call."

I gave her the thumbs up sign. Jess sat down in the one chair that fit inside my cramped office. "Tell me about the summerhouse."

Jess blinked. "Why do you want to know about it?"

Damn millennials and their curiosity. "I'm meeting a friend there later today."

"You agreed to meet a friend somewhere

you didn't know existed?"

I sighed. "It's complicated, Jess, and I don't have a lot of time to explain it. But if you can tell me where the summerhouse is and what it looks like, I'd greatly appreciate it."

She raised her eyebrows. "Sure, but it seems like a strange place to hang out with a friend."

I motioned with my hand for her to continue. "Less commentary on my social calendar and more information about the summerhouse, please."

"Okay, okay," said Jess. "Frederick Law Olmsted constructed the summerhouse in the late 1800s. I forget the exact year. It's on the west lawn of the Capitol, Senate side."

I tried to imagine the geography in my mind. "Close to the Senate park?"

She nodded vigorously. "You got it."

"What exactly am I looking for? What type of building is it?"

"If you're looking for it, you won't miss it," she said. "It's red brick octagon built into the landscape."

"And why would Olmsted decide to construct something like this on the Capitol grounds?" I asked.

"You know Olmsted," said Jess. "He

designed Central Park and the Biltmore, too. As a landscape architect, his goal was to beautify and adorn the Capitol grounds. The summerhouse was an added bonus, a place for visitors to rest and relax during a hot summer day."

"I guess it was well before air conditioning. These days, the tourists find refuge in the Capitol Visitor Center," I said.

"Or they grab a drink at Bullfeathers," said Jess. "That's what I prefer to do."

"Good point. Thanks for your help, with the summerhouse and the picnic." Smiling, I added, "Good luck with Oliver."

She scuttled out of my office and back to her cubicle. I picked up the phone, remembering Patsy had instructed me to call Detective O'Halloran. Luckily, he answered the call on the first ring.

"O'Halloran here," he said.

"Detective, this is Kit Marshall. I got a message to give you a ring."

"So good of you to check in, Ms. Marshall. I played phone tag with your best friend today," he said.

"Sorry about that. It's been a busy day. But I'm afraid I still don't know who killed Melinda Masters. There's a lot of motives, yet I'm not quite sure who did it."

"We're having difficulty figuring out who

could have done it, Ms. Marshall."

O'Halloran was driving at something specific. "What do you mean, Detective?"

"We have an alibi problem in this case," said O'Halloran. "I'll be more explicit. Everyone seems to have one."

"That could be a problem," I said slowly. We'd been headed in the wrong direction during the entire investigation. I massaged my forehead. If we came up empty handed, Chairwoman Jackson's opinion of my boss would head south.

"Sure is. I'll run it down for you. We have a pretty small window for the time of the murder, so we were able to chase down whereabouts more precisely." I could hear O'Halloran flipping through the pages of his notebook. "Let's see. The Honorable Bridget Cartwright was with her chief of staff, Clay Donovan. Steve Song from the Architect's Office was with the Comptroller Gordon Romano."

"What about Grant Dawson?" I asked.

"I'm getting to him. He was a little harder, but when we went back and interviewed the catering staff, they were able to corroborate his whereabouts. He was still at the Botanic Garden, but he wasn't inside the glass solarium where Melinda was strangled."

"Great," I murmured. "Back to square

one." I heard O'Halloran chewing on the other end of the line. "Afternoon snack?"

More chewing. "Someone gave me a leftover donut from this morning. I needed a sugar boost."

Stereotypes were bad, yet sometimes they were altogether appropriate. "I guess you'll need it if our suspect list is wrong." I glanced to the edge of my desk, where Clarence was sleeping peacefully.

"Anything else to report, Ms. Marshall?" he asked.

"There is something important, Detective. Let me tell you what happened today." I recounted the suspicious incident on the Mall this morning during our jog and then the threatening note on Clarence's collar.

"Ms. Marshall, that would imply we haven't been barking up the wrong tree," said O'Halloran.

"Correct, Detective. Otherwise, why would the killer bother to issue a threat?"

"Quite right." I heard a big gulp on the line, which probably meant he was washing down his donut with a swig of coffee. "It's impossible to know. Be careful. I don't like the fact that someone got close enough to send a warning. If the killer can get to Clarence, he or she can get to you, too."

I shivered. Detective O'Halloran was

right. That also meant the murderer would have a clear path to Doug, Sebastian, and Meg.

"I have one more lead to chase down today." I explained to him why I wanted to meet with Marty Buchman.

"Sounds safe to me," said O'Halloran. "Buchman has no connection to Masters. He wasn't on the invite list at the Botanic Garden. I'm not sure he'll have much to add to the investigation, but what the hell. You might as well see what he has to say. Be sure to call me if it turns out to be important to the case."

"Understood, Detective," I said. "By the way, do you like picnics?"

After O'Halloran answered in the affirmative, I invited him to our barbecue tomorrow afternoon. That way, he could give a report to my boss and Chairwoman Jackson in person.

"There may not be too much to tell them about. At least we'll be doing it while eating burgers and hot dogs," said O'Halloran.

"My thoughts exactly, Detective. I'll see you tomorrow."

I ended the call and thought about the information he'd shared. Something wasn't right. Either we were totally off base or someone was lying.

Turning back toward my computer, I scrolled through my email. I suddenly realized I hadn't told Detective O'Halloran about the entry in Steve Song's calendar I'd seen: "Romano — Taft C."

Should I call him back? It was such an obscure reference, I doubted O'Halloran would have an immediate answer. Now that I thought about it, "Taft C" sounded like a meeting room in a hotel. Thank goodness there were only one hundred thirty-two hotels in Washington, D.C. It shouldn't take more than a month to determine which one had a room named "Taft C."

Instead of tackling the impossible, I dove into my long list of unanswered work emails. Two hours later, with only brief breaks to pet Clarence, I exhaled in relief. My inbox cleared, I could focus on my meeting with Marty Buchman at the mysterious summerhouse. At half past five, it was time to depart the office.

I looked around for Meg to say goodbye, but she was nowhere to be found. Instead, I found Jess at her cubicle.

"I'm leaving to meet my friend at the summerhouse," I said. "I'll see you a little before noon tomorrow for the picnic."

She gave me a "thumbs up" in return. Then I remembered Clarence. Should I take him to the summerhouse? In general, the Capitol grounds was dog friendly. But I had no idea if Marty liked dogs or if the historic summerhouse had a dog restriction. Best not to risk it.

"Jess, please ask Meg to watch Clarence for a bit. I'll be back to the office in about an hour," I said.

Jess nodded and took Clarence's leash. "He can hang out with me until Meg comes back. She said something about going to the restroom to put on makeup."

I raised my eyebrows. Was Meg primping for Trevor's arrival? Wonders never cease.

"Have Meg text me if there's a problem," I said.

As I was walking across Independence Avenue onto the East Capitol lawn, I realized I'd never told Doug that I'd reached Marty.

"Drat." He had planned on riding home with Clarence and me.

I texted him my plans and told him to meet me at the office in Cannon around six-thirty. How long could this meeting with Marty Buchman take? After it was over, I could collect both my husband and my dog, and we could depart for home, eager to start the weekend in relative peace with hopefully good news at home from Sebastian on his job search.

I wrapped around Southwest Drive and crossed in front of the Capitol's West lawn. In the distance, I spotted the infamous statue of James Garfield. So much had been made of this statue, yet I'd never really taken time to scrutinize it.

The sculptor John Quincy Adams Ward had portrayed President Garfield as a regal leader, his left foot slightly tipped over the base, as if to portray Garfield as "on the move." The information provided by the Architect of the Capitol explained that the three reclining figures below the main statue represented the different phases of Garfield's career. Ward had taken inspiration from Michelangelo's tomb in Florence.

It was an impressive piece of artistry. Had Melinda Masters lost her life over this statue? I certainly hoped not. The monument seemed to give this corner of the Capitol grounds a certain gravitas. As much as I admired James Madison, I wasn't sure it was appropriate for James Garfield to lose his revered spot.

I kept walking around the drive circling the Capitol and began to traverse the ascending Northwest drive slope. When I got closer to Constitution Avenue and the Senate park fountain, I kept my eye open for the summerhouse. Suddenly, I spotted an arched red brick structure built into the landscape. I certainly hoped this was it. Although it was on the cooler side for July, the walk had been a chore.

I scrutinized the summerhouse as I approached. It resembled a tomb, with a half oval opening popping out of the surrounding hillside. Ivy had grown over the octagonal structure, concealing its presence even further. If Frederick Law Olmsted had truly wanted a cool refuge for tourists during the summer, he'd succeeded. The earth shielded the structure from the brutal sun, and the almost invisible location of the summerhouse certainly limited the number of visitors who would actually find it.

The wrought-iron gate was open so I stepped cautiously inside the structure. My eyes immediately focused on a fountain at the center of the structure. I was just about to inspect it when I heard a familiar voice behind me.

"You should always watch your flank, Ms. Marshall."

I turned around to find Marty Buchman sitting on a stone bench directly behind me.

"Marty!" I exclaimed. "You scared me. Why would you do something like that?"

"Sorry, kid." He had on his straw fedora,

conveniently covering the top half of his face. "But we need to be invisible."

I joined Marty on the bench, sitting directly underneath a large barred window overlooking a grotto with a small stream flowing through. I looked through the metal grille. "Picturesque. I never knew this place existed."

"You're not the only one. Why did you think I suggested we meet here?" Marty peered underneath the brim of his hat. "It was locked up so I had to use my skills to open one of the iron doors." He motioned toward a heavy linked chain that sat on the ground with a lock next to it.

"With luck, I won't have to add breaking and entering to my repertoire of Capitol Hill accomplishments." I scrutinized the summerhouse interior. "I like playing tourist, but couldn't we have just had another drink at the speakeasy?"

Marty grabbed my arm. "You don't get it, do you?"

Instinctively, I pulled away. "What don't I get, Marty?"

"This murder is serious business. It's not just about a jilted lover or a political hack who got angry at his opponent." Marty frowned.

"You think it's about money. You're still

following the lead about the improper contracts," I said.

"Not just money, kiddo." He spread his arms wide. "Big money. I'm talking millions of dollars in contracts and kickbacks to match."

"I'm game to listen. To tell you the truth, I got nothing. We chased down a couple of suspects, but they all have alibis, so I'm not sure where to turn next."

"I hope you didn't tell anyone you came here to meet me." Marty blinked rapidly.

I shook my head. "No one except Detective O'Halloran. He's guilty of eating too many donuts, but he'd never hurt a fly."

Marty reclined on the stone bench and let out a big breath. "I chased down my original source who claimed there was corruption in the Architect's Office. Enough years had gone by, and the guy isn't looking for federal contracts anymore. He was willing to dish and pass along the names of other companies who felt they got a raw deal."

"If there was a lot of unhappy bidders on contracts, why didn't something happen?" I asked. "Wouldn't that make the Architect of the Capitol look bad?"

Marty smiled. "Only if the Architect was worried about getting caught."

I rubbed my chin. "By whom?"

"When bidders think a contracting decision was decided unfairly, they can file a protest," said Marty. "Do you know who reviews those decisions?"

I shook my head. I prided myself on knowing congressional process and procedure, but bureaucratic minutiae wasn't a strong suit.

With a gleam in his eye, Marty leaned forward. "The Government Accountability Office, kiddo."

CHAPTER TWENTY-ONE

I gasped and covered my mouth. "G-A-O? Why do they handle protests?"

Marty shrugged. "They've done it for over eighty years."

"What do you think happened?" I asked.

"I'm not a homicide detective, but I am a competent investigator. The fix has been in for a while. Not every contract protest, mind you. The Comptroller General was smarter than that. Let's just say the Architect had the latitude to do whatever he wanted for a long period of time."

"He? You don't mean Melinda Masters."

"No way," said Marty. "In fact, I think the problems started when Masters got nominated for the position. The previous Architect had been there for some time, as you know."

"It's a ten-year term, right?"

"Yes, but he sought reappointment and got it," said Marty. "He ended up serving fifteen years in office."

My eyes widened. "I didn't realize it was that long."

"Do you know where the previous Architect of the Capitol lives these days?" he asked.

"I heard he went south," I said. "Hilton Head?"

"Not even close," said Marty. "Try Palm Beach. The average home price is three point six million dollars."

"Hard to imagine how someone saves that on a government salary. Does he have a story about how he affords such expensive digs?"

"I checked into it," said Buchman. "Some bull crap about inheriting from a rich aunt. But when I looked into the public records, I couldn't find any evidence of inheritance. There's something fishy about it, and I'm not trying to come up with a clever pun about Florida."

"Let's break this down." I turned to face Marty on the bench. "How is this tied to Melinda's death?"

Marty adjusted the rim of his hat so he could see me clearly. "I'd say the previous A-O-C had a pretty desirable arrangement. He fixed certain contracts and took payouts. There's always a threat of a bid protest. But the Comptroller General was on the take, too. He probably took a cut of what the Architect got for kickbacks. Or something like that."

"Gordon Romano was profiting from looking the other way. Then, his sugar daddy decided to retire to Florida," I said. "What happens next?"

Marty shrugged. "All of a sudden, the extra cash wasn't coming in for Romano. My guess is that he decided to find out if Melinda Masters would continue the legacy of her predecessor."

"That's why he developed a romantic relationship with her."

"Hard to say on that one," said Buchman. "She was a looker. But sure, it couldn't hurt. Maybe Romano thought if they grew close, he'd have a better chance persuading her to join his contracting scheme."

"What about Steve Song?" I asked.

"Might have been in on it. You have to figure there was more than one person in the Architect's Office who knew about the shenanigans. Or at least he stayed silent."

I told Marty about the strange note I found on Steve's calendar, "Romano — Taft C."

"Was Steve trying to meet Romano at a hotel inside a conference room?" I asked.

"It seems like a strange place to liaise about a crime."

Buchman's forehead wrinkled. Then he snapped his fingers. "It's not a hotel conference room. But I do think they were meeting to talk about the murder."

"But where?" My voice was almost dovetailing into a whine. "It's a code word."

"Not exactly, Ms. Marshall. I do think you need to brush up on your Capitol Hill geography," said Buchman with a teasing sparkle in his eye.

"Taft C refers to something around here?" I asked.

"If I'm right, it's shorthand for the Taft Carillon," said Buchman. "Another property of the Architect of the Capitol. It's north of the Capitol on Constitution." Marty pointed in the right direction.

"I didn't know Taft was important enough to get a presidential memorial."

"Not William Howard Taft," corrected Buchman. "The carillon was erected in memory of Senator Robert Taft. You've heard the bells ringing on the quarter hour. You just didn't know it was in honor of Taft." Marty chuckled.

"Why would they meet there?" I asked.

"It's nearby and obscure enough. I'm sure Steve Song secured a key for the inside of the carillon where no one could see them."

"Steve Song and Gordon Romano were each other's alibis," I said slowly.

"This meeting might have been about getting their stories straight," said Buchman.

It was starting to come together. I replayed my conversation yesterday with Gordon Romano. Something bugged me about it. Marty's revelations helped it fall into place.

"When I spoke with Romano yesterday, he mentioned that Melinda Masters had been strangled with a vine at the Botanic Garden," I said. "But that detail had been left out of the press by the police. They didn't want visitors to the Botanic Garden to think the plants could be weaponized."

Marty rubbed his chin. "There's a chance the police might have told him about the vine. But maybe not. It's a good catch."

"You've been really helpful, Marty. Right now, the case against Romano is circumstantial. I wonder if the police could get Steve Song to flip on him if they applied some pressure. Or vice versa."

Buchman stood. "Seems like the right idea. You should call your Capitol Hill police contact and get him cracking on it. My gut tells me Song might have gotten dragged into this somehow. I bet if the police gave him an easy out, he'd go for it."

I nodded. "I'll do that later this evening."

Buchman motioned for me to leave the summerhouse. "After you, Ms. Marshall."

"Actually, Marty, I think I'm going to sit here by the grotto for a few minutes and chew on what you told me."

He tipped his hat. "No worries. It's a protected oasis in the midst of a very chaotic place. I'm glad I could introduce you to it. By the way, don't forget to secure the chain and the lock on your way out." He pointed to the ground. "I may break the law from time to time, but I try to put everything back in place when I do."

I laughed. "That's fair. Don't worry, Marty. Other than contacting the police, I won't say a word to anyone about what you found out. If this turns out to be true, I want to make sure you get the exclusive story."

Marty smiled, turned, and exited the summerhouse. I fished around my purse for my phone. It was already half past six. Doug would be wondering where I was. I'd better let him know I'd be a few minutes late.

My fingers started to type out the message when I heard a rustling immediately behind me. I turned around and peered through the barred window. With the exception of water trickling down the stream, everything was still.

I went back to my text message, ready to hit send when I felt the uncomfortable sensation of eyes watching me.

"Is someone there?" I said, feeling silly for talking to an empty building.

In a split second, a man emerged from the shadows, turned the corner of the entrance, and slammed the iron gate behind him.

"You're right about one thing, Kit Marshall. You aren't going to say a word to anyone about what you just heard."

CHAPTER TWENTY-TWO

"Comptroller Romano." I forced my voice to remain even. "What a coincidence to run into you here."

Romano laughed bitterly. When Meg and I had chatted with him earlier in the week, I'd considered him an attractive middle-aged man. Now, his face was contorted with anger, making me think of those childhood comic book villains who tragically transform into evil versions of themselves.

"There is no such thing as coincidences in Washington," said Romano. "Only good luck and bad luck. And I'm afraid you've had a stroke of the latter this evening."

"I take it you weren't taking a stroll on the Capitol grounds this evening and came upon the summerhouse." I stood and took a step forward, shifting my eyes back and forth around the hexagon enclosure. The other exit routes were gated and locked. The summerhouse had no roof, but there was no way I could boost myself over the wall from a bench, especially if he tried to stop me. The only way out was the unlocked gate, which Romano currently protected like Fort Knox.

"I don't have time for leisurely walks. But I was out early this morning and followed you and your friend along the Mall. You two had no idea I had eyes on you," he said. "The dog is the smartest of the bunch."

It was hard to argue with Clarence's intelligence, which was quite impressive for a canine. Nonetheless, I resented the implication. "I suppose you were the one who put the threatening message on his collar."

Romano grinned from ear to ear. "I figured you deserved at least one warning. I'd send you a message and if you backed off, then I'd forget your meddling. But you kept it up, meeting with your merry band of amateur sleuths and ambushing Song over in the Architect's Office."

"Steve is your accomplice, then," I said.

So far, Romano hadn't brandished a gun or a knife. What was his game plan? Clearly, this wasn't a confessional. I wished I'd told Doug or Meg where I was meeting Marty. They'd never think of looking for me at an obscure place like the summerhouse.

"I never said that, Ms. Marshall." Romano

shook his finger at me. "You wouldn't make a very competent analyst at G-A-O. Too many assumptions."

"Then why did you meet with him yesterday at the Taft Carillon? I gather that's what 'Taft C' stood for."

"Your friend the reporter got the location right," said Romano. "It's a perfect place for clandestine meetings, by the way. Not that you're going to have the opportunity in the future for that kind of activity."

I had my answer. Romano was planning to kill me. But how?

Romano continued. "Song might be greedy, but he doesn't have the guts to kill anyone. When the previous Architect retired, I continued my convenient arrangement with him. Song continued to fix the outcome of contract bids, and I continued to make sure protests weren't successful. The companies who benefited treated us quite generously over the years."

"How long has this been going on?" I asked. "Bridget Cartwright knows there's something fishy. You can't kill everyone who uncovers your crimes."

Romano sighed. "No, I can't. But Cartwright will shut up as soon as several of my patrons make generous donations to her campaign coffers. Others won't be so lucky.

As soon as I take care of you, I'll make sure the reporter disappears. Luckily, no one will miss him."

"You won't get away with this." I didn't bother to hide the desperation in my voice. "If you come after me, I'll scream. Someone will hear me."

"Doubtful, Ms. Marshall. It's a summer Friday evening at the United States Capitol. Everyone has left for Dewey Beach or happy hour. This place is deader than a doornail." He snickered. "No pun intended."

I needed to stall for time. "You killed Melinda because she wouldn't join your moneymaking scheme."

"I always knew there might be a problem when a new Architect was selected. When it was an attractive woman, I figured I could win her over. It worked. You may not agree, but I'm actually quite charming." He flashed a toothy smile, which almost caused me to retch.

"Maybe personally, but Melinda Masters wasn't corrupt," I said.

"That's correct. After we developed a rapport, so to speak, I floated a few possible contract proposals coming her way that could be quite lucrative if she greased the wheels. But she didn't bite."

"In fact, I bet she threatened to expose

you," I said.

"Not in so many words, but she did give me reason to be nervous," said Romano. "And there was no way I was going to let her take me down."

"You'll spend the rest of your life in federal prison once you're discovered."

"That's where you're wrong. After I empty my offshore bank account, I'm going to spend the rest of my life in a tropical location that doesn't have an extradition agreement with the United States. Not a bad retirement plan, in my humble opinion."

"Detective O'Halloran knows I'm here. It will be better if you just let me go. Another murder isn't going to help when the police catch you," I said.

"I don't see it that way." Romano pointed to the chain used to lock the gate. "I'm afraid I didn't come fully prepared this evening. Amazingly enough, I seem to find useful weapons when I need them. That strangling vine really came in handy a few days ago."

He reached inside his suit jacket and pulled out a pair of rubber gloves. "A murderer should never leave home without these." He shook them in my direction as he put them on. "I noticed your reporter accomplice touched this chain when he picked the lock. His fingerprints are all over it. He'll take the rap for your death, and with some creativity on my part, I'm sure I can convince the police he killed Melinda, too." Romano bent down and picked up his makeshift weapon. "It will make perfect sense when he's discovered dead. An apparent suicide seems to fit the storyline well, don't you think?"

Now I knew what was coming. He planned to strangle me, pin the murders on Marty Buchman, and then make his death look like a suicide. There was one wrinkle in his plan. He'd have to outsmart me, and I wasn't planning on going down without a fight.

The door behind him was closed but unlocked. If I could entice him to move away from it, I'd have a chance to escape.

"You'll have to come and get me." I moved behind the stone fountain in the center of the summerhouse.

"Ms. Marshall, it's best if you don't make this difficult," said Romano. But my ploy worked. He took a few steps forward.

Then, I heard a familiar sound in the distance. It was a dog barking. Not just any bark, but the all-too-familiar yap of a beagle mutt. Clarence was somewhere on the Capitol grounds. Unless he'd somehow managed to run away, that meant either Doug or Meg was with him. Thank goodness Sebastian hadn't been successful in training Clarence to stay quiet.

It was now or never. The longer I stayed inside the summerhouse with Romano, the more likely I'd end up like Melinda. My purse was still on the ground near the bench.

"Oh, I plan on making this very difficult," I said.

I moved swiftly to the left and shoved my hand inside my purse. Once I found what I was looking for, I dashed around the fountain in the opposite direction. My unpredictable move caught Romano off balance. As I charged toward him, he tried to throw the chain around me so he could pull me in. But I was ready for that move. It was time to test those burpees. I hit the ground flat. Before he had a chance to reach down for me, I lifted up his pant leg and stabbed him hard with the fancy fountain pen Sebastian had given me last night.

"YOW!" Romano screamed in pain.

The moment's hesitation was all I needed. In one swift move, I was on my feet again. I swung open the door and sprinted down the path across the Capitol lawn. I'd only run fifty feet before I heard the barking again. Clarence turned the corner, pulling on his leash, with Doug, Trevor, and Meg in tow.

"Don't let him get away!" I pointed back to the summerhouse. "Gordon Romano is inside, and he tried to kill me!"

Doug put his arm around me. "Calm down, Kit. He's not going anywhere. We already alerted Detective O'Halloran. The police are surrounding this area. He won't get far."

Clarence growled softly to get my attention. I bent down and he planted a sloppy kiss on my cheek. In return, I scratched his ears and gave him a big squeeze.

"Clarence, promise me you'll never change."

Three staccato barks acknowledged my request.

CHAPTER TWENTY-THREE

"Can you pass the mustard?"

"Surely," I said, passing the yellow bottle across the picnic table. "Would you like relish, too?"

"Nah," said Detective O'Halloran. "I'm a purist when it comes to hot dogs." He took a big bite of his frank, chewing with a glowing smile of contentment.

"We're glad you were able to join us, especially given everything that's happened," said Doug.

"Romano's being difficult," said O'Halloran. "We have our best people working on him. In the meantime, we picked up Steve Song last night, and he sang like a canary. That's going to make our job a lot easier."

Meg had polished off a sizable cheeseburger and now was working her way through a plate full of potato salad and baked beans. I caught Trevor eyeing her. If he wanted to date Meg, he'd better get used to her appetite. With yesterday's confusion, I hadn't gotten a full debrief from Meg about their conversation, but Trevor had given me a "thumbs up" sign when he arrived at the picnic. Life was about to get even more interesting.

"Did Steve help Romano murder Melinda Masters?" I asked. "As I said in my police statement, I got the impression from Romano during our brief interlude that he didn't."

"We don't think so," said O'Halloran. "Song is likely an accessory after the fact. Romano met him at the Taft Carillon to insist Steve serve as an alibi for him. Song says he resisted, but Romano held the shady Architect of the Capitol business over his head. He had no choice but to corroborate Romano's story and provide him with an alibi after the reception finished."

"Congratulations are in order to Capitol Hill's top-notch detectives," announced a familiar voice. Chairwoman Rhonda Jackson approached our table. Maeve Dixon was two steps behind her.

"Thank you for joining us today." I moved over on the bench so there was room for Jackson to sit.

"No need to make room for me," she said.

"I'm only dropping by for a brief announcement."

Meg and I exchanged blank expressions. Why would Chairwoman Jackson come to our office picnic to make an announcement?

Maeve said in a loud voice. "Everyone, please gather around."

With similar looks of confusion on their faces, staff and invited guests moved closer to our picnic table.

"I would have made this announcement next week in your office, but when I heard you had a picnic planned, I thought the timing couldn't be better," said Chairwoman Jackson. "On Monday, I plan to announce my run for the United States Senate. Given that I'm not as young as I used to be," she paused briefly to smile, "I am resigning from my seat in the House of Representatives to campaign full time."

A collective gasp could have been heard two picnic pavilions away. I snuck a peek at Maeve Dixon. She was smiling broadly behind Jackson. Something else was up. After the surprise wore off, everyone applauded Jackson. Several shouted, "Good luck" and "Congratulations, Senator!"

Jackson motioned for silence. "Of course, this means I will not serve as the chair of the House Administration committee any longer. That's why I am here today."

My mouth fell open. I glanced at Doug, who had broken into a wide grin. Even he understood the significance of Jackson's next words.

"I've spoken with the leadership in the House, and the Speaker agrees with my recommendation. Maeve Dixon will succeed me as chair of the committee. Please join me in congratulating her." Jackson enveloped Meg in a hug.

The entire crowd erupted into clapping, whoops, and hollers. I sucked in a quick breath. Given Maeve's short tenure in Congress, her elevation to a committee chairmanship was extraordinary. It also meant her stature and public profile would rise considerably.

I stood and walked over to my boss, sticking out my hand. "Congratulations, Congresswoman. I mean, Chairwoman Dixon."

She took my hand and drew me in for a brief hug, whispering in my ear, "I'm counting on your help, Kit."

I drew back and nodded. The staff had lined up behind me to offer congratulations, so I returned to my seat on the picnic bench.

Sebastian shook his head. "Never a dull moment. Everyone on the west coast thinks Washington is boring. It couldn't be further from the truth!"

Trevor adjusted his glasses. "Maelstroms of controversy seem to coalesce around your sister, so her orbit may not be the most representative." He paused, beaming at Meg. "However, I admit that the chaos does have its benefits."

"Speaking of good news, how did your interviews go yesterday?" asked Meg.

Sebastian ran his fingers through his bushy hair. "Looks like I might need to get a trim. I was offered a tech position at a worthy nonprofit. As long as my salary negotiations go well, I should start in about a week."

Sebastian had told me about the job earlier this morning. Between his decision to relocate and Maeve's promotion, I couldn't stop smiling.

"Do you still plan to continue your protesting?" asked Meg.

Sebastian nodded. "In the evenings and on weekends." Then he winked in my direction. "If I have time, of course. It seems like I might have to add amateur sleuth to my list of extracurricular activities."

"Without Sebastian's help, I wouldn't have gotten away from Gordon Romano," I said. "Not only did he give me the pen I used to stab Romano, but thanks to him, I was able to do a burpee to escape!"

Doug raised his glass of lemonade. "Three cheers for my brother-in-law and newest Washington, D.C. resident." Everyone joined the toast and raised plastic cups in appreciation.

There was one remaining detail that bugged me, and in the midst of the confusion last night after Romano had been apprehended, I didn't have a chance to ask about it.

"Clarence's big mouth also helped save the day. If I hadn't heard him, I might not have had the courage to break free from Romano. How did you know where I was?" I asked. "I didn't tell anyone where I was meeting Marty Buchman."

"But you did, Kit," said Meg. "Remember, you asked Jess about the summerhouse and she told you the location. When you didn't show up to meet Doug at our office, Jess overheard and let us know where you'd gone."

Trevor spoke. "After you were ten minutes late, we decided to take a walk to find out what was going on. I didn't think Marty was a bad guy, but you never know."

"It turned out Marty had it all figured out," I said. "Did anyone notify him about Romano's arrest?"

Trevor nodded. "I gave him a call this morning. Since he knows the background already, he has a big leg up. As we munch on hot dogs and hamburgers, Marty is typing up his story and selling it to the highest bidder."

"Good for Marty," I said. "Maybe he'll finally get that Pulitzer."

"Speaking of investigations, what about all the wrongdoing in the Architect of the Capitol's office?" asked Meg. "Won't that be under Maeve's jurisdiction as chairwoman now?"

Congresswoman Dixon must have overheard Meg's comment because she interjected herself into the conversation. "I've already had several discussions about it this morning. We've decided that Representative Bridget Cartwright will take the lead on chairing a special subcommittee to investigate the matter."

"That should keep her busy for a while," muttered Meg.

"It shall," said Maeve, with a sparkle in her eye. "And in exchange, she's going to drop her campaign to add James Madison to the Capitol grounds. President Garfield is safe. At least for now."

"A high-profile investigation about government corruption will get her much more attention than replacing a statue," said Doug. "Sounds like the perfect political solution."

"Sometimes things really do work out," I said. "But we're going to have a busy agenda going forward. And I know exactly what your first action as committee chair should be."

Maeve's eyes twinkled with interest. "Tell me. I'd love to hear what you think I should focus on, Kit."

"Making sure we have an accurate calendar about when the next corpse flower blooms," I said, laughing. "Those flowers are downright deadly."

ABOUT THE AUTHOR

Colleen J. Shogan has been reading mysteries since the age of six. A political scientist by training, Colleen has taught American politics at several universities and previously worked on Capitol Hill as a legislative staffer in the United States Senate and as the Deputy Director of the Congressional Research Service. She is currently the Assistant Deputy Librarian for Collections and Services at the Library of Congress. Colleen lives in Arlington, Virginia with her husband Rob and their beagle mutt Conan.

CPSIA information can be obtained
at www.ICGtesting.com
Printed in the USA
BVHW031020180921
617023BV00004B/5

9 781432 891817